Rosemary for Remembrance

Tales from Grace Chapel Inn®

Rosemary for Remembrance

Sunni Jeffers

Guideposts
NEW YORK, NEW YORK

Rosemary for Remembrance

ISBN-13: 978-0-8249-4753-8

Published by Guideposts
16 East 34th Street
New York, New York 10016
www.guideposts.com

Distributed by Ideals Publications
535 Metroplex Drive, Suite 250
Nashville, Tennessee 37211

Guideposts, Ideals and *Tales from Grace Chapel Inn* are registered trademarks of Guideposts.

Library of Congress Cataloging-in-Publication Data

Jeffers, Sunni.
    Rosemary for remembrance / Sunni Jeffers.
        p. cm. — (Tales from Grace Chapel Inn)
    ISBN-13: 978-0-8249-4753-8
    1. Bed and breakfast accommodations—Fiction 2. Sisters—Fiction.
    3. Pennsylvania—Fiction. I. Title.
    PS3610.E36R67 2008
    813'.6—dc22

                                        2008013849

Cover by Lookout Design Group
Interior design by Cindy LaBreacht
Typeset by Nancy Tardi

Printed and bound in the United States of America

10 9 8 7 6 5 4 3 2 1

Acknowledgments

This book is dedicated to my sister-in-law Sue and to her sister-in-law Aunt Jan. Special thanks for information on spinning, crocheting and quilting, and especially for your prayers. You're the best! Also, many thanks to the spinners, knitters and crocheters of the Pend Oreille Fiber Arts Group, who allowed me to join them for an amazing day with the Northwest Regional Spinners Association at Bear Paw Camp. I learned a lot about spinning wool and raising sheep. Thanks to Ruth Logan Herne, Mary Jarvis, Wanda Jollymore and Heidi Wulfraat of the London-Wul Fibre Arts for advice on lambing and spinning. Any errors concerning spinning, crocheting and lambing are strictly mine. My cows are much easier, I do believe.

—Sunni Jeffers

Chapter One

Icy rain pelted Louise Howard Smith as she tugged at the door of Time for Tea. The force of the wind made the door hard to open. Inside, Samuel Bellwood saw Louise's struggle and hurried to her aid. His gentle smile, which always seemed at odds with his immense size and strength and his rugged farm clothing, was as welcome to her as his help.

"Thank you, Samuel."

Franz Liszt's *La Lugubre Gondola* played over the shop's stereo system. *A sad lament for a dreary day*, Louise thought. She spied Wilhelm Wood, the store owner, behind the counter. "Good morning, Wilhelm." She slipped off the hood of her raincoat and gave her head a little shake. Droplets of water fell from her short silvery bangs. "What a day!"

"Not fit for man or beast," Wilhelm said. "Good tea weather, but no one wants to venture out to buy it, and I can't blame them. I have half a mind to leave Acorn Hill and head for Brazil for the rest of the winter."

"That does sound appealing right now," Louise replied, then she turned to Samuel. "We don't see you often enough, Samuel. I hope Rose is well."

"Oh yes, she's fine. I came to town to buy feed and left her minding the farm. The errand is really an excuse to look for a gift. We have an anniversary coming up. Forty years."

Samuel ran a hand through his sandy hair. "I can't remember the last time we had a real anniversary celebration. Every year something happens at the farm, and I completely forget what day it is. She fixes a fancy dinner and tries to make the day special, but the farm demands a lot of attention. This year, I thought I'd get an early start, so that at least I have a nice gift for her. I thought maybe one of Wilhelm's jazzy tea sets or something. I don't know. Maybe you could suggest something?"

Looking down from his considerable height, he gave Louise a hopeful look.

"A tea set would be a fine gift, Samuel. I'm sure she would love it. Perhaps you also could take her out to dinner, so she doesn't have to do the cooking."

Samuel shook his head. "I've tried that before, but it never seems to work out. And I want to surprise her. What was the best anniversary you and Eliot ever had, Louise?"

"That's easy. It was the year we renewed our vows. We had a small ceremony in the chapel at the university, and then we had a lovely luncheon for our families and a few close friends. I don't know if I can explain, but there was something deeply moving about professing our love all over again."

"Rose would like that."

Louise smiled and nodded. "I'm sure that she'd be very pleased and touched if you reaffirmed your love that way."

Samuel looked at his feet. "Yes, but I wouldn't know how to start planning such a thing."

Louise's heart turned over for this dear man. "If you would like to do it, Samuel, I would be honored to help you."

He looked up. The hopeful light in his eyes warmed her. "You would?"

"Absolutely. When is your anniversary?"

"February fourteenth."

"Truly? What a wonderful anniversary date. And that means we've nearly six weeks to plan this ceremony."

"It has to be a secret."

"We'll do our best. You'll have to avoid mentioning anything to Rose that relates to our plans. Sometimes it's hard not to let something slip in a conversation."

"That won't be hard. I'm not one to chitchat."

Louise could believe that. In fact, she couldn't remember ever before having such a lengthy conversation with Samuel.

The steady, cold rain continued as the Grace Chapel board members converged in the meeting room at the church Tuesday evening. Alice Howard arrived first, followed by her aunt Ethel Buckley and Lloyd Tynan, the Acorn Hill mayor. Florence Simpson arrived next.

Lloyd helped Ethel and Florence remove their raincoats before he removed his own. Though Ethel wore a heavy wool sweater beneath her coat, she shivered in the cold room. "Could we turn up the heat in here?" she asked. "I'm chilled to the bone."

"I'm sorry, Ethel," Rev. Henry Ley said, entering the room. He had a dark mark on the cuff of his white shirt. His nose was smudged where he'd pushed up his glasses. "The old furnace is ch-ch-chugging away as hard as it can. I checked the filter. It looks f-fine. Just overworked." As the associate pastor, Rev. Ley often took care of minor maintenance in the chapel.

"It's the damp weather," Fred Humbert said as he came in behind Henry. "We're in for a lot more of this rain and ice." Fred was an amateur weather prognosticator and, more often than not, his predictions were correct. If the locals wanted to know when to plant a garden or to have an outdoor event, they went into Fred's Hardware Store and asked for a forecast.

"I'd rather have snow," Florence said. "At least you can see it and shovel it. This icy rain is treacherous, and the dampness ruins my hair and makes my foot ache." Florence did look a little droopy, which was unusual. She never appeared in public without carefully applied makeup and professionally coiffed hair. She hobbled over to a chair and sat down.

Alice assumed the bunion on Florence's right foot was acting up again. As a nurse, Alice was aware of how the damp, cold weather affected people. Many of her Potterston Hospital patients had been complaining recently of aches and pains in their joints and extremities.

Cyril Overstreet arrived, looking quite dashing in his long overcoat and fedora. Cyril amazed Alice. Although he seemed a bit slower than usual, for a man in his eighties, he was quite spry.

Sylvia Songer and June Carter came in together. The luscious scent of warm apple pie filled the air as June placed a deep-dish pie in the middle of the table. Sylvia put down paper plates and plastic forks.

"I just took this out of the oven," June said. She owned the Coffee Shop, and her pies were legendary. "I thought everyone could use some cheer."

Patsy Ley came in with a fresh pot of coffee and cups. "Here's coffee to go with that pie," she said.

"Well now," Fred said, grinning broadly, "This is a treat." He rubbed his hands together. "Thank you, ladies. Let's get this meeting under way. Henry, will you lead us in prayer?"

Everyone sat down, and Pastor Ley asked the Lord to bless their meeting.

They ate as they discussed church business. Lloyd suggested they have someone take a look at the church's furnace and see if it needed maintenance. Fred said he would look into it and order parts if needed.

When they had gone through everything on the agenda, Fred asked, "Do we have any new business?"

"I do," Ethel said, raising her hand. "As the Committees

Director, I have a suggestion from the Seniors Social Circle. We have decided the church needs a midwinter social event for women."

"Like a tea?" Sylvia asked.

"No, no. After my annual Christmas tea, another tea would be redundant," Florence said. Her tea party was one of the finest social events in Acorn Hill.

"A women's retreat was mentioned as a possibility."

"What for?" Cyril asked with a wry smile. "So a bunch of ladies can get together and gossip?"

"Now, Cyril, that isn't why women have retreats," June said, wagging her finger at him. "The older I get, the more I realize the value of my friendships with other women. You men are wonderful, but we gals need each other. We have a lot of ladies in Acorn Hill who are tied down by young families or jobs or health issues, and a retreat would give them a chance to get reacquainted and to discover they're not alone. I think it's a great idea."

"Well," Cyril said, "I'm not saying I'm against it, mind you. Just doesn't make any sense to me. But the Bible does say the older women should counsel the younger women."

Patsy Ley sat next to her husband. She wasn't part of the board but recorded the minutes of the meetings. Alice saw her nudge her husband. He sighed and cleared his throat.

"I think the l-ladies should have their r-retreat." He glanced at Patsy, who smiled approvingly. "M-may I suggest, er, an outreach t-to all the l-ladies in A-Acorn Hill?"

Alice said, "What a wonderful idea, Henry."

"Excellent idea," Sylvia agreed. Sylvia owned the local fabric store. "Several young mothers from various churches come to my store to take classes, and they have a great time together. I'm sure many of them would be interested in a retreat. Perhaps we could have a craft time as well as an inspirational speaker."

"I know of a wonderful speaker," June said. "My niece from Chicago speaks to women's groups. I could ask her, if you'd like."

Fred stood. "Ladies, we don't need to plan the details here and now. Just set the date."

"We considered a Valentine's theme, so mid-February," Ethel said.

"All right. All in favor of the Grace Chapel women sponsoring a retreat say aye."

The consent was unanimous. As the ladies began tossing ideas around, Fred declared the meeting adjourned.

"We must have a planning meeting," Ethel said. "I propose that the ladies on the board form the initial committee."

When everyone agreed, Florence stood. "The planning committee can meet at my house on Friday," she said. "I'll prepare a small luncheon."

Alice saw a disgruntled look pass over Ethel's face. "We'll need to meet more than once. Grace Chapel Inn is available for meetings too," Alice said, referring to the bed-and-breakfast she and her sisters had created from their family home.

"Yes, thank you. We can hold the first meeting at Florence's house, then subsequent meetings at the inn," Ethel said decisively.

Alice hoped Ethel and Florence would not compete to plan the retreat. The two were friends, but each liked to be in charge.

When Alice returned to Grace Chapel Inn, she entered through the kitchen door and was greeted by the sweet, buttery scent of something baking. She pulled off her coat and hat and rubbed her hands together.

"*Brrr.* That wind cuts right to my bones."

Alice and her sisters had run Grace Chapel Inn in their Victorian home since the death of their father.

"Come sit down. I've made tea and butter horns," Jane Howard said.

Alice joined her sisters at the kitchen table. "I'll have tea, but I'll pass on the butter horns. June brought an apple pie to the meeting."

After Jane passed her a mug of tea, Alice held it in both hands, enjoying its warmth while deeply inhaling the pleasing aroma. "*Ahhh.* Now this is what I needed. There's nothing as comforting as hot tea. Thank you."

"Anything interesting happen at the meeting?" Jane asked.

"As a matter of fact, yes. Aunt Ethel proposed that Grace Chapel host a Valentine's retreat for all the women in town."

"Really? What fun," Jane said.

"A retreat close to Valentine's Day could be a problem," Louise said.

"Why is that?" Alice asked.

"Samuel Bellwood wants to plan a surprise for Rose for their fortieth anniversary, which happens to be on Valentine's Day."

"And that would affect the women?" Alice asked.

"Many of them. You see, I suggested that he surprise Rose with a ceremony to renew their vows. He asked me to help."

"Oh, Louise, what a fabulous idea," Jane said. "I'd love to help too. Where will the ceremony be held?"

"We haven't discussed details yet. This is all very preliminary and secret. Rose is not to find out."

"I won't breathe a word," Jane said.

"Nor will I," Alice said. "Maybe we can convince Aunt Ethel to change her dates. I don't know how we'll do that, though, without giving her a reason."

"True, which presents a problem," Louise said. "Unfortunately, she loves a good secret, and the telling of it."

"Don't forget, we are fully booked for the inn's Valentine Special weekend too," Jane reminded them.

"I hope neither of these events conflicts with that," Louise said.

"Perhaps you could join the committee and help them select the date, Louise," Alice suggested.

"I suppose I could do that. I'll talk to Aunt Ethel tomorrow. My goodness. Between the retreat and the Bellwoods' anniversary, things will get very exciting. Now if only the weather will cooperate."

"Yes," Alice said. "We'd better start praying for sunshine in February."

"Amen to that," Jane said.

Chapter Two

The next morning, the sun punched a tiny hole in the clouds. Though it wasn't full sunshine, it was enough to lift Louise's spirits when she looked out her third-floor bedroom window at the frosted trees sparkling in the light. She said a little prayer of thanksgiving for the break in the rainy weather.

As always, Louise dressed with care. She wore a light-blue sweater set adorned with her signature pearl necklace. Her flared brown wool skirt moved gracefully as she descended the stairs.

She smelled the ham and potatoes before she reached the kitchen. As they had no guests staying at the inn, Louise didn't go to the dining room to set the table. Laying a letter to her daughter Cynthia on the registration desk, she went into the kitchen.

"Good morning, Jane . . . Alice." She poured a cup of coffee for herself. "Did you see the sunshine?"

Jane turned toward her, flipping her dark ponytail over her shoulder in the process. Louise thought her sister looked young enough to be her daughter when she wore her hair pulled up in the youthful style. It was hard to believe she was fifty.

"You mean that pinprick of light through the blanket of clouds?" Jane teased.

"That pinprick of light reminded me that the sun is up there, no matter how many clouds there are."

"That's easy to forget when the days are so gloomy," Alice said.

The door from the outside to the kitchen opened, and Ethel stepped in.

"Yoo-hoo. Good morning, girls," she said. "Did you see the sunshine?"

"Good morning, Auntie. We were just talking about it. I hope that's a sign of brighter weather ahead," Jane said. "Have you had breakfast?"

"Yes, I had a bowl of oatmeal, but I'd be happy to join you for a cup of coffee. Is it that special blend from Africa?" Ethel removed her jacket and sat at the table.

"One of them. This one is from Ethiopia. I think you'll like it," Jane said, handing her a cup.

"What brings you out so early this morning, Aunt Ethel?" Alice asked.

"I thought I'd take advantage of the break in the weather," she said. "I wanted to tell you the exciting news, if Alice hasn't already told you. The ladies of Grace Chapel are hosting a retreat for all the women in Acorn Hill."

"What a wonderful idea," Louise said, glancing at Alice.

"Terrific," Jane said. "That'll perk up things around here. When will it take place?"

"The weekend after Valentine's Day."

"That'll be a busy weekend, so close to the holiday," Jane said.

"I haven't heard of anything going on," Ethel said, as if nothing could happen without her knowledge.

"Since Valentine's Day is in the middle of the week, some families will be celebrating on the weekend. Perhaps you should move the retreat to March," Louise suggested.

Ethel just sipped her coffee, ignoring Louise's comments.

"Louise is very good at organizing events, Aunt Ethel. She would be a big help on your committee," Jane said.

Ethel seemed to ponder this idea. "Why don't you come to our planning meeting on Friday? I'm sure the others would love to hear your thoughts."

Louise glanced at her sisters, who gave her encouraging nods. "I'd be happy to. Where and when?"

"Our first meeting is at Florence's house. It's nice of her to invite the committee for lunch, but you know how domineering she can be. I don't want her getting the idea this is her retreat. After all, I am the Committees Director. Alice was kind enough to suggest we meet at the inn after the initial meeting."

"That would work better for me, so I could be on hand if we have guests arriving or checking out," Louise said.

"An excellent point. That settles it. We must meet here." Ethel looked so gleeful that Louise almost retracted her comment. She disliked encouraging her aunt's competition with Florence.

"I'm looking forward to Florence's luncheon," Louise said. "She entertains so graciously. With both of you on the committee, the retreat will be a great success, Aunt Ethel."

"Thank you," Ethel said as she rose from her chair. "I must be running along now. I have a great deal to do before Friday."

After Ethel left, Louise said, "I do wish Aunt Ethel and Florence would stop competing, and try to agree on the retreat plans."

Jane shook her head. "Those two? Agreeing is about as likely as spring arriving tomorrow."

All three sisters turned and looked out the window. The sunshine had disappeared. A light fog had descended to obscure the backyard. Spring rarely appeared in Acorn Hill before mid-March, and this year looked like no exception.

∞

Jane glanced around the sanctuary of Grace Chapel. The Wednesday night service never drew as many as the Sunday morning service, but tonight's attendance was unusually sparse. Between the weather and the letdown after the holidays, people weren't venturing out. Louise was minding the inn, while Alice was in the church's Assembly Room with the ANGELs, a group of middle-school girls that she led during the Wednesday night service.

A young couple walked up the aisle and sat in the pew across from Jane. They were the Caseys, Blair and Kristin. He was the new large-animal veterinarian. Jane caught Kristin's eye and smiled. The young woman smiled back.

What a handsome couple, Jane thought. He looked like an all-American football star: tall and blond with square shoulders and a pleasant face. His fair coloring contrasted with his wife's jet-black hair and dark-chocolate eyes. *Stunning*.

When the service was over, Jane stepped across the aisle to greet the Caseys. "It's great to see you again. You're brave to come out in this weather."

"Toughening up," Blair said, smiling. "Once I get my practice established, I will be busy most winter evenings. It seems like the difficult deliveries usually happen in the worst weather and at night."

"I suppose that's true," Jane said. "How's your practice going? Are you starting to get busy yet?"

"Not really. It'll take time for the local farmers to trust me."

"Blair is a wonderful vet, and animals love him. I hope people start giving him a chance to prove it soon," Kristin said.

Kristin's soft southern drawl made Jane think of Melanie in *Gone with the Wind*. "You need introductions, and I can help with that," Jane said. "I know! Come to dinner after church Sunday. I'll invite some other friends as well, and you can meet some new people then."

Kristin's eyes lit up. "We'd love that, wouldn't we, darling," she said, taking her husband's arm.

"That's very kind of you," he said. "We'd be honored to come. Thank you."

"It'll be our pleasure." Jane was already thinking of whom she would invite to join them. She liked the Caseys. They had stayed at the inn a few months ago while they looked for a house. At the time, Acorn Hill had no large-animal veterinarian. He figured it was the perfect place to open a clinic for all the horses, cattle, sheep and goats in the area.

The plan seemed to be a good one, but right now Jane felt sorry for them. Coming from the South and spending their first winter and holidays away from family and warm weather required that they make a huge adjustment. A little encouragement and a few friendly faces would certainly help.

Just after one on Thursday, as the Howard sisters sat at the kitchen table sipping their after-lunch tea and coffee, there was a knock on the door. Louise went to answer it and found Samuel Bellwood.

"I hope I'm not interrupting you," he said. "I was in town for supplies and I thought I'd take the opportunity to speak to you."

"You're not interrupting. We've finished. Come sit with us and have a cup of coffee," Louise said. "I told my sisters about your upcoming anniversary."

"Good. Thank you," he said, taking a seat. "I've been thinking about your suggestion. I like your idea, Louise, but I don't know how to go about making all the arrangements."

"Events like weddings and renewals are more a woman's realm," Louise said. "Jane, Alice and I would be delighted to help you."

"Yes, we're excited about your anniversary," Jane said, handing him a cup of coffee and offering him a dish of warm cranberry-apple crisp with cream sauce, which he accepted.

"Thank you." He swallowed some coffee and set the cup down. "What do I do?"

"First let's figure out what you want," Louise said. "This must be meaningful for you as well as for Rose. It could be the simple act of renewing your wedding vows in front of your family and a few close friends, or it can be like a wedding. It can be in the church or your home or somewhere else."

Samuel looked a bit alarmed and shook his head. "So much to think about. I don't know."

"What do you think would please Rose?" Louise asked.

"Nothing so formal as a church. I think in our home would be best. We had a simple wedding with just our families there. I want to honor her in front of our family and all our friends who have been so important in our lives."

"What if you do a ceremony followed by a reception?" Jane said. "I could put together a really nice reception."

"I will be happy to help you with the ceremony," Louise said.

"I'll help my sisters," Alice said. "And I can do the invitations."

"First, we must set a date," Louise said. "Your anniversary falls in the middle of the week. It'd be better to celebrate on a weekend so more people can attend."

"You're right. Samantha wants to be here, and our sons all work during the week. What do you suggest?"

"It could be the weekend before or after, but the inn's Valentine Special is the weekend before, so after would work better for us," Jane said.

Samuel rubbed his chin. "That's fine. I surely don't want to inconvenience you. Let's go with the Saturday after."

"All right. Could you make a guest list?" Louise asked.

"I don't know who to ask. I'll have Samantha call you from college. She'll know who to ask, and she has all the out-of-town addresses on her computer. Let's be sure that everyone knows it's a surprise. Oh, and no presents. We have more stuff than we need now."

"People will want to congratulate you," Alice said. "We can stipulate cards only."

Samuel cleared his throat. He started to speak, but stopped and cleared his throat again.

"I can't tell you how much I appreciate this. I can shear sheep and bale hay, but I don't know anything about putting on a party. With you doing the planning, I know we can do something special for Rose."

Jane reached over and patted Samuel's hand. "You and Rose have always been good to everyone in town, helping young people with 4-H and the fair, opening your farm every Christmas for your wonderful living nativity. This is a chance for us to give a little bit back to you."

"Jane's right," Alice said. "We'll make this a very happy occasion for both of you."

"I think we have a good start, Samuel," Louise said. "Oh, one more thing: Rose should have a special dress. If you'd like, I'll check at the dress shop to see if Nellie has something. Otherwise, we could ask Sylvia Songer to make a dress."

"Go ahead and do what you think best. You know better than I do what she'd like. I think it should be something blue. That's Rose's favorite color."

The color of Samuel's eyes, Louise thought. "I'll be happy to. And you should think about what you want to say to Rose. It can be something personal, or you could do the traditional wedding vows. You could ask Pastor Thompson to help you with that."

"Good idea." Samuel seemed relieved that he could leave all the details to the sisters and all he had to do was talk to the pastor, another man. With that settled, Samuel picked up his spoon and enjoyed the cranberry-apple crisp as they continued to chat. Then he thanked them and stood. Reaching into his pocket, he took out several hundred-dollar bills, which he handed to Louise.

"This should get you started. I expect to cover all the expenses, so let me know how much more you need. I want Rose to have the best."

That said, he donned his hat, then left.

Louise looked at the money in her hand, five hundred dollars. That would give them a good start, but the anniversary surprise would cost much more. She would put together a budget for Samuel, to make sure that he understood and agreed.

She looked out the window to watch him drive away. Across the yard, she saw Ethel at her window. She would certainly want to know why Samuel Bellwood had visited the inn, an odd occurrence, for sure. If Ethel learned his mission, they wouldn't have to send out invitations. Everyone in town would know, including Rose Bellwood.

Chapter Three

The retreat committee sat around the large antique table in Florence Simpson's formal dining room. A hint of the lovely wood could be seen beneath the white lace tablecloth. Small salad bowls holding Waldorf salad on crisp lettuce leaves were at each place. The delicious scent of hot chicken casserole filled the air, as Florence served liberal portions onto fine china luncheon plates.

"This looks wonderful, Florence," Sylvia Songer said and the rest murmured their agreement.

As soon as everyone was served, Florence carried the empty casserole dish to the kitchen.

When Florence left the room, Ethel began to speak.

"I am so pleased you could all come to this preliminary meeting," she said. "When I brought the retreat suggestion before the church board, they unanimously approved the plan. I proposed that we hold the retreat in conjunction with Valentine's Day. That only gives us six weeks, so we need to get busy."

"Aunt Ethel," Louise said. "Don't you think we can wait until Florence rejoins us?"

"She was at the board meeting, so she already knows this part," Ethel said with a defensive air. "I thought we could save time by filling in everyone else on the basics."

Florence came back and sat down.

"Louise, would you ask the Lord to bless our time together?" Ethel asked.

"Certainly." She bowed her head. "Heavenly Father, we ask Your blessing that we may be productive and pleasing to You in all we do and say. Bless this meal and bless Florence and Ronald for their hospitality. In Jesus' name. Amen."

As everyone began eating, there were numerous exclamations about the food. Everyone wanted Florence's chicken recipe, and she graciously promised to pass it along.

"We should have a recipe exchange at the retreat," June Carter suggested.

"That's a great idea," Sylvia said. "You can give us your recipe for blackberry pie."

June laughed. "Not on your life. No one would come to the Coffee Shop for my pie if I did that."

"We could open the retreat with a potluck, and everyone could share her recipe for the dish she brings," Patsy Ley said. "That way, the women could copy the recipes they like. I'll organize that if you'd like."

"Ladies, let's get back to the purpose of this meeting," Ethel said. She reached down to the tote bag next to her chair and pulled out a notebook. "Patsy, you are in charge of the potluck and recipe exchange. Now I have a list of other details we must discuss. First the dates. Valentine's Day falls on a Tuesday. I suggest we hold the retreat the following Friday night, all day Saturday, Saturday night, then end with breakfast on Sunday morning. That way we can still get to church."

"A lot of people will be celebrating Valentine's Day that weekend, since the holiday falls during the week," Louise said. "Perhaps we should consider waiting until March, when nothing else is happening." Her argument sounded weak, even to her own ears. She tried to think of a better reason.

"If we want to include younger women, to give them a

break and some encouragement, I think we should limit the retreat to two days," June said. "Husbands might be willing to watch the children for one night, but two is stretching it. Besides, if you want to keep the February dates, the women might want to go out with their husbands Saturday night when they can find a babysitter. We could begin on Friday morning, say after school starts, and end on Saturday morning. That gives us time for a nice retreat and still allows for families or couples to spend time together."

Louise could have hugged June.

"Most husbands have a hard time knowing what to give their wives for Valentine's Day. We could suggest that they take over for their wives for that time as a gift," Sylvia said.

"All right," Ethel said. "We can advertise it that way. That brings us to the next important item. Where shall we hold the retreat?"

"We should stay close to town, so those who cannot stay overnight can still attend," June said.

"What about Rolling Hills Youth Camp?" Sylvia suggested. "Shelly Hackenbauer, the camp administrator, came into the store last week. She told me that since they added the winterized facilities last fall, they are trying to keep the camp booked year-round."

"The camp would be perfect," Louise said, and the others agreed.

"Sylvia, will you contact Shelly and see if we can reserve those days?" Ethel asked. At Sylvia's nod, she went on with her list. "Now we need to decide what kind of program we want."

"My niece is quite well-known as a retreat speaker," June said. "She talks about family relationships, which would be perfect to attract the younger women."

"What are her credentials?" Florence asked.

"Shannon is a family counselor with an inner-city counseling clinic in Chicago. She works with children and families, and gives seminars and workshops at churches and conferences. She has a Web site if you want to find out more about her."

"She sounds like an excellent choice," Ethel said. "Shall we go ahead and contact her?" she asked the group. When the committee agreed, she scribbled a few sentences on her notebook, then looked up. "That takes care of the dates, where to hold it, and the program. What else do we need?"

"We need some fun activities that will help the women get to know each other, and also something interesting to attract them. Perhaps a craft demonstration," Sylvia suggested.

"That sounds like your department," June said. "You give all kinds of craft classes at Sylvia's Buttons."

"I do, but many of the women have already taken my classes. They might want something else. Perhaps Jane could show them how to make jewelry or something. She is so talented."

Louise knew Jane couldn't take the time to do something at the retreat and put together Samuel's anniversary surprise for Rose, but she didn't want to give away that secret. At least not until the invitations had gone out. "I believe Jane will have her hands full. The holiday weekends are so busy."

"Yes, that's true," Ethel said. "We'll just have to come up with something else. Let's all think about that and see if we can have some suggestions at our next meeting. I think that covers it for today. June, please call me if your niece can speak, and Sylvia, let me know about the camp. When those things are settled, we can begin advertising." Ethel put away her notebook.

"Our next meeting will be at Grace Chapel Inn a week from today at noon."

"Well, we've accomplished quite a lot," Florence said. "I think we deserve some dessert."

Once again, the committee agreed.

Sunday afternoon Jane carved the corned beef that had cooked while they were in church and arranged the slices on a platter, which she slid into the warming oven with the bowl of red cabbage and onions. When the corn casserole was almost ready to come out of the oven, she heard Rev. Kenneth Thompson's baritone voice in the entry hall, then more voices. Alice poked her head into the kitchen.

"Our guests have arrived. May I help you?"

"Oh dear. I should have had this ready so I could introduce Kristin and Blair to everyone."

"I'll be happy to do that."

"Great. Thanks, Alice. I'm just about finished. Could you take out the tray of hors d'oeuvres while you're at it?"

A few minutes later, Jane carried a bowl of fried apples to the table. Louise had extended the table to its full length and covered it with a lemon-yellow tablecloth.

Alice helped Jane bring out the rest of dinner while Louise invited the guests to the table. Rose and Samuel Bellwood sat across from Kristin and Blair Casey, and Nia Komonos sat next to Kristin. They were already discussing the wonders of the Internet. Kristin designed and maintained Web sites for several large organizations; Nia, the town's librarian, did extensive research on the Internet.

Jane set the platter of meat on the table, then sat down at the head. She asked Rev. Thompson to say a blessing.

He bowed his head. "We offer thanksgiving and praise for Your provisions, Lord. Bless this meal and the sweet fellowship of friends. In Jesus' name. Amen."

He looked up and said, "I feel especially blessed today. Corned beef is a favorite of mine, and I haven't had any for months."

As Jane passed him the platter to start the food around,

Samuel Bellwood said to Blair, "Jane tells me you have a lot of experience with large animals."

"I grew up on a dairy farm down south. We also kept horses and raised hogs and sheep several years. I worked for the local vet through high school and summers during college and vet school. He taught me a great deal." Blair grinned. "I'm probably more comfortable around animals than people."

Kristin looked at Blair with a rueful smile. "Unfortunately, that's close to being true. After he graduated from UGA veterinary college, Blair worked at an animal clinic in Atlanta not far from my parents' house. That's where I met him. I took my cairn terrier to the clinic, and Blair examined her." Kristin's smile faded. "She was really old and had cancer." Kristin gave her husband a look of grateful adoration. "Blair was so gentle with her. When she died, I think he was as upset as I was." She turned to them and smiled. "That's why I fell in love with him. But Blair hated the city. We moved to Acorn Hill so we could live in a small town where he could start a veterinary clinic."

"Did you grow up in Atlanta, Kristin?" Rose asked.

"Yes. I'm a city girl. My grandma lived in the country, or at least I always thought it was the country. I guess it was more like suburbs. It was nothing like this. And I've never lived in a cold climate before," she said with a little shake of her head, making her shiny black hair shimmy and cascade over her shoulders. "I ordered sweaters and a wool coat through a catalog, figuring I just needed to add a layer of clothes to be comfortable, but the wind here cuts right through them. I don't know how y'all stand it."

Jane felt a pang of compassion for the lovely young woman. "I lived in San Francisco for several years, so I understand the trauma of moving to a small town. You are experiencing culture shock along with the weather changes."

"That's true," Nia agreed. "I wanted to live in a small

town, but I didn't realize how much different it would be. I think it helps that I'm on a mission. I plan to turn Acorn Hill's library into one of the best in the state, so I have plenty to keep me busy. And I do a lot of genealogy research. That takes up many hours each week. Do you have a hobby?"

"Not really. I've thought about taking up knitting or crocheting, and I want to experiment more with cooking."

"Rose teaches knitting and crocheting at Sylvia's Buttons. You'll have to join one of her classes. She makes gorgeous sweaters from the wool of the merino sheep they raise," Nia said.

"Really?" Kristin turned toward Rose. "Do you sell your sweaters?"

Rose glanced at Samuel, then said, "Sometimes. The farm takes up too much of my time. I make sweaters for gifts and for the grandkids." Rose pushed her brown hair behind her ear. "Why don't you come to one of my classes and I'll teach you to make your own?"

"Are you starting a new class?" Jane asked. "Perhaps I'll come too. My crocheting needs a lot of help."

"You have so many talents, I don't know how you find time to do all you do," Nia said, then turned to Kristin. "You should see the amazing jewelry Jane makes."

"Really?" Kristin turned her wide-eyed gaze to Jane. "I admire anyone who can make things. I don't have any talent."

"Now, sweetheart, that's not true," Blair said, clasping his wife's hand. "You do amazing things with the computer."

"Anyone who can create Web sites and graphic art has a lot of talent," Jane said. "I bet you'll discover you have many other talents as well."

"I hope so. I hate to admit to y'all, but I've been really bored lately."

"That's partly the time of year. After the holidays, we start thinking about spring, but it takes its time getting here," Alice said. "Did you hear that the ladies of Grace Chapel are planning a retreat for all the women in Acorn Hill? That'll help give us a break from the winter doldrums. We'd love to have you come, Kristin. You, too, Nia."

"It's going to be delightful," Ethel piped in. She had been talking with Lloyd and Rev. Thompson, but she had the ability to tune in to several conversations at one time. "We are planning a potluck and recipe exchange and a craft time."

"Sounds like fun. I'd love to come if I can," Nia said.

"You can make this corn casserole, Jane, and share the recipe with all of us," Ethel said.

"Great idea," Lloyd said.

Jane said, "I'd sure be happy to share it."

When everyone had finished, Jane and Alice cleared the table and brought in dessert. Blair and Samuel were leaning forward, deep in discussion about the digestibility and the caloric and mineral content of various sheep feeds. Kristin, Nia and Rev. Thompson were discussing the differences between city and country living. Ethel was leaning back, talking behind Samuel to Rose, telling her all about the retreat plans. As Jane placed a spice cake on the table, she heard Rose promise to help with the retreat preparations in any way she could.

Chapter Four

The last inn guests checked out at eleven o'clock Monday morning. Louise glanced at her watch, then picked up the telephone and dialed the number for Sylvia's Buttons.

"Hello, Sylvia, it's Louise Smith. I'm sorry to ask this on such short notice, but I must talk to you. Would you have time to get together during your lunch hour?"

"Yes, certainly. Shall we meet at the Coffee Shop?"

"This is something that I'd like to keep private. Could you come to the inn? Jane made a pot of soup."

"Now you've whetted my curiosity and my appetite. I'll be there in an hour."

"Thank you. And please use the front door." Louise said good-bye and hung up the receiver. She knew her last comment sounded mysterious, but she didn't want Ethel to see Sylvia arrive and decide to join them.

Louise went upstairs to help her sisters with the guest rooms.

"Sylvia is coming for lunch," she told them. "I hope she'll agree to make Rose's dress."

"Nellie didn't have anything?" Jane asked.

"Nothing suitable in blue, and the manufacturers are working on their spring and summer lines now, so she couldn't order anything."

"I hope Sylvia can do it," Alice said. "There's not much time."

"I'm finished here," Jane said as she coiled the cord of the vacuum cleaner. "I'll go make corn bread to go with the soup."

"I'm sorry to put an extra burden on you today, but I didn't want to talk to Sylvia in a public place."

"Not a problem, Louie. Now you owe me one."

Louise raised an eyebrow. She tried to frown, but her smile spoiled it. "You're in on this scheme, too, but I'll concede. With all you do around here, I owe you more than one favor."

"I don't do any more than you and Alice, but I'm not about to turn down an IOU, so I'll just get going while I'm ahead." She put the vacuum away and bounced her way down the stairs. Louise watched her go and shook her head.

"Where does she get all that energy?"

Alice laughed. "She's fifteen years younger than you are."

Louise sighed. "Yes, and she always will be."

"As I recall, you were very energetic at her age, and you still keep an active schedule. Jane just bounces more than you do."

Louise laughed. "You're right. I never was the bouncy type. So what can I help you with?"

"Not a thing. We're finished up here. I'll help you set the table."

"Let's eat in the kitchen," Louise said. The kitchen was cheery and more casual.

The heat from the simmering soup had fogged the windows, making the kitchen even more intimate. The corn bread was baking in the oven while Louise and Alice set the table.

Sylvia arrived right on time, tapping on the front door before entering. Louise went to greet her. Sylvia's cheeks were red.

"Did you walk? You look like you're freezing. Let me take your coat and hat."

Sylvia slipped off her fleece-lined coat and knit hat and handed them to Louise. She removed gloves and rubbed her hands together. *"Brrr.* It's nippy out there."

"Nippy? That's an understatement. Come to the kitchen. It's warmer there."

"Hi, ladies. Yum. What kind of soup? It smells delicious," Sylvia declared as she entered the kitchen.

"It's navy bean and ham," Jane said. "I added a touch of maple sugar, which gives it that wonderful smell."

Sylvia handed Jane a white paper bag. "I picked these up at the Good Apple Bakery. They're peach turnovers, fresh out of the oven. Clarissa said to say hi."

"Wonderful. I didn't make dessert." Jane placed the turnovers in the warming oven.

When the soup was dished up and Louise had asked a blessing on their meal, she wasted no time satisfying Sylvia's obvious curiosity.

"I have a favor to ask of you, on behalf of Samuel Bellwood," Louise told Sylvia.

Sylvia's forehead wrinkled in a perplexed way. "What does Samuel want?"

"He wants you to make a dress for Rose."

Sylvia's eyes widened knowingly. *"Ahhh.* For their anniversary, right?"

"Well yes, but how did you . . ." Louise asked.

"Rose is teaching classes for me and selling her sweaters through the shop so she can surprise Samuel on their anniversary. It is their fortieth, you know."

"What is she planning?"

"She's saving for a second honeymoon. She's been planning this for months. She already made reservations and paid for half of the trip."

"Oh dear. That could interfere with Samuel's surprise," Alice said.

"What surprise? He isn't planning a trip, too, is he?"

"No. He wants to have a ceremony to renew their wedding vows," Louise said. "That is why he wants a special dress, but he doesn't want Rose to know about it. He wants to surprise her."

Jane laughed. "This is getting really interesting."

Louise raised one eyebrow. "It is getting really complicated. The women's retreat is planned for the same weekend. Do you know when Rose scheduled her trip?"

"The same weekend. Rose told me she got a better deal by waiting until after Valentine's Day," Sylvia said.

"Oh no," Louise said with a groan.

"There must be a way we can make all of these events work together," Sylvia said. "They'll spend Saturday night at a hotel in Philadelphia and fly to Hawaii the next day. They don't have to leave for Philadelphia until late afternoon, so the ceremony could be earlier in the day. But what about the retreat? Is that why you tried to get it moved to March, Louise?"

"Goodness. I hope I didn't give anything away."

"No. You didn't, though I didn't quite follow your logic for the change," Sylvia said with a laugh. "Will this be a small affair or a social event?"

"Samuel wants to invite all of their friends and relatives," Alice said.

"I see," Sylvia said. "This will take careful timing."

"Indeed it will," Louise said. "We're helping coordinate everything, and Jane's catering the reception."

"This is so exciting!" Jane said. "It's just the thing to drive the winter blues away."

"Speaking of blue. Samuel wants Rose's dress to be blue. Can you make it, Sylvia? I know there isn't much time,"

Louise said. "I checked with Nellie, but she didn't have anything appropriate."

"Rose has helped me so many times with classes, and the Bellwoods do so much for everyone, I'd love to make a dress for her. Tell Samuel that I'll only charge him for materials. I'll look through my pattern books and find some possible styles. Should I show them to Samuel and let him pick the dress?"

"I think he would rather let us choose. He seemed happy to put all the details in our hands, didn't he?" Louise said.

Alice chuckled. "That's the impression I got."

"Me too," Jane said as she got up. She put the warmed peach turnovers on a platter and carried them to the table. "Oh, by the way, Kristin Casey and I are going to sign up for Rose's next crocheting class."

"Are you sure you want to take that class? Rose is teaching how to make layettes. Maybe you and Kristin would rather take a later class, when she teaches how to make a shawl."

Jane laughed. "I want to take *this* class, so I can be in the thick of things. I have a feeling it's going to get very fascinating as Valentine's Day gets closer. I'll just have to donate my class project to the church nursery. But I'll check with Kristin."

When Jane rang Kristin's doorbell for the third time the next morning, she berated herself for not calling first. It appeared that Kristin was not at home. Jane looked for a place to leave the apple kuchen she'd brought as a gift. She didn't want to leave it on the porch where animals could get into it.

Jane walked around the side of the house toward the back door. As she passed a window, she noticed a light on inside. She saw a movement, then a face appeared in the window. It was Kristin. She opened the window.

"Jane! Gracious, I didn't hear you. Come to the kitchen door."

When Kristin opened the back door, Jane saw that the pretty young woman was wearing an oversized flannel bathrobe and bulky socks on her unshod feet.

"I'm sorry. Did I wake you?"

Kristin looked startled, then looked down at her apparel. She laughed, but Jane could see her embarrassment. She held the door wide open for Jane to come inside. "I wasn't expecting anyone to see me this way. My mama would have a fit. 'A lady always dresses as if she is expecting company,' she used to say." Kristin's drawl thickened as she imitated her mother. "Mama wouldn't come to the kitchen to make breakfast until she had on a dress and makeup. If y'all wait just a minute, I'll get some clothes on."

"Don't change on my account," Jane said. "We aren't formal around here. I just wanted to say hi and bring you something." She held out the kuchen.

"Oh wow, how nice. Thanks. Please sit down. You're my first visitor." She glanced at the clock. "Good grief, I didn't realize it was so late. I got up early and started working and time just got away from me. I do that sometimes."

"I'm interrupting your work. I should have called."

"No, really, I'm glad you're here." Kristin ran a hand through her hair. "Wait here. I'll be right back." She turned and whisked out of the room, leaving Jane standing in the kitchen.

Jane looked around. The Caseys had rented an old farmhouse just outside town. Blair was excited to find a house with a barn and shop building where he could set up his veterinary practice. The kitchen needed upgrading. The stove enamel had deep scratches and permanent stains. The black backing showed in spots through the faded green linoleum. The Formica countertops had knife cuts and chips from years of use. As a chef, Jane noticed the deficiencies, but still she approved of Kristin's decorating. Bright floral curtains hung over the windows. The walls were freshly painted lime green and the cabinets were painted light yellow, making the room cheery.

Kristin returned a short time later, wearing jeans and a flowered shirt.

"Much better," she said. "Would you like a cup of coffee?"

"If you have it already made."

"This stuff is mud. It won't take a minute." She poured out the dregs of a pot and filled the carafe with cold water.

"I really apologize for dropping in on you like this. My sisters tell me I'm too impulsive."

Kristin started the coffeepot and turned to Jane. "I'm glad you came. I . . ." She looked down. "It gets pretty lonely out here, since I work at home, I mean." She sat down across from Jane. She looked uncomfortable.

"I can't imagine what it must be like to make so many changes all at once," Jane said. "Moving away from your family, getting settled in a house, trying to start a business . . . I know it was hard enough for me when I returned to Acorn Hill, and I was moving back to family. I already knew most of the people in town, but I still felt like the stranger."

Kristin looked up. "That's just how I feel, like I don't belong. And I miss my mother terribly."

Jane suspected she might be about the same age as Kristin's mother, a thought that gave her a bit of a start. "I imagine your mother feels the same way."

Kristin's eyes filled with tears. She sniffled. "She does. She says she'd come visit if she could, but my daddy had an accident and he can't get around very easily. She can't leave him right now. Long distance gets expensive. Besides, I need to keep the phone line clear for veterinary calls, so I can't call her all the time."

Kristin looked down. "I keep in touch by e-mail, and that helps. We e-mail several times a day. I'm on the computer anyways. But it's not the same."

"I suppose not. You can run your Web-design business from here?"

"I can now that we got a satellite dish. But work doesn't keep me as busy as I'd like." She laughed nervously. "I didn't realize how long the days could be. With Blair gone most of the time trying to build his practice, it gets pretty lonesome out here."

Jane felt sorry for this young woman who was so hungry for a friend.

Kristin's brow furrowed. "I guess I've been pretty sheltered. I went away to college but lived with my aunt and uncle off campus. I was living with my folks when I met Blair. I'd moved back home until I could get established. That never happened. We got married and had an apartment a mile from my parents' home. Then we moved up here. I want to fit in, Jane, but I don't know what to do."

"Actually, I came to tell you about Rose Bellwood's class. You said you were interested in learning to crochet."

"Yes, I want to take it. When does it start?"

"Friday morning, but Sylvia told me it is a class to make baby things, like blankets and booties."

Kristin's eyes lit up. "I'd love to make a baby blanket. I'm hoping . . . we want to start a family. That was one of the reasons we decided to move to Acorn Hill. It seems like the perfect place to raise children."

"You're right about that. I loved growing up here, and it hasn't changed much."

Kristin got up to fix a tray with the coffee and a plate with slices of the apple kuchen. She brought it to the table and sat down. She took a bite of the sweet bread.

"This is delicious! You're so talented. Everything was so good on Sunday, and y'all were so sweet to introduce us to your friends."

"They enjoyed meeting you and Blair."

"I was wondering—I don't want to be a pest—but could I come watch you cook sometime? I really want to learn. I don't want you to go to any trouble. I'd just watch and take notes. Or maybe I could help you." She looked flustered. "I mean if it wouldn't be too much trouble."

Jane reached over and put her hand on Kristin's. "I'd be delighted to have you come cook with me. In fact, I'll probably need some help. It's a big secret, but I'm going to be catering a reception for Samuel and Rose's anniversary in February. Perhaps you could help me and learn a few things in the process."

"Really? I'd love to."

"I usually take at least one afternoon a week to experiment with new recipes. If you'd like to come over after lunch on Thursday, we can spend a couple of hours baking."

"Super! I can't wait to tell my mom. She's been worried about me. She thinks we should move back home and Blair should go to work for the veterinary hospital there. They offered him a job, but he really wants to have his own practice. He says I just need to get out more and find things to do. I suppose he's right. If I'm going to be a mother, I need to learn to stand on my own two feet."

"You're going to do just fine." Jane stood and carried her empty coffee mug and plate to the sink. "I have to get back, but I'll see you Thursday afternoon."

"I can't wait!" Kristen said as she led Jane to the front door.

Jane noticed the furnishings looked secondhand, and no two pieces or styles matched, but Kristin had done a great job of arranging the eclectic mix in the popular shabby-chic style. Blair had been right when he said Kristin had artistic talent. Jane intended to help Kristin develop her other talents. She looked forward to watching her young friend blossom as winter turned to springtime.

Chapter Five

As Alice hung up the telephone, hesitant piano notes came from the parlor. One of Louise's students was struggling with a simplified version of a classical piece. Alice wasn't sure what the girl was playing, but she needed a lot of work before the spring recital in May.

A student's first year was often painful for Louise, but through her unfailing patience and her excellent teaching methods, she had developed some very fine pianists.

Heading for the kitchen, Alice debated whether to share the results of her phone conversation with Jane now or wait until Louise finished. She glanced at her watch. Ten minutes of the lesson were left.

The tart smell of fresh sliced apples and cinnamon greeted her as she entered the kitchen. Jane and Kristin were leaning over the table rolling out piecrusts. Alice remembered the day Jane tried to teach her the secret of perfect piecrusts. She had shown Alice how to roll the dough between two sheets of plastic cut from kitchen trash bags. "The trick to tender, flaky piecrust," she'd said, "is to roll out the dough very thin without handling it a lot." When Alice had tried to flip the plastic bags to turn over the rolled dough, she'd strewn lumps of crust all over Jane.

Jane looked up and saw Alice watching them. "We're almost finished here," Jane said. "I had Kristin call and invite Blair for dinner. We've made enough food for an army."

"Hi, Miss Howard," Kristin said. The young woman's dark hair was curled in wisps all around the headband that was meant to keep it out of the way. She had a dusting of flour on her nose, which wrinkled as she smiled.

"Please call me Alice. It smells wonderful in here. What have you been cooking?"

"Jane taught me how to make meat loaf. Now she's teaching me to make piecrust. I never knew there were so many tricks to cooking."

Jane laughed. "Kristin has already mastered things that took me months of practice."

Kristin blushed. Alice thought she was one of the prettiest girls she'd ever seen.

"I'm really clumsy," Kristin said, "but Jane's a great teacher."

"That she is. I thought I'd make a cup of tea, if I won't be in your way."

"Why don't you make a pot? We'll have these in the oven by the time the water boils, and we'll be ready for a break." She turned back to Kristin. "Now remove the top plastic and lift your dough from the bottom, with the plastic bag that is still attached, like this." She demonstrated, lifting the dough and turning it into the pie pan.

Kristin followed Jane's instructions. Her dough crumbled a bit as she placed it in the pan. "Oh no. It's falling apart."

"No problem. It crumbles because it is short, and that's good. It will be light and flaky. Just pat it together with a little water like this." She demonstrated. "There. See? Now sprinkle a little sugar on the bottom. That keeps the filling from making the bottom crust soggy. Now, put in the filling and top with the other crust."

They heaped pie filling into the pan and added the top

crust. Jane showed Kristin how to crimp the edges around the pie. Jane's edge looked perfectly uniform, while Kristin's looked uneven, but Jane praised her student. They assembled another pie, then brushed the tops with milk and sprinkled sugar on them before putting them in the oven.

"You did a beautiful job with the pies," Alice said to Kristin. "I don't even try. My pièce de résistance is canned cherry pie filling over ice cream."

"Do I hear talk of dessert?" Louise said, entering the kitchen. "Apple pie, I presume? It smells heavenly."

"Jane has been giving me a cooking lesson," Kristin said.

"Tea's ready." Alice brought the teapot to the table that Jane had just wiped clean. Kristin carried the cups.

"Good. I could use a cup," Louise said. "I'm beginning to despair of my last student learning the basics. I'm thinking of recommending that she try the cymbals."

Alice laughed and handed Louise a cup. "I heard her murdering something. But you've done wonders with worse students."

"I love to hear you play in church, Mrs. Smith. You make the hymns come alive."

"Thank you, Kristin. And please call me Louise."

"All right. Y'all are so kind. I really enjoyed Sunday afternoon and today." She took a sip of tea. "I had been feeling so lonely. Now I'm excited to start the crochet class tomorrow, thanks to you."

"Speaking of excitement, I have some to share," Alice said. "I just spoke with Samantha Bellwood." She turned to Kristin to explain. "You see, Kristin, the Bellwoods have an anniversary on Valentine's Day—"

"I told Kristin about it," Jane said. "She's going to help me with the cooking."

Alice glanced at Jane, at first surprised that she would ask a novice to help her. Then Alice smiled. Jane was the perfect person to help this young woman settle in. "Wonderful.

The Bellwoods' daughter Samantha is away at college, so she's delighted we're going to help her dad with the arrangements. She is going to send a list of names and addresses for all their family members to your e-mail, Jane. Then we can send out the invitations. Samantha didn't really know whom in town to invite. She promised to list those she could think of and asked us to add anyone else we feel should be invited."

"Do you need any help? I could design the invitations on my computer if you'd like." Kristin said.

"I was thinking of something simple," Alice said.

"I can make whatever you want, and I purchase ink and paper in bulk, so it wouldn't cost much."

"Samuel is paying all the expenses, but we couldn't ask you to donate your professional talents," Louise said.

"Of course you can. I really want to help. Besides, Jane is donating her time to teach me to cook."

"We'd love to have you help us with the invitations," Jane said. "Samantha can come home for the ceremony, I hope."

"They are having a Valentine's dance at school, and she already promised to go, but it's on Friday night, so she will leave right afterward."

Louise plunked down her teacup. "She shouldn't drive alone from Philadelphia at night. Her mother would have a fit."

"She's not," Alice said. "One of her brothers is going to bring her."

"Good. That reminds me. We must see if the boys want to be involved in the plans," Louise said.

"The Bellwoods have four sons as well as a daughter," Jane explained to Kristin. "The boys are all grown. Caleb and Ben have families of their own. Travis and Joshua aren't married. They all live in the area, but they are awfully busy with their own farms and jobs. We can ask, but we shouldn't put them on the spot."

"As a matter of fact, Samantha talked to Caleb's wife Gretchen, and they want to make an anniversary quilt for Samuel and Rose. They want friends to make quilt squares, and Gretchen will put them together as a gift."

"But won't that be difficult?" Jane asked. "Not everyone knows how to quilt. Do they want a certain pattern?"

"Samantha described what they want. People will be given cloth squares. They can embroider the squares or use fabric paint. They can write congratulatory messages or draw a representation of some favorite memory of the Bellwoods."

Kristin sat up straight. "If anyone has a favorite photo of them, like their wedding picture, I can transfer it to a cloth square."

Louise frowned. "I can't imagine a picture on a quilt."

"I think that's a terrific idea! Perhaps Gretchen might want to put the wedding picture in the middle of the quilt," Jane said. "They do it on cakes now, and I've seen it done on T-shirts, but I never thought about a quilt."

"Goodness, technology is amazing," Alice said.

Louise shook her head. "This is all beyond me. I'll have to see it to understand it."

Seven women crowded into the back corner of Sylvia's Buttons, where folding chairs were set up for Rose's crochet class. Jane and Kristin took seats in the front. Jane introduced Kristin to a couple of younger women from church who were about her age. Haley Gorman was obviously pregnant and due soon. Mila Babin was wearing a maternity smock, but that was the only sign that she was pregnant.

Betsy Long sat next to Kristin. Jane introduced them. Betsy was a friend of Hope Collins, who was a waitress at the Coffee Shop.

"My sister is having a baby," Betsy said. "A girl. It's her

fourth. The other three are boys, so she's very excited. I thought I'd give a try at making a layette."

"What a sweet idea," Kristin said. "By the way, that's a gorgeous sweater you have on."

"I bought it from Rose. She spun the yarn from the wool of their sheep." She stood and turned around so they could see the intricate pattern in the hand-knit, oatmeal-colored sweater.

"I hope she has some more," Kristin said. "I'd love to buy one."

"She has a whole table of them over there," Betsy said, pointing to the far wall. "And some more at Nellie's dress shop. I think she is taking orders too." Betsy leaned close and lowered her voice. "She's trying to raise money for a trip, you know, but it's supposed to be a secret. Something about a second honeymoon. I think that's so exciting."

Kristin glanced at Jane, who winked at her but said nothing.

At that moment, Sylvia clapped her hands to get the ladies' attention. "Most of you know Rose already," she said. "With her help, I know you are going to make wonderful layettes. I have all the supplies you'll need, and I'll be glad to help you select your materials. We carry Rose's fine and superfine homespun merino wool as well as synthetic yarns. And don't forget, we have some of her hand-knit sweaters and scarves for sale. I'll turn the class over to Rose now." Sylvia stepped aside and Rose took over.

"Thanks for the commercial, Sylvia." Rose passed out plastic bags. "Everyone take one," she said. "Inside is a pattern with instructions, an F-gauge crochet hook and bit of fine yarn. This is the yarn weight we'll be using for the blankets. We'll use a superfine yarn for the cap, booties and mittens. You'll need to purchase the yarn you want. I didn't include that in your supplies, because everyone has a different preference. I make all my baby items out of merino wool, because it is very soft . . . and because I raise merino sheep," she said, grinning.

Everyone laughed at that.

"Now, take out the sample yarn and crochet hook. Does everyone know how to make a chain stitch?"

"I don't," Kristin said.

Rose came over to help Kristin.

"Does anyone else need help?" Sylvia asked.

The barely pregnant young woman raised her hand, and Sylvia went over to help her.

"Each of you will crochet a square. Start by chaining twenty single crochets, then we'll reverse to add a row," Rose instructed. "We want to end up with twenty-three rows."

Rose showed Kristin how to chain a row. Kristin's stitches were clumsy and her hook slipped off, so she pulled it out and started over.

When they all had their chains, Rose showed them how to reverse and add a row.

Kristen inserted the hook into a stitch and pulled it through. She ended up with a large loop. "That's good," Rose said. "Now pull it snug, then make the next stitch."

Kristin managed eight stitches of varying tightness, then she dropped a stitch and pulled several loose. "My fingers feel like wood sticks," she said to Jane.

Rose came back over and bent to look at Kristin's work.

"For a first try, you're doing just fine. And the beauty of crochet is that there's only one stitch to lose, and you can always pick it up. Here. Let me help you." Rose took the yarn and crochet hook from Kristin and picked up the dropped stitches for her, then handed it back. "There. After we've checked your gauge size, you can take it apart and use it to practice. You'll feel comfortable with it in no time." Rose left to help some of the others.

Kristin let out a short laugh. "I sure hope Rose is right. At this rate, I might finish this project by the time I have a teenager."

"I know this doesn't feel natural to you yet, but you'll be whipping out rows in no time," Jane said, realizing suddenly how out-of-place Kristin must feel. She knew that Kristin would make her way, adjust to her new home and make friends. But until that happened she needed a mentor. Jane said a silent prayer for her young friend and one for herself, that she would do the things that would encourage Kristin. Then she looked over and smiled. "Look at you! Your square is nearly finished. And it looks great."

Kristin laughed. "It looks . . . lopsided. But I think I have the hang of it."

Rose came back. "Let's see what you've got."

Jane scrambled to finish her square while Rose looked at Kristin's. "The first part is tight, which is very common when you are learning," Rose said, "but the last half looks good. I think this is the right gauge for you. Take this home and practice with the square before you begin the blanket, and you'll do fine."

Jane finished her last stitch and handed it to Rose.

"Looks good. Stick with this size, unless you want a looser blanket."

"I'll use this one. Kristin and I are going to look at your sweaters too. Betsy's is beautiful."

"Thank you. I try to make each one slightly different, so you won't find one just like hers, but I'm pleased with the way they came out."

"I'm glad you're finally selling some of your work. You could sell your quilts too."

"Actually, I have a few for sale. Since Samantha went away to college, I have a little more free time. And I have an incentive. I'm saving for a special occasion."

"Betsy told us. I hope you don't mind," Jane said.

"Oh no. As long as Samuel doesn't find out. At least not until our anniversary."

"Have you considered selling your sweaters and quilts over the Internet?" Kristin asked. "I design and manage Web sites. I would love to help you."

"Bless your heart. I can't really afford to advertise."

"I wouldn't charge you. It wouldn't take much time. If you decide to go into business, then we could work something out, but right now things are slow and I'd be happy to have something to do," Kristin said.

"You make it sound like I'd be doing you a favor. I know better than that," Rose said, "but I'd love to have your help. I'll trade you services. I'll give you some of my merino wool for your layette. I'll show you what I have after class and you can pick."

"Thank you!" Kristin said. She looked so excited that Jane wondered if perhaps Rose was the one to mentor Kristin. But she knew Rose was busy, and it wouldn't hurt Kristin to have two mentors. After all, being a mentor really meant being a friend, and Jane certainly could do that.

Chapter Six

It was eleven o'clock when Jane got home from the crocheting class. Louise had set the table for the retreat committee's lunch and was standing at the kitchen counter, preparing a green salad. Jane pulled off her wool scarf and coat, hanging them on a hook by the door. She set her bag of yarn in the corner.

"I'm ready for this cold to go away."

"It is unusually cold, isn't it?" Louise said. "I just put your penne, chicken and pancetta dish in the oven. I'm sure it will be a hit today."

"Thanks for helping. I know you're busy with the ladies' meeting and guests checking in."

"The guests won't arrive until later, and I'm happy to help. How was the class?"

"Good. I'm glad I went. I think Kristin and I are going to become good friends, but I had an odd revelation."

Louise wiped her hands on a towel and turned to her sister. "Really? What kind of revelation?"

"Kristin is young enough to be my daughter. Suddenly I saw myself as the older woman. You know, the mature woman who is supposed to help the younger woman."

Louise chuckled. "What a daunting realization. I catch a glimpse of that every so often with Cynthia. We have become such good friends that I don't always think of her as my daughter. Then she'll ask for advice or say something that triggers a memory and I suddenly feel old. However, I doubt Kristin thinks of you as older. You view life through youthful eyes. Younger women relate to you. I've noticed that with our guests. Kristin needs a friend, and I think you fit the bill perfectly."

Jane laughed. "Thank you, Louise. I feel much younger already." She hugged Louise before she put on her apron and got to work, knife in hand, preparing a loaf of crusty Italian bread for garlic toast.

Watching her, Louise marveled at the transformation. Her little sister suddenly became the serious professional chef. Louise shook her head. The various elements that made up Jane Howard were as complex as a piano concerto, and just as lovely. The Lord had lavished talents and a love for people upon Jane. Kristin was about to be blessed.

Ethel entered the kitchen from outside. "When is this cold going to end?" she said. She removed her heavy wool coat and hung it on a hook next to Jane's coat. "I hope no one else has arrived yet."

"No. You're the first," Louise said.

"Good. I want to check the table to make sure everything is perfect." She bustled out of the kitchen.

"Oh boy. I'm glad it's you and not me taking part in this committee," Jane said.

"Yes, well I'm counting on your lunch to put everyone in a good mood." Louise looked toward the dining room. "I hear voices. They're early, but I'd better go join them. Let me know when you're ready to serve. I'll come help you."

Jane chuckled and nodded as Louise went through to the dining room.

Sylvia, Florence and Ethel were standing in the entry hall, talking. As Louise approached, they turned toward her.

"Louise, what do you know about the Bellwoods' anniversary plans?" Ethel asked.

Ethel's displeased frown and accusing gaze warned Louise to weigh her answer. From Florence's smug expression and Sylvia's look of dismay, it appeared Florence had told Ethel something about Rose and Samuel's surprises. Louise raised one eyebrow.

"What about the Bellwoods' anniversary?" Louise asked.

Ethel shot a sharp glare at Florence. "Florence says they are planning a Valentine's celebration for their anniversary. Is that why you liked the idea of ending the retreat early?"

"I'm sure Rose and Samuel are not the only ones who wish to celebrate Valentine's Day on the weekend," Louise said. "I was under the impression that we wanted to include the younger women in the community in our retreat. Some of them will want to celebrate with their husbands on the weekend."

"I want to know about Rose and Samuel. Are they planning a big party?"

Louise looked to Sylvia for help, but she pursed her lips and shook her head. No help there. Louise sighed. Ethel would find out when she received an invitation, and she knew enough to be curious. She would not be content until she unearthed every detail, so she might as well know the whole story now. Unfortunately, Florence and Ethel thrived on discovering and revealing every tidbit of local news. Louise doubted either could keep a secret.

"The Bellwoods' anniversary is Valentine's Day. Samuel wants to *surprise* Rose with a celebration. I don't know what you've heard, Florence, but Samuel wants to honor Rose with a special celebration. They've done so much for everyone in Acorn Hill, they deserve to have a successful anniversary. Alice, Jane and I are helping him. You will receive an invitation soon. Please, *do not* tell anyone else about this. If Rose finds out, it'll spoil the surprise for both of them."

"Louise Smith, how dare you insinuate that I'd give away Samuel's surprise!" Ethel wore an injured expression. She raised her nose in the air. "*I'm* not like *some people* in this town." She glared at Florence.

"Ethel Buckley, you old hypocrite. You're just upset that I found out before you did," Florence said. She gave Ethel a haughty look and turned to Louise. "You can be sure if the story gets out that it will *not* come from *me*. I wouldn't wonder if your aunt spills the beans, though."

"You already *spilled the beans*," Ethel shot back. "And what's this about Rose also making secret plans? Florence is spreading that rumor too."

"Rose is also planning a surprise for Samuel. If you want to help, you could purchase one of her sweaters or her knit scarves. But this is *not* public knowledge. I know neither of you wants to spoil the Bellwoods' plans."

Ethel raised her chin. "My lips are sealed. Furthermore, I shall call Rose this afternoon and buy a sweater from her."

"So shall I," Florence said.

"Ladies," Sylvia said. "Don't call her. Samuel might answer the phone. I have a supply of Rose's sweaters at my store, and all of the proceeds go to Rose."

"You can expect me this afternoon," Ethel said, crossing her arms over her chest.

"I'll go directly from here to buy a sweater," Florence said, leveling her gaze at Ethel.

∽

Alice rubbed her gloved hands together. Her breath huffed out in a cloud that instantly froze into tiny ice crystals that seemed to hang suspended in the air. The wool ski hat kept her head warm, but her nose had gone numb. She stomped her feet as she and Vera Humbert hurried along Hill Street. It was Saturday, the best morning for Vera, a fifth-grade teacher, to walk during the school year.

"Let's stop for a cup of tea to warm up," Vera suggested. "I'll treat."

"You talked me into it," Alice said. She loved her walks with Vera, and they had braved the weather all winter, but this damp, frigid cold was more than Alice could handle for very long.

Vera opened the door to Good Apple Bakery, and they hurried inside and shut the door. A rush of warm air and sweet, rich smells enveloped them. The sound of clanging pans came from the back, but not a soul occupied the chairs and tables in the front. Alice and Vera removed their hats and gloves.

"Seems we're the only brave ones out this morning. Or perhaps we're the only ones foolish enough to go outdoors in this cold," Vera said.

Clarissa Cottrell, the bakery owner, came from the kitchen carrying a pan of hot caramel-pecan rolls. She moved a bit slower than usual. Alice guessed the cold weather was aggravating her arthritis.

Clarissa's eyes lit up when she saw them. "Good morning. I'm so glad to see you! I was beginning to think the town was deserted. Let me guess. You want two cups of tea. Or I have hot spiced cider and hot chocolate."

"I believe I'll have the cider for a change. And I bet those rolls just came out of the oven," Vera said.

"Sure did. Would you like one?"

"Yes, please, one for each of us," Vera said.

Alice smiled. "Well, I guess you just twisted my arm, but I'll stick with a cup of tea."

"Have a seat. I'll bring it to you in a moment." Clarissa disappeared in the kitchen and reappeared with a pot of tea for Alice and a mug of steaming cider for Vera. She next brought two warm rolls and set them down. Butter melted over the pecans and caramel frosting.

"I'd love to stay and chat, but I have bread in the oven. Make sure you warm up completely before you go back out in that weather. I heard on the radio that it might go as low as ten degrees today."

"No wonder we're freezing. Thanks, Clarissa," Vera said. She took a bite of the rich sweet roll. "*Mmm.* This makes it worth braving the cold."

Alice watched Clarissa disappear into the kitchen, then turned to Vera. "I'm glad no one else is here. I want your advice." Alice told Vera about the anniversary party and the plans for a quilt. "Samantha and Gretchen want me to ask people to make quilt squares. I can include that request on the invitations, but I'm not sure what to ask for. Since you're an expert quilter, I thought you could give me some advice."

"How many invitations are you sending out?"

"Close to one hundred."

"I'd guess more than half of them won't participate. You might get about forty squares."

"Kristin Casey suggested making a few squares out of photographs of the Bellwoods. She can scan the pictures onto her computer and print them onto cloth. We thought their wedding photo would be perfect for the center square."

"What a wonderful idea! So it'll be like a memory quilt."

"I suppose so. Have you made one before?"

"None like you're describing. I can't wait to see how it comes out. I'd love to help put it together."

"I'll let Gretchen know. I'm sure she'll be happy to have some help. Now, what do I ask for in the invitations?"

"If the center square will be their wedding picture, it'll probably be larger than the other squares, I imagine." Vera got a pen from the counter by the cash register and started sketching on a paper napkin.

"I've been trying to picture what this quilt will look like. I used a pattern for the little bit of quilting I've done, so all the squares were uniform," Alice said. "This won't be as structured." She took a sip of tea. "I'm worried that this could turn out to be quite a hodgepodge."

"Do you remember when Rose taught my class to make a quilt? The children each made a square and the class raffled it off to raise money for a needy family at Christmas."

"Oh yes, I remember. The quilt was beautiful. If this turns out half as nice, Rose will love it."

"Yes, she'll love it. In fact, I predict it will become a precious treasure, because it will be an expression of love."

"You're right. So how do we proceed?"

"Give everyone a fabric square, that way there'll be some uniformity. And offer suggestions about how to create a design. The quilt square should represent what the Bellwoods mean to the creators of the squares. They could embroider a design or a saying. They could appliqué something on the squares or draw a picture with fabric paints. The squares should be cut from two-hundred-count muslin. A twelve-inch square would be a good size."

The front door whooshed open, and the mailman came in. Clarissa came out front.

"Nasty day to be out, Norbert. Take a cup of hot cider with you."

"Thank you, Clarissa. Don't mind if I do. Would you have any of those peach turnovers today? I'm almost finished with my route, and it sure would taste good for my lunch."

Clarissa put two turnovers in a sack and handed them to

Norbert. When he tried to pay for them, she waved him away. "You're doing me a favor. There's no one here to eat them today."

"Thanks." He turned to Alice and Vera. "Good day, ladies. I hope you don't have far to go. It's beginning to blow out there." He hunched his shoulders and went back out. A cold blast of air swirled in before he pulled the door shut.

"Can I get you anything more?" Clarissa asked.

"No, thank you," Alice said.

"We're doing fine," Vera said, "but we're not quite ready to go out in that cold."

"Stay as long as you want. Just holler if you need anything. I'll be in the back. The pep club ordered donuts for the high school basketball game this afternoon. As soon as they pick them up, I'm closing and going home." Clarissa went back into the kitchen.

Alice said to Vera, "Where were we? Oh yes. The fabric. I'll see what Sylvia has that we can use."

"Have you talked to her about the project?"

"No. She is involved with another project for the Bellwoods' anniversary." Alice considered whether to tell Vera and decided the two surprises were practically public knowledge. Besides, Vera was the soul of discretion. "As you know, Samuel is planning a surprise for Rose, but Rose is also planning a surprise for Samuel, and the rest of us are getting involved in both surprises and trying to help them each keep their secrets. It's quite exciting."

"I heard that Rose is selling her hand-knit sweaters and scarves. She's never made things to sell before that I can remember. Is that part of it?"

"Yes. She is saving for a second honeymoon. I believe she has already made the reservations. They leave for Philadelphia the Saturday after Valentine's Day and fly to Hawaii the next day. Samuel won't discover the surprise until they leave for

Philadelphia." Alice grinned. "She said it'll be too late for him to back out then."

"I can't imagine Samuel going on a vacation willingly. Especially with a flock of pregnant ewes."

"Lambing season isn't until March, and I think one of their sons is going to stay at the farm while they're gone."

"So Sylvia is helping Rose sell her sweaters."

"That's not all. Sylvia is making a dress for Rose. Of course, that's a secret from Rose as well."

"Goodness. Isn't the anniversary celebration on the weekend of the women's retreat?"

"It is. So that's one more thing to work around. Louise is helping Samuel plan the event and is on the retreat committee. Jane is catering the reception and will help out with the retreat food."

Vera shook her head. "You and Jane and Louise always manage to get stuck in the middle of these things. Let me know how I can help. It sounds like you'll have your hands full."

The door flew open, and Lloyd Tynan came in.

"Alice, Vera," he said by way of greeting. "I see you had the good sense to get out of the cold. Ethel called me, concerned when you hadn't returned from your walk. And here you are, safe and warm."

"Have you been out looking for us?" Alice asked.

"Not exactly. I told her I would keep my eyes open. I was driving by and saw you through the window, so I stopped. May I give you ladies a ride home?"

Alice looked at Vera.

Vera nodded.

"Thank you, Lloyd. We've had enough cold for one day."

Vera took their empty plates and cups to the back, paid Clarissa and told her that they were leaving. Then she and Alice wrapped up in their coats, hats and gloves and followed Lloyd.

The short walk from the Good Apple Bakery to Lloyd's car assured Alice they had made the right choice. The brisk wind had turned the cold into a sharp knife that she felt through her jeans. As she climbed into the warmth of the back seat, she thanked God for friends like Lloyd Tynan and for her nosy but loving aunt Ethel.

Chapter Seven

Early Sunday evening, Jane and Alice were sitting in the living room reading. Cheery flames danced in the fireplace. The last weekend guests, grandparents of a Franklin High School student, had just left, having extended their checkout time so they could attend their grandson's choral program. The telephone rang as Louise filed the paperwork. Sylvia Songer had fabric samples and patterns for Rose's dress to show her, and Louise invited her to come over.

As soon as she hung up, Louise went to the kitchen to start water for tea. She arranged a plate of Jane's linzer cookies and shortbread and set it on the kitchen table, then went to the parlor.

"Sylvia is coming over with dress patterns," she told her sisters. "I put water on for tea."

Jane stretched. "Sitting here is so cozy and warm, I almost fell asleep." She put a bookmark in her book, set it on the table next to the couch and stood.

Wendell, the family's very spoiled gray tabby cat, was curled up in Alice's lap, purring contentedly. Alice laughed. "I must admit I've been nodding off. I read the last two pages three times, and I still couldn't tell you what it's about."

"It must be exciting," Jane said. "Wendell certainly is enjoying it."

Alice looked down. One of Wendell's ears twitched, but his purring continued uninterrupted. "I hate to disturb him. Perhaps he'll get up when Sylvia arrives."

Several minutes later, they heard a knock on the kitchen door. Wendell stretched his neck and cuddled closer to Alice. Louise hurried away to let Sylvia in, and Jane followed.

Sylvia came into the kitchen carrying two plastic bags. She set them on the counter and removed her scarf, hat, gloves and coat, then rubbed her hands together.

"Come sit at the table and warm up," Louise said.

The kettle whistled, and Jane filled the teapot with water.

Alice came into the kitchen. "Wendell didn't want to get off my lap, but I couldn't miss this."

She went to the sink and washed her hands, then joined the others. Sylvia laid several patterns on the table and a pile of fabrics in various shades of blue. Just then they heard a tap on the door as it opened to let in a blast of cold air.

"Yoo-hoo." Ethel Buckley came into the room. "It's freezing out there."

"Why did you come out in it then, Aunt Ethel?" Jane asked.

"Oh, I saw Sylvia arrive, so I brought this over to see if she could help me repair it." Ethel pulled a wrinkled dresser scarf out of her pocket and held it out. The lace edging on the old embroidered cloth was torn and frayed. "It belonged to my mother, you know."

What Louise knew was that Ethel couldn't resist finding out why Sylvia would visit them on Sunday evening, after dark, in inclement weather.

"I believe I can match this, Ethel. Bring it down to the store, and I'll look through my vintage trims."

"Yes, I'll come by tomorrow." Ethel turned to see the pattern covers. "What lovely dresses. Who are these for?" She looked at each of them. "These must be for a very special occasion." She gave Sylvia a questioning look.

Louise knew Ethel wouldn't be satisfied until she knew about the dress. She already knew about Samuel's surprise. "These are patterns for a dress for Rose," she said. "Sylvia's going to make it as part of Samuel's surprise for Rose. He wants blue. We must choose a style and fabric."

"Well, I can help you with that." Ethel sat at the table. She had taken Jane's chair.

Jane raised her eyes and shook her head. Louise shrugged. Jane carried the teapot to the table and got out an extra cup for Ethel. Then she pulled the counter stool over to the table and perched on it so she could see.

Louise poured the tea and passed the cookie plate. Ethel helped herself to one of each cookie. The others each took one. Then Sylvia passed the first pattern to Louise.

"I picked three different types of dresses. One tailored and two dressy," she said. "For the V-neck princess-style dress, I chose this acetate and spandex material." She handed Louise a shimmering, ice-blue fabric.

Louise fingered the cloth. Brocaded flowers gave it a rich texture and contrasted with the shimmer of the iridescent fabric. "Beautiful. Rose would love this one."

Louise passed it to Jane, who fingered it, then passed it to Alice, who looked at it and passed it to Ethel.

"The next pattern is also very dressy," Sylvia said, passing another pattern to Louise. "The bodice crosses like a wraparound that attaches to the skirt by a beaded cummerbund. The sleeves and overskirt would be this sheer silk georgette. The lining is satin." She handed Louise two pieces of material.

The sheer silk and shiny satin reminded Louise of a dress she'd worn when she'd performed a piano concerto during her college days. She had felt like a celebrity that night, and Eliot had called her beautiful.

"The bodice and waist would be trimmed with these clear crystal beads," Sylvia said.

Louise looked at the delicate beads and studied the picture. "This looks like a lot of work."

"It does have more detail than either of the others," Sylvia said. "The last pattern is a scoop-necked, sleeveless sheath with a peplum jacket. It's basically a classic suit, but the side-slits in the dress and the satin trim on the jacket make it dressy. And I found a wonderful merino wool that I thought would please Rose." She handed the pattern and a piece of baby-blue wool to Louise.

The fine wool felt as soft as a cloud. The color reminded Louise of a summer sky. The pattern showed a matching blue satin collar and piping around the jacket, satin-covered buttons, and a satin tie belt and bows around the jacket's flared cuffs.

"The first pattern is the dressiest. I vote for it," Jane said.

"I have no fashion sense," Alice said, "so I leave the choice to the rest of you. They're all very pretty."

"Yes, they are," Jane agreed. "And you did a wonderful job in picking the styles and fabrics, Sylvia."

Ethel cleared her throat. "If I may give a word of advice . . ." She waited until everyone looked at her. "I can tell you what Rose would prefer."

Louise looked at Ethel over the top of her glasses. "You can? How do you know?"

"Rose is a farmer. She's married to a farmer. She grew up on a farm. I was a farmer's wife." Ethel looked at them as if that settled it.

Louise mentally shook her head. She failed to see the logic in Ethel's thinking.

"So which one would Rose like, Aunt Ethel?" Jane asked.

"Why, the wool suit, of course. She raises sheep, after all. And the suit is practical. She might find an occasion to wear it again. Those other dresses would be lovely for a city girl, but not for out here in the country. Definitely the wool outfit." Ethel sat back and folded her arms.

"You have a good point," Alice said. "Rose would like something practical."

"But this is a very special occasion," Jane objected. "It isn't a time to be practical. The V-neck dress would look so pretty on her."

Louise looked at both patterns again, then reached for the material. She loved the ice-blue brocade, but it had a sophisticated look that didn't seem quite right for Rose. Samuel would like the suit. Rose would love the soft wool. The V-neck dress would be the simplest to make, but Ethel was right. The suit had Rose's name written all over it. She'd prefer it for the very reasons Ethel stated. "You're right, Aunt. Sylvia, will you have time to make the wool suit?"

"Yes, and I agree. I think the suit is the right choice. I'll make the dress and jacket in muslin first. I thought I'd tell Rose it's for an out-of-town customer who's her size and ask Rose to try it on for me."

"Wonderful. That's technically true. Rose does live outside of town, and she's one of your customers," Louise said.

Ethel stood. "Well, I must be getting home now. I'm glad I could help you girls decide on the dress. Good-bye." She took one more cookie, stuffed the dresser scarf back into her coat pocket, put on her coat, hat and gloves and went out the back door.

"Ethel's really getting into the spirit of this surprise, isn't she?" Sylvia said after she'd gone.

"Seems to be. I know she loves a good tidbit, but she loves romance even more, and this is a very romantic surprise," Jane said.

"That reminds me, we need to discuss the other surprise," Louise said.

"Oh, the quilt," Alice said. "Sylvia, I know you are busy with this dress, but we need your help on one more project. Rose's daughter-in-law Gretchen and Samantha came up with the idea to make a memory quilt for Samuel and Rose. They want people to make squares, and Gretchen will sew them into a quilt."

"Great idea, but that's a big project with only five weeks to put it together."

"Yes, it is. Vera suggested that we request the squares in the invitations, saying that we'll provide fabric squares and instruction sheets for everyone who wishes to participate. We were wondering if you have appropriate material in stock. Samantha suggested that people could embroider the squares, do appliqués or draw pictures with fabric pens."

"I have muslin, which works well in my beginner classes. I also have instruction sheets. I'll just make more copies," Sylvia said. "I have all kinds of pens and paints and liquid embroidery. It's silly for people to buy those things to make one quilt square, though. What if I set up an area where people can work on squares using my supplies? If they want to use appliqués or cut shapes out of remnants to iron on, they can buy those."

"Sylvia, you are so generous. Are you sure you have time for all that?"

"Maybe you and any other volunteers can come to the store and cut squares. That's the most time-consuming part of it."

"I'll help," Alice said.

"I'll help too," Jane said.

"Someone has to mind the inn," Louise said. "I would be happy to help if you care to bring the supplies here."

"Great idea," Jane said. "We'll have a cutting party. How about Tuesday afternoon?"

"I work at the hospital on Tuesday," Alice said.

"Then we'll wait until you get home. Four o'clock on Tuesday. All right?" Louise asked.

"Good. I'll make a pumpkin roll to go with our coffee."

"And tea," Alice said.

"In that case, I will come by after I close the store," Sylvia said.

∽

Thursday afternoon, when Kristin came to the inn for a cooking lesson, Jane noticed that she seemed unusually quiet. Jane was experimenting with a creamy spinach-and-turkey lasagna.

"The possibilities with leftover turkey are unlimited, but most people only think of turkey soup or hot turkey-and-gravy sandwiches. Sometimes I make a turkey-and-stuffing casserole, but this recipe gives turkey a completely different taste," Jane explained.

After she added lasagna noodles to a large pot of boiling water with a dash of olive oil and stirred gently to make sure they didn't stick together, she put several tablespoons of butter in a saucepan over a low flame.

"While the pasta cooks, we'll make white sauce. The trick to smooth sauce is constant stirring and adding the thickener and liquid gradually, until you achieve the desired consistency." She handed Kristin a wire whisk. "Stir the butter while I add flour."

Kristin soon had a thick paste in the pan. Jane began adding milk, a little at a time. "I try to balance my Alfredo sauce by using a combination of milk and half-and-half. It isn't quite as rich as sauces using cream, but it still has great taste and texture. Keep stirring. It will blend and thicken as you whisk it.

"That looks good. Now we add a mixture of cream cheese and fresh grated parmesan and asiago cheeses and our spices. I've used oregano, basil, Italian parsley, a dash of marjoram and nutmeg."

"That's a lot of spices. I just buy Italian spice in a jar."

Jane laughed. "Store-bought spices work fine, but I love to use fresh spices when I can. I grow most of these and freeze them or dry them myself. They usually hold their flavor through the winter."

"You only use them one winter? My mom had spices in her cupboard for years."

"Spices don't spoil, but they do lose some of their flavor and intensity. Now we're ready to drain the pasta and assemble our lasagna."

As they worked, Jane could still sense Kristin's underlying distress. She tried to cheer her up, telling her about some of her early experiments with cooking.

"I remember learning to make cream soups," Jane said. "I started with a chicken-broth base. Then I decided to create my own recipe using pumpkin with onion and apple cubes. I spiced it with curry. For cream, I used sour cream. Unfortunately, I mashed the cooked pumpkin when I should have pureed it. The soup tasted great, but the texture was, well, my husband called it slime soup. Unfortunately, he was right."

"How awful," Kristin said. "I probably would have given up cooking."

Jane grinned. "I admit I was discouraged, but I loved cooking. I love creating something beautiful and tasty. With other forms of art, people can take it or leave it, but everyone has to eat. My art may not last, but it is enjoyed."

"I never thought about cooking that way. My grandmother makes all kinds of desserts with pumpkin. Did you ever make pumpkin soup again?"

"As a matter of fact, I kept experimenting until I was satisfied with the results. It became a standard when I cooked for the Blue Fish Grille in San Francisco."

"That's cool."

They layered the pasta, grated mozzarella cheese, turkey

slices, and fresh spinach, basil and arugula leaves with the sauce as they talked. Jane topped the dish with a breadcrumb-and-parmesan mixture and put it in the oven.

"There's something so nice about working on food together. My first introduction to cooking was snapping green beans on my grandmother's front porch," Kristin said. "She always cooked them in a big pot with bacon or ham. Gran fixed fried chicken, mashed potatoes and gravy, beans and coleslaw and biscuits every Sunday afternoon. All my aunts and uncles and cousins came. I really miss that."

"Speaking of Sunday dinner," Jane said, "Rose Bellwood invited us to dinner next Sunday after church. She said she'd invited you and Blair too. You're in for a treat. Rose is an excellent cook. Have you been to their house yet?"

"Not yet. I'm really looking forward to going. Blair said they have a great farm."

Jane laughed. "Leave it to a man to see the farm and not the house. You'll love it. The style is folk Victorian, which has most of the features of a Queen Anne, only not as formal. Most country folk didn't bother with architects. They just got a carpenter and built a house. The Bellwoods have fixed it up beautifully and added wings to it over the years as their family grew."

"Blair wants a farm. Me, too, I guess."

"You're not sure?"

"I thought I was. I mean, when we were planning to have a family, a farm seemed like the perfect place to raise children." Kristin's chin began to quiver. Tears filled her eyes. She turned away from Jane.

Jane instinctively reached out and put her arm around her. "What's wrong, Kristin? Are you and Blair having problems?"

"N-o-o-o. I just . . . I went to the doctor and I . . . I found out I can't have children."

Kristin let Jane envelop her in a hug as she began to sob.

"I'm so sorry," Jane said as she held Kristin. "I can only imagine what a blow that was."

After a few moments, Kristin stepped back and wiped her eyes. "I'm sorry," she said as she struggled for control. "I didn't mean to drown you."

"Have you told Blair?"

"Not yet. I haven't told anyone, except you." Kristin fidgeted with the apron tied around her waist. "Blair will be so disappointed. He wants a big family." She sniffed. "So do I."

"Oh, Kristin, don't give up. Lots of people have children after they've been told they couldn't, and there are other options. I don't know what plans God has for you, and it might not be your own children, but He has something very special for you. The Bible says, 'For we are God's workmanship, created in Christ Jesus to do good works, which God prepared in advance for us to do' (Ephesians 2:10). I know it looks bleak right now, but God is faithful. And I'm going to pray for you."

"Thank you, Jane. I'm so glad we've become friends."

She gave Jane a big hug.

Help me, Lord, Jane prayed silently. *Show me how to help Kristin.*

Chapter Eight

Kristin slid into the seat nearest Jane the next morning just before the crochet class started.

Jane reached over and squeezed her hand. "I didn't know if you'd make it today," Jane said softly.

"I almost didn't. Then I thought that since I already bought the yarn and I want to learn to crochet, I might as well make a baby blanket. If it comes out all right, I can give it to someone."

"Good for you. That's what I plan to do. I thought perhaps the church nursery could use it."

Kristin looked sad for a moment, but then she cheered up. "I'll give mine to the nursery too."

Rose started the class by demonstrating the shell stitch they would be using. Kristin had chosen a bright lilac with light orange for the trim. Jane's blanket colors were sunflower yellow for the body and raspberry for the trim. The other women had chosen pastel colors, with lots of pinks and blues. Jane leaned over to Kristin.

"I'm glad to see I'm not the only one who likes bright colors."

Kristin followed Jane's gaze around the room. She looked at Jane and giggled. "I'm not very traditional."

Jane laughed. "Neither am I. But our blankets will certainly brighten the nursery."

They worked diligently for the duration of the class, with Rose periodically checking on everyone's progress. When the class was finished, Kristin went to look at fabric. Jane stopped to chat with Sylvia. Rose packed up her things and came to the counter.

"I see the sweaters have sold. Shall I bring more?" she asked Sylvia.

"That would be great. I've been getting requests for them. Rose, I wonder, could you do me a favor before you leave?"

"Sure. What is it?"

"I'd like you to try on something for me. I'm making an outfit for an out-of-town customer. She's a size eight."

"I'm a size eight."

"Perfect," Sylvia said. "I made a trial pattern out of muslin. I want to be sure it's right before I start cutting the fabric. Jane, would you mind staying around to give me your opinion? My customer described what she wants, and I think it'll work, but I don't want her to be disappointed."

"All right. Call me when you're ready. I'll be with Kristin."

Sylvia led Rose to a fitting room.

Kristin was unrolling a bolt of fabric on a cutting table when Jane walked up to her. Big sunflowers covered the quilted fabric.

"That's pretty. What are you making?" Jane asked.

"Placemats. I thought I'd cut them in flower shapes for the kitchen table." She held her hands apart over the fabric to get an idea how it would look. "What do you think?"

"The sunflowers are perfect for your kitchen."

"I thought so too."

"Jane, we're ready," Sylvia said, poking her head out of the fitting room. "Are you in a hurry, Kristin? I can cut that fabric for you in a few minutes."

"That's fine. I can wait," Kristin said.

"Come on back and see what Sylvia is making," Jane told her.

"I don't want to intrude."

"You're not. Come on."

They followed Sylvia to the dressing room where Rose stood in front of a mirror. She was wearing a plain tan dress, turned inside out so the seams were on the outside of the dress.

Kristin looked skeptical.

Jane frowned. "Tan is not your best color, Rose."

Rose laughed. "I agree. What color will it be, Sylvia?"

"Blue, and the fabric will drape better than this muslin. I'm more concerned with the fit right now." She checked the shoulders and the way the sleeveless dress fit beneath the arms.

"It feels good," Rose said. She looked over her shoulder at her image in the mirror. "What's the occasion?"

Sylvia looked at Jane. Jane shrugged.

"I think she's going to be in a wedding ceremony," Sylvia said.

"Oh. Don't you think the dress is too simple?" Rose turned one way, then the other, looking at the dress in the mirror. "I suppose the side slits will make it dressy."

"There's more," Sylvia said. "I want to make sure the dress fits before I have you put on the jacket. It needs a tuck in the back." She took straight pins from the pincushion at her wrist and made the back seam tighter.

"Looks fine," Jane said. "Let's see the jacket."

Sylvia held out another unfinished, inside-out muslin garment, and Rose put it on. Jane tried to envision the stylish outfit they had chosen for Rose's anniversary dress. The muslin shell looked totally unappealing. She tried to picture the lovely suit on the pattern envelope and to superimpose it on Rose.

"It seems to fit." Jane tried to think of something else to say . . . something complimentary, but nothing came to mind.

Sylvia stepped forward and pinched some fabric at the waist. She pinned a small tuck on each side. Then she stepped back and eyed it critically.

"That looks better," Kristin said.

"Are you sure this is what she wants?" Rose asked. "It seems very plain for a wedding."

"These are just the basic pieces." Sylvia said. "Imagine this in a soft blue fabric, then put a contrasting collar and trim and nice buttons on the jacket. The fabric and finishing touches will make all the difference."

Rose frowned at herself in the mirror. "Well, maybe it'll work. I love blue. Blue and white were my wedding colors." She laughed. "Everyone thought I should have red and white since it was Valentine's Day."

"I hope she likes it," Sylvia said, frowning. She shot a concerned look at Jane.

"She will," Jane said, nodding her head thoughtfully. "I can almost picture it."

"I wish I could look at something plain and see the possibilities," Kristin said. "You are all so talented. I really admire you."

Rose turned toward Kristin to respond, then jumped. "Ouch." She laughed. "I forgot about the pins. Are you finished with me?"

"Let me put a couple of marks at the hem length."

Sylvia took her yardstick and chalk, and marked lines front and back and on both sides. She stood. "There. Let me help you take that off."

Rose gingerly slipped out of the mock jacket while Sylvia held it. Jane and Kristin left so Rose could get dressed.

"That seems like an odd outfit for a wedding ceremony," Kristin told Jane. "I guess I'd have to see the pattern."

Jane looked around. They were alone in the front of the

shop. She leaned close to Kristin. "The dress is for Rose's anniversary, but we couldn't tell her that."

Kristin's eyes widened. "Oh." Then she giggled. "I can't wait to see the finished dress."

"I can't either," Jane said.

The women's retreat committee was due in a half hour, so Alice and Louise were in the kitchen putting together the luncheon that Jane had prepared earlier. When Jane came in from her crochet class, Kristin was with her.

"Something smells delicious," Kristin said. She was carrying a laptop computer.

"That's Jane's casserole," Alice said.

"Kristin gave me a ride home so that she can talk to you, Alice, and I am very grateful," Jane said. "It's freezing out there. Walking to class was enough for me. I'll take over the salad plates so you two can talk," Jane said, removing her coat and putting on her apron. She turned on the faucet to wash her hands.

Kristin set her computer on the table, then removed her gloves, tucked them in her pocket and hung her coat next to Jane's on a hook. She rubbed her hands together. "I'm never going to get used to this cold."

"Would you like a cup of tea or coffee to warm up?" Louise asked.

"I'd love a cup of coffee."

"I'll get it," Alice said. "And a cup of tea for me." Alice fixed two cups and carried them to the table.

"I brought a sample invitation for the Bellwoods' anniversary party." Kristin pulled a folder out of her computer case and took out a sheet of cream-colored stock paper. "I can do these on any color." She handed the paper to Alice. Jane and Louise came to peer over Alice's shoulder.

"I put a sprig of rosemary on the invitation. Since rosemary stands for remembrance and fidelity, and this is their anniversary, I thought it was appropriate. I don't know what the Bellwoods' background is, but I was looking up unique wedding customs to make the invitations special, and I found a custom of decorating with a rosemary wreath. It's a Moravian custom for the bride to make a rosemary wreath the night before her wedding."

"That's perfect," Jane said, clearly delighted. "Rose loves traditions. She decorates with Moravian stars at Christmas. I'll see if Craig Tracy can order rosemary sprigs through his florist shop, and we can make a rosemary wreath for a decoration."

"What a wonderful idea," Alice said. She picked up the printed paper and held it up. Upside down in the upper left quarter of the paper was a scripture quote in beautiful script lettering surrounded by a border of rosemary sprigs.

"I printed it that way so it can be folded like a greeting card."

"I see." Alice turned the paper and read,

"Arise, my darling,
my beautiful one, and come with me.
See! The winter is past;
the rains are over and gone.
Flowers appear on the earth;
the season of singing has come"
(Song of Solomon 2:10–12).

The invitation portion was printed right side up in the lower right quarter of the paper, also inside a border of rosemary sprigs and printed in lovely script.

Samuel Bellwood requests the honor of your presence
To witness the renewal of his wedding vows
To Rose, his beloved bride of forty years.
On February 18 at 11:00 AM
At the Bellwood home.

R.S.V.P. to Louise Howard Smith

This is a surprise for Rose, so please keep the secret.
No gifts please, but if you would like to participate
in a memory quilt for Rose and Samuel,
contact Alice Howard at Grace Chapel Inn.
(The quilt is a surprise for both Rose and Samuel.)

"The invitations are beautiful. Kristin, I don't know how to thank you," Alice said.

"You have all been so nice to Blair and me, I'm happy to do it. In fact, we might not have moved here if you hadn't given us such a warm welcome when we stayed at the inn."

"I'm sure you'll find that nearly everyone in Acorn Hill is friendly," Louise said.

"It's partly my fault that I haven't met more people," Kristin said. "I work at home, and with Blair being gone so much establishing his business, I get lonely." She smiled and shrugged. "I'm not outgoing like Blair. Usually I like working alone, but now I feel isolated."

"That's called cabin fever," Jane said. "With the inn, we have so many people coming and going I never feel alone." She chuckled. "Sometimes a little peace and quiet would be welcome."

"Why, Jane, I thought you thrived on having people around," Alice said.

"Most of the time. And right now I hear voices. I'd better get this lunch ready to serve."

Louise went out to greet the committee members, and Kristin asked, "May I help?"

"Sure," Jane said as she took a large casserole dish out of the oven. "Pop those rolls in the oven. As soon as the women are seated, you and Alice can carry out the lunch plates."

Jane spooned fruit compote into sherbet dishes and topped them with dollops of creamy dressing, then placed the dishes on small salad plates with thin, crisp homemade crackers. Just then Louise poked her head in the doorway.

"Everyone is here. May I help you serve lunch?"

"Kristin and I will bring it out right away," Alice said.

Alice introduced Kristin to the ladies as they served. She had met many of them at church.

"You must come to our retreat in February," Florence said.

"I'd love to come," Kristin told her.

"Good. Do you want to help with crafts or with food?" Florence asked.

"She doesn't have to help with anything," Ethel said. "She can just come."

"I'd be happy to help any way I can," Kristin said.

"Good." Florence gave Ethel a smug look.

"We'll get the lunches now," Alice said to move Kristin away before Ethel could reply.

Jane had a basket of assorted rolls ready for the table, and plates of hot chicken casserole and minted peas and carrots. When everyone had been served, Alice, Kristin and Jane ate in the kitchen.

"I'm sure the ladies would welcome us to the table, but I don't want to chance getting roped into the planning," Alice said.

"Wise woman," Jane said.

"This is so good," Kristin said, taking a bite of the chicken casserole.

"It's one of our mother's recipes," Jane said. "It's good, old-fashioned comfort food."

"Was she a great cook like you?"

"According to Alice and Louise, she was a wonderful cook. She died when I was born."

"I can remember her sitting down with her cookbook after a luncheon or dinner party and making notes," Alice said.

"Really? How neat. My mom doesn't like to cook. I wish I had something to remind me of her. We e-mail back and forth, but of course that's not like being together." Kristin's gaze grew wistful. "You know, it's funny. I work with computers and spend most of my time on the Internet, but e-mail is so impersonal. When Mom sends me a letter, I read it over and over, just to see her handwriting. It makes it seem like she's right here." She laughed. "That sounds silly, doesn't it?"

"Not at all," Alice said. "I love getting letters, and I know letters are therapeutic for people who are sick. I've seen patients go from miserable and hurting to cheerful when they get a note or a card from someone. I remember when we found our father's journal after he died. It comforted me to read his words in his own handwriting."

"I felt the same way, and so did Louise," Jane said. "And speaking of Louise," she said, popping up out of her chair, "I bet they're ready for dessert."

Chapter Nine

Jane, Alice and Kristin cleared the table and served the caramel-apple bread pudding. Then, as Kristin and Alice ate their dessert in the kitchen, Jane went to the office computer and copied the addresses Samantha had e-mailed to her onto a disk. She brought the disk into the kitchen and gave it to Kristin.

"Great," Kristin said. "I'll run a mail merge and print the addresses on the envelopes. I'll use a script that looks like handwriting, and it will only take a few minutes."

Alice shook her head. "Amazing."

"Everyone is going to be thrilled to get these invitations," Jane said.

"You're right," Alice agreed. It seemed everyone in town wanted to be in on the Bellwoods' surprises.

"Do you have time to look at the Web site I developed for Rose?" Kristin asked.

"Sure." Jane said, pulling her chair next to Kristin.

"I think it turned out well, but I want a second opinion. And a third, if you'll take a look too, Alice." Kristin took out her laptop and booted it up. A screen saver showing a handsome old brick house surrounded by a wrought-iron fence and beautiful magnolia trees and azalea bushes appeared.

"That's lovely," Alice said.

"That's my parent's house, where I grew up."

"It's beautiful. No wonder you miss it," Jane said.

Kristin brought up another picture, a muted gray-and-white picture of a snow-covered driveway bordered by a wooden fence and two large, winter-bare maple trees. Lovely, but stark compared to the first scene. A sign on one side announced Bellwood Farm. In the background, the house looked charming. Superimposed over the picture were the words *Homespun Creations by Rose.*"

"That's the Bellwoods' driveway," Alice said. "Did you take that picture?"

"Yes. I wanted to capture the flavor of their farm, but I didn't want to intrude, so I just took it from the road. Do you think it's all right?"

"I think it's beautiful," Alice said.

Kristin showed them another page with pictures and descriptions of Rose's handmade sweaters, hats, throws, scarves, quilts and other items. Next to each item was a box for indicating a purchase.

"Very professional," Jane said. "Of course you *are* a professional, but you've captured Rose's nature here. She'll love it."

Kristin beamed. "Thanks. I designed the shopping pages to accommodate Rose's unique items. Since all of her creations are one of a kind, when an item is bought it will be removed from the page automatically."

"That's perfect," Jane said.

"You said that you aren't creative, Kristin, but the invitations and this Internet site are truly works of art," Alice told her. "You may not realize it, but God is blessing others with your gift."

"Do you really think so?" Kristin asked.

"My, yes. Don't you agree, Jane?"

Jane nodded.

Kristin's eyes grew luminous with tears. She threw her

arms around Alice and hugged her, then drew back, looking embarrassed. "I'm sorry. I'm just . . . Thank you."

Alice smiled, her heart warmed by Kristin's gratitude. "You're welcome, but I only spoke the truth. We're the ones who are grateful for your help."

Alice pulled into the Bellwoods' driveway seconds after the Caseys. She took a moment to compare the farm entrance with the picture she'd seen on Kristin's computer screen.

"Lovely, isn't it?" Jane said from the backseat.

"Yes, it is" Louise said, "but if we sit in the driveway much longer, we'll be late."

"Sorry," Alice said. "I guess I was woolgathering." She stepped on the gas and proceeded up the driveway.

"Woolgathering is the Bellwoods' job, not ours," Louise replied with an arch smile.

Blair and Kristin were waiting for them in front of the large porch. As the sisters walked up the steps, the front door opened and two little boys burst through the door and rushed past them.

"'Scuse me," one said.

"Hey, Miss Jane," the other shouted as he ran by.

"Hey yourself," Jane called after the disappearing figure. She laughed watching them run around the corner. "Too bad we can't bottle that energy."

"Oh dear," Rose said from the doorway. "I hope you'll excuse my grandsons. They get carried away when they're together. Come in out of the cold."

Inside the glass-enclosed entry porch, the temperature jumped from frigid to comfortable. When they were all in and the door shut, Rose opened the front door to the house.

"I'm so glad you could come. Let me take your coats," she said, holding out her arms in welcome. Her smile took away the rest of the chill.

As Blair helped Kristin remove her coat, she looked around. The house branched off in three directions from the foyer. A wide stairway led upstairs on the right. The left side led to the dining room and kitchen, and in front of them, the living room was set apart by four slender columns of light-gray ash that supported matching ceiling beams. She turned to Rose. "I love your house."

As they went into the living room, three men stood. Samuel came forward, smiling broadly.

"Hello, ladies. Welcome, Kristin, Blair . . ." Samuel shook their hands. "I'd like you to meet our sons." Two young women wearing aprons came out of the kitchen. "And our daughters-in-law," Samuel added. With an affectionate smile, he held out his hand to include them.

Caleb, their eldest, stood an inch shorter than his father and looked like a young Samuel. His wife Gretchen was tall and sturdy with a joyful countenance. Benjamin was several inches shorter than his brother and had Rose's dark hair. His wife Daylene also had dark hair. They made a striking couple.

"Joshua and Travis can't make it for dinner," Rose said. "They are involved in an outreach program at their church in Potterston. Since they are both single and handy with tools, they get asked to help with a lot of programs."

"Blair, come visit with us while the ladies gab in the kitchen," Samuel said.

Blair looked at Kristin as if he wasn't sure he should leave her. She smiled at him and followed the women to the large country kitchen.

"Everything is almost ready," Rose told Kristin, "but we can visit and let the men have a few minutes to themselves. Caleb and Ben both farm, and Caleb is active in the grange, so I want Blair to get to know them."

"May I help you with anything?" Kristin asked.

"My helpers and I have done most of the cooking. You just sit at the table and keep us company while we finish."

"Mom said Jane and Kristin are taking her crochet class," Gretchen said over her shoulder. She'd gone to the sink to wash bowls and measuring cups. "She's a great teacher, isn't she?"

"Yes," Kristin said. "Have you taken her classes too?"

"That's how I met Caleb. Rose taught a class for 4-H. I was fifteen and I decided to make a tablecloth for my hope chest." Gretchen laughed. "What a disaster. I came to the farm for a private lesson and had to go out to the barn to find Rose. I left a gate open, and I ended up having to help Caleb and Dad chase lambs around the farm. Caleb thanked me for helping them. Can you imagine? Well, I fell in love right there, but I was afraid to come back after that fiasco."

"Caleb told me afterward that she was the prettiest sheep-herder he'd ever seen," Rose said. "I had already decided that she was a very nice girl, so I was quite happy when he waited for her to grow up."

"Did you finish the tablecloth?" Kristin asked.

"No. I left it here. I was too embarrassed to come back and get it."

"She abandoned it," Rose said, "so I rescued it."

"Mom gave it to me as a wedding present, all finished. It's gorgeous."

"What about you, Daylene? How did you and Ben meet?"

"Nothing so interesting," Daylene said. "We met at college. Ben was quarterback for the football team, and I was a cheerleader. He was voted homecoming king. I was one of the princesses, but my prince was dating the queen, and so Ben and I ended up together." She smiled dreamily. "We started going steady and got married right after Ben graduated."

"Now if I could just find such wonderful brides for my two bachelor sons, I'd be a happy woman," Rose said.

Love and the affection of comfortable relationships shone between Rose and her daughters-in-law. They worked together in the kitchen with the ease of long practice.

"I'm going to tell the boys to wash up," Rose said. "It always takes them twice as long as the adults," she added. Having raised four sons, she understood her grandsons well.

Gretchen and Daylene watched her leave the kitchen, then they hurried over to the table and sat down. They leaned forward like conspirators.

"We want to talk about the anniversary celebration. We feel so out of the loop. Dad just says 'talk to Samantha' or 'talk to Louise.' Poor man, he wants everything to be perfect, but he doesn't have a clue what to do."

"We don't mean to leave you out," Alice said. "We'd love to have your help and input."

"Absolutely," Louise said. "Perhaps we can arrange a time to get together and plan the details. Whenever is convenient for you."

"I want to help, but we're right in the middle of calving season. I'm already bottle-feeding two calves, and we still have seventeen births to go. Caleb needs me at home. I hardly leave the farm this time of year," Gretchen said. "When calving season ends, we go into lambing season. We came today because no births are imminent, and Caleb has a teenager helping on weekends. He's there today, so he can call us if we need to leave."

"I want to help too, but I work full-time at the feed store in Potterston," Daylene said. "Between work and taking care of Ben and the boys, I don't have time for much else."

"I'm afraid if it were left to us, nothing would get done, but we want to help," Gretchen repeated. "Mom and Dad deserve a special day and lots of friends to help them celebrate."

"Perhaps you can help me with cooking for the reception," Jane said.

"I can do that," Gretchen said.

"I can buy a ham or something and some dessert items," Daylene suggested.

"That would help a lot," Jane said. "Perhaps you could order something through the Good Apple Bakery. I'm sure Clarissa wants to do something for the reception. You might check with Hope at the Coffee Shop too. Why don't I put together a menu and let you look it over and make suggestions. Then we can plan from there."

"Wonderful," Daylene said.

"What about the quilt Samantha suggested? She said the idea came from you, Gretchen," Alice said.

"Yes, and I want to do that. I can work on it at night if we get the squares back in time."

"The invitations go out this week. Kristin made them on her computer," Alice said. "We hope we'll get enough people contributing quilt squares to make a decent-size quilt."

"Even if it's just big enough for a wall hanging, Mom will love it," Daylene said. "And we'll make squares. I intend to have each of the boys make one."

"Me too," Gretchen said. "And Samantha said she will send one."

"Kristin volunteered to make squares out of photographs," Alice said. "The center square could be their wedding picture if we can get a copy to scan."

"Wow, what a neat idea," Daylene said. "We have one hanging in the house. Where do you live? Maybe I can drop it off on my way to work."

"We're in the old farmhouse about two miles out on Village Road, on the left," Kristin said.

"I know where that is. I'll bring it tomorrow."

"I've some old family pictures. I'll give them to Daylene so she can drop them off too," Gretchen said. "This is getting so exciting. I can't wait."

"Can't wait for what?" Rose said, coming into the kitchen.

"You all look like you're planning some big secret. Is somebody getting married or something?"

"Or something," Gretchen said. They were saved from further explanation when three of the boys burst into the kitchen, wanting to know if dinner was ready.

They all helped Rose get the food to the dining-room table, which had been extended to its full length and which had a card table added at one end. A long quilted tablecloth in cheerful reds, yellows and greens covered the tables. Pinecones holding crayon-decorated name cards sat at each place. The artwork showed the grandsons' talents.

The boys occupied the card table. The adults sat five on each side with Samuel at the head of the table. Their conversation centered on farming. Blair had visited Caleb's and Ben's neighboring properties, which were several miles from Bellwood Farm.

By the time they finished dessert, and Caleb's and Ben's families left to get back to their farms, the women had moved forward in planning the anniversary surprise without revealing anything to Rose, and the younger Bellwoods had invited Blair and Kristin to visit their farms.

Chapter Ten

Monday morning, Kristin came to the inn carrying a box of envelopes and unfolded invitations. Alice was sitting at the table making a to-do list for the week. Jane was kneading bread dough. Her hands were covered with flour, so Alice hurried to let Kristin in the back door.

"Goodness, that's quite a stack. Put them on the table."

Alice had just shut the door, when Ethel opened it and stepped in. "Good morning," she said in her usual cheerful singsong voice. "I saw Kristin carrying those boxes and thought you might need some help."

"That's very nice of you, Auntie," Alice said. "We do have a stack of invitations to work on, and Jane is up to her elbows in dough. Louise is upstairs. I'll call her."

Alice found Louise in a guest room.

"I'm almost finished stripping the beds. Do you need me?"

"Kristin has arrived with the invitations. They have to be folded and stuffed into envelopes. Aunt Ethel came over to help, so I'm sure we can manage without you. We don't have anyone checking in today, so if you don't mind, I'll help you clean the rooms later."

"Yes, the cleaning can wait. I want to help with the invitations. I'll take the laundry down and join you in a moment."

Alice scooped up the towels. "I'll get these for you."

Ethel was already folding the invitations when Alice and Louise came into the kitchen. She looked up from her task. "Kristin has done a lovely job. Look at these." Ethel handed a folded invitation to Alice.

"These came out beautifully," Alice said. She passed it to Louise.

"Very elegant. What can I do?" she asked, sitting down.

"You could seal the envelopes," Kristin said. She was inserting a folded invitation into a preprinted envelope.

"I have just the thing," Louise said. She left the room and returned with a rectangular glass dish with a sponge in it. She dampened the sponge, then set to work. Alice put postage on the sealed invitations.

Jane covered her bread to rise, then cleaned up and made fresh tea and coffee. While the coffee brewed and the water heated, she rolled out some extra dough, cut it into small squares and dropped them into hot fat. They puffed up as they cooked. In minutes she had a plate full of little doughnuts lightly dusted with powdered sugar.

"Yum, those smell delicious," Kristin said. "You made those from bread dough?"

"Yes. They won't be as sweet as real doughnuts, but they're great with coffee," Jane said. "It looks like you're almost finished."

"Just in time," Ethel said, folding the last card with a flourish. She handed it to Kristin. "We wouldn't want to get grease on the invitations, but those doughnuts must be eaten while they're warm."

"You're right, Aunt Ethel," Alice said. She put a stamp on the last invitation, then went to get the teapot. Jane brought the coffee to the table.

Alice handed cups of tea to Louise and Ethel. She picked up her cup and inhaled the warm, comforting scent of

Darjeeling tea. "The perfect ending to a job well done. I'm so relieved to get those invitations ready. Thank you, Kristin."

"You're welcome." Kristin took a sip of Jane's gourmet coffee and ate a doughnut. "*Mmm.* Your coffee is wonderful, and these remind me of the beignets my grandmother made. She was from Louisiana. That's one more thing I miss about home."

Alice saw a hint of sadness return to Kristin's eyes. She said a silent prayer that the young woman would begin to see Acorn Hill as her home and her husband as her family.

"How do you plan to keep Rose from discovering the surprise celebration?" Ethel asked as she picked up another doughnut. "You have to decorate the house and take all the food out there."

"Somehow we must convince her to attend the retreat," Louise said.

Ethel smiled brightly. "I have just the answer. Why don't we ask her to demonstrate spinning her yarn and to show the women how to make something simple? The whole group couldn't attend at once, so we could schedule her for several sessions. Then she'd have to stay for a good length of time."

"That's a wonderful idea, Aunt Ethel," Alice said. "We were trying to find a craft for the retreat, so your suggestion would solve two problems."

"You could ask her to give a personal testimony too," Kristin said. "She inspires me. I think all the women would like to hear about her life."

"Kristin, you have the best ideas. I am the Committees Director. I know Pastor Thompson wants some new groups to form. Would you like to help me plan activities?" Ethel asked.

"I'm not sure what my schedule will be for the next few months, so I'd better not take on anything more right now," Kristin said. "Perhaps if you still want me, I could help out later."

"You're wise to consider before you take on responsibility," Louise said. "There's always time to get involved."

"It's just that I might go home to spend some time with my parents next month," she said. "Mom misses me, and I really miss her."

"You'll be here for the anniversary, won't you?" Ethel asked. "It'll be the affair of the year for Acorn Hill. Besides, you are helping with the retreat, aren't you?"

"Oh yes. I'm looking forward to the retreat and the anniversary. I wouldn't miss them for anything."

"Good. Besides the potluck recipe exchange, we will need lunch on Friday and breakfast on Saturday."

"Oh no. I'm not good at that kind of thing. Maybe I could bring something, like chips and dip or sodas. I'm just learning to cook." She sent Jane a grateful smile. "I could take all the recipes from the potluck and make recipe booklets for everyone."

"That would be wonderful, Kristin," Louise said. "Perhaps we could include other things from the retreat, like part of the speaker's message so the women can look back and remember."

"Oh yes, and I can bring my digital camera and put photos in the booklet. It'll be fun!" Kristin exclaimed.

"Don't worry, Aunt Ethel. I'll help with the meals," Jane offered. "I have several breakfast casserole recipes that can be made ahead and baked at the last minute. That with some fresh fruit and breakfast breads will make a lovely meal. Lunch could be sandwich fixings, chips and cookies."

"Good. I will leave that in your hands, Jane. Well, I must be going. Lloyd is picking me up for lunch. At this rate, I'll never be ready in time." Mayor Lloyd Tynan was Ethel's special friend, and they spent a lot of time together.

After Ethel left, Louise shook her head. "I don't know how she does it, but she managed to load you up again, Jane. And Kristin too."

Jane sighed. "Oh well, I'll just have to delegate some of the retreat cooking."

"And don't worry about me," Kristin said. "These projects won't take long, and I won't commit to anything after the retreat and anniversary party. I don't know what I'll be doing after that."

"Do you know the words to 'The Servant Song' by Richard Gillard?" Louise asked.

When Kristin shook her head no, Louise recited:

"Brother, let me be your servant.
Let me be as Christ to you.
Pray that I might have the grace
To let you be my servant, too."

"God has a unique purpose for each of us," she said. "Just because we can do many things, it doesn't mean we must say yes to everything. That would rob someone else of the joy of serving and keep us from fulfilling our own purpose." She glanced at Jane.

"Ouch. I admit it. I'm guilty."

"I never thought of it that way. I wonder what my purpose is," Kristin mused.

"If you ask, God will reveal it to you," Louise told her.

"I pray, but I never hear an answer," Kristin said.

"Sometimes we don't know how to listen," Alice said. "But God still answers us, even if we don't realize it. He works through other people and circumstances. Sometimes, looking back, I can see how He was working all along."

"I don't see how He can answer this one." Kristin looked at Jane, then turned back to Louise and Alice. "I thought my purpose was to be a wife and mother, but the doctor told me I probably won't ever have children." Tears filled her eyes.

Louise's heart ached for Kristin. She couldn't imagine life without her precious daughter Cynthia. "I don't know what God has in store for you, Kristin, but we'll pray for you."

"Have you considered adopting a child?" Alice asked. "I work with a doctor who's on the board of an adoption agency. I could introduce you to him."

"I don't know." Kristin shook her head. "I don't know what to think. I just assumed I would have my own children. I've never known anyone who was adopted. What if the child didn't like me? What if we didn't bond as a family?" She gave Alice a helpless look.

"Adopting a child is a serious step. It requires a lot of prayer and commitment from both parents. Talk to Blair and give yourself time to seek God's answer for you," Alice said. "I never had a child, but I love children. God has answered my prayers by giving me young patients to care for at the hospital and the ANGELs group of girls at church. They continually fill my life with joy."

"I'll pray about it."

"Would you like us to pray with you?" Louise asked.

"Yes."

Louise bowed her head. "Heavenly Father, You know that Kristin desires to have a family. We don't know Your plans for her life, but we know they are good. Reassure her of Your love, Lord. Give her peace that You have heard her prayers and will answer. Guide her, Lord, in the way You want her to go and give her joy. In Jesus' name. Amen."

"Thank you," Kristin said quietly. She stood, her head still bowed as if in prayer. "I must go now. I'll mail the invitations on my way home." Kristin put on her coat and gathered her things.

"Thanks for helping me get these ready," she said. "I'll see you in church Wednesday night." She hurried out the door as if someone were chasing her.

"Goodness," Louise said as they watched her leave. "I hope I didn't scare her away."

"No, dear," Alice said, patting Louise's shoulder. "You gave her much to think about. She must do that alone."

"You're awfully quiet, Jane. What are you thinking?" Louise asked.

Jane stood and picked up the empty cups. "I want to help her, but I feel so inadequate. Yet I believe that God brought her into my life for a reason. I just hope I'm doing the right things to encourage her."

"You are the perfect person to relate to Kristin," Louise assured her. "You are full of life and joy in spite of the trials you've faced in your life. You love the Lord and other people, and it shows. Kristin is drawn to you by the light that shines out of you."

"Do you really think I can help her?"

"Absolutely," Louise said, "and I'm never wrong." The superior look she gave Jane over the rim of her glasses did the trick. Jane began to laugh and soon she was joined by both her sisters.

Chapter Eleven

Jane stood at the stove, stirring a batch of pralines. The heat rising from the burner warmed her, while the rich combination of melted butter, cream and brown sugar delighted her senses. The mixture had almost reached the soft-ball stage when the telephone rang. Louise and Alice were not at home, so she reached for the phone with her free hand.

"Grace Chapel Inn. Jane speaking."

"Hello, Jane, this is Nia Komonos. I just received my invitation to the Bellwoods' anniversary party. I'll be there. Is there anything . . ."

"Nia, I'm so glad that you can go and I'd love to chat, but I'm making candy and I'm at a critical point."

"I understand completely. I'm at the library. Call me when you get a chance."

"Okay. Thanks. Bye." She hung up the phone and grabbed a potholder to remove the pan from the burner. The phone rang again. She started to put down the pan, but resisted the urge to answer. Stirring with one hand, she added the premeasured vanilla and chopped pecans. The timing was everything.

The candy mixture began to thicken, then clouded, becoming the color of caramel. Tipping the pan, she quickly dropped spoonfuls of the hot mixture onto parchment paper to cool. The phone rang again, and as Jane continued to drop spoonfuls of candy on the paper, it rang once more.

Jane scooped out the last of praline mixture just in time. The batter was getting hard. She set the pan in the sink and filled it with hot water to soak before she removed her apron and went out to the reception desk to hear the telephone messages. She hit play.

"Hi, this is Carlene Moss," came over the answering machine. "I just got my invitation to the Bellwoods' party and I'll be there. I'd like to do a quilt square. Call me when you get a chance. Thanks. Bye."

The answering machine announced message number two. A man's voice came over the machine. "Wilhelm Wood here. I have an idea for the anniversary party. Call me." No good-bye.

The final message started. "Hi, Alice or Louise or Jane . . . This is Betty Dunkle at Clip 'n' Curl. I am so excited about the Bellwoods' party. It was so sweet of them to include me. Oh, I know it's a surprise. I won't tell. But I'll be there. Oops. Customer. Gotta go. Bye." Click.

Jane jotted down the messages and returned to the kitchen. The phone rang as soon as she got there. She picked up the receiver.

"Grace Chapel Inn, Jane speaking. May I help you?"

"Hi, Jane, this is Nellie Carter. I'm calling about the Bellwoods' anniversary party. I definitely want to attend. What a wonderful way to celebrate. I'd like to make a quilt square. What do I do?"

"Sylvia has the fabric squares, instructions and supplies at her store."

"Great. I'll drop by there when I take my lunch break. I'll let you go. I'm sure you are busy."

The back door opened, and Louise shouldered her way in carrying two grocery bags.

"Bye, Nellie." Jane hung up and took a bag from Louise. "Do you have more out there?"

"No, this is it." Louise set the other bag on the counter. "I thought I'd never get out of the General Store. Everyone wanted to talk about the Bellwoods' anniversary. The invitations arrived in the mail today. I hope I can remember everyone who said they'd come. Let see, there's Florence Simpson, although she said she'll send a formal reply. Patsy Ley said she and Henry will be there. Justine Gilmore is very excited about attending and wants to help. She'll do a quilt square. She said Josie would help her with the design."

Louise removed her coat and hung it by the door. "Is the water hot? I need a cup of tea. This cold weather is not letting up."

"I'll make a pot," Jane said, reaching for the kettle. "Stand by the stove. It's nice and warm."

Louise held her hands over the warm stovetop and rubbed them together. "I saw Kathy Bentley in the post office. She and the doctor will come, and she wants to make a square. I stopped at Nine Lives Bookstore and, of course, Viola plans to attend and will make a square. I haven't seen so many smiles and such excitement since Christmas. I even feel more cheerful."

"No, Louie, not you," Jane said in mock disbelief. Louise laughed. The teakettle whistled.

"Let's have a cup of tea and sample your pralines," Louise said. "That'll sweeten you up too."

"If you insist. Then I have some calls to return. The phone rang off the hook right in the middle of making the pralines. I had to let the answering machine take messages."

"I'm glad you did. Burning the pralines would be criminal." Louise filled the tea ball with loose tea, poured water over it in the pot and carried everything to the table. Jane picked up the plate of pralines just as the telephone rang. She looked at Louise, at the plate, then sighed. She handed the plate to Louise and answered the telephone as she saw the back door open and Ethel step inside.

"Your beloved aunt is here," she announced. "Oh, excuse me, you're on the phone." Ethel put a gloved hand to her mouth. Then she spotted the plate of pralines and made a beeline for the table.

Jane raised her eyebrows but responded to the caller.

"I'll put you on the list, Lorrie. I'm glad you can make it. Stop by Sylvia's Buttons to get the quilt square and instructions." Jane finished the conversation and hung up. She jotted Lorrie Zell's name on the list she had started.

"Cup of tea, Aunt Ethel?" she asked.

"Thank you, Jane. You are so considerate." She took a bite of her second praline. "These are lovely, dear."

"Thank you. It's one of Mother's recipes."

"Your mother made these at Christmas. Well . . ." she said, pausing for dramatic effect, "I spoke with Rose, and she's delighted to present a spinning demonstration for the ladies' retreat. I assured her we would finish in plenty of time for her to leave for the trip she is planning. She seemed surprised that I knew about it, but I told her everyone in town knows except Samuel, and he'll never learn about it from me."

Louise choked on her tea, and Ethel reached over and patted her on the back without a pause in her report. "Rose hesitated to give a personal testimony. However, I convinced her that she'd do a wonderful job. I scheduled that for after breakfast on Saturday. That way she cannot leave early." Ethel beamed, pleased with her accomplishment.

She turned to Louise. "You mustn't drink so fast. You young people are always in such a hurry."

Jane was afraid that her sister would choke again, but Louise took a breath and said, "I can't believe you consider me a young person."

"You must be young, because I'm still in my prime," Ethel said, "and I'm older than you are."

Ethel never revealed her age. The sisters estimated their father's younger sister to be in her midseventies, a good ten years older than Louise. Ethel's bottle-red hair, her energy and youthful style made her seem years younger.

Jane grinned. "Then we are all youngsters," she said. "That suits me just fine. Good job getting Rose to help with the retreat, Aunt Ethel. That will give us the time we need to prepare Samuel's surprise. And from the calls we've been getting, everyone in town plans to help them celebrate."

Ethel's face lit up. "Oh, this is so romantic."

Alice wound her way through the aisles to the back of Fred's Hardware. She had stopped on her way home from work, hoping to talk to Fred, but she didn't see him. She found a rental brochure on the counter and picked it up. She was looking through it when Vera appeared beside her.

"Hi. We got our invitation. It was beautiful. Of course, Fred and I will be there." She looked over Alice's shoulder at the form. "What are you looking for?"

"I want wedding supplies for the anniversary, but I don't know exactly what."

"I have a book of wedding things we can order. Just a minute." Vera went around the counter and pulled a catalog from the bottom shelf. She put it on the counter and opened it to party supplies.

"Good. I feel completely helpless here," Alice said.

Vera laughed. "Samuel told Fred you'd be in and said to put everything on his account. Don't worry too much about the budget. Fred intends to discount the costs. Samuel told Fred not to let Rose see the bill, but she works so closely with Samuel that it's going to be hard to keep her from finding out."

"I know. I feel like a secret agent," Alice said.

"Okay, let's see what you need."

Alice showed Vera her list. Then they thumbed through the catalog pages together. Alice was amazed at all the choices that were available.

"We can rent the tablecloths, silverware and the decorative arch. What about serving dishes, like platters or chafing dishes?" Vera asked.

"That is Jane's department. I'm sure she has that well in hand."

"If she needs anything, have her call me." Vera helped Alice choose candles and nice plastic plates and glasses. By the time they finished, Alice had crossed most items off her list. She straightened.

"You're a lifesaver, Vera."

"I'm glad I could help. I'll put in the order now so we'll be sure to get everything in time," Vera said. "And I talked to Sylvia about the quilt squares. She's had thirty-three people come to get squares already. I'm going to spend a couple of evenings at her store helping people make their squares."

"Wonderful. Thank you. I feel much better now. I must admit wedding planning is not my forte."

"Perhaps not, but you always help so cheerfully. You have no idea how much you bless people with your generous spirit, Alice."

Alice knew that she always received far more than she gave. A wave of gratitude swept over her for friends like Vera. The weather outside might be frigid, but the joy of belonging in a town like Acorn Hill warmed her from the inside out.

Jane stopped Alice when she came in the door, before she could remove her coat and gloves.

"I've been waiting for you. I was just thinking about flowers for the anniversary. Have you had a chance to order any yet?"

"No. I just stopped at Fred's and ordered decorations.

That was trying enough. Thank goodness Vera was there to help me." Alice sighed. "Do you have any ideas? I'd appreciate your advice."

"Do you have time to go with me to Wild Things?" Jane glanced at her watch. "It's four thirty. Craig's still open."

"Good idea. Then I can cross that off my to-do list too. Maybe Louise would want to go with us."

As if on cue, the kitchen door opened, and Louise walked in. "I'm glad that's my last lesson for the day. My students couldn't sit still for thirty minutes today."

"We're going to Wild Things to order flowers. Would you like to come help us?" Jane asked.

"Oh yes. Perhaps we can get an arrangement for our table. Let me put on my coat."

Darkness had descended by the time they entered Wild Things. In the midst of the tropical paradise, Jane felt the tensions of the day drain away. Lacy ferns cascaded from hanging baskets, and delicate violets and cyclamen bloomed on shelves. Craig Tracy, the owner, had decorated for Valentine's Day. Pots of bright red kalanchoes and gerbera daisies bloomed next to miniature roses in shades of red, pink and white. More containers held lacy spider chrysanthemums, hydrangeas and sweet-scented gardenias. Red and white heart-shaped balloons bobbed overhead. Red-satin-covered boxes of candy, plush stuffed animals and gift baskets sat on the shelves. Roses, carnations, mums, lilies, gladiolas and daisies, all in myriad colors, filled the display cases.

As the door closed, Craig came from the back room. When he saw them, he smiled broadly.

"Good evening, ladies. It isn't often I see all three of you together in here. Is this a special occasion?"

"You could say that," Alice answered, stepping to the counter. "We're here to order flowers for the Bellwoods' anniversary. Did you get your invitation?"

"I did and I'll be happy to attend," he said. "Do you have a plan in mind for the flowers?"

"Samuel requested that they be blue and white," Louise said.

"I ordered a white archway for the ceremony. Could we put baskets of blue and white flowers on either side of it?" Alice asked.

"Let's see . . . for blue, I can get these bearded iris." Craig opened the flower case and took out one lovely blue ruffled iris. "And delphiniums. For white, there's Shasta daisies, chrysanthemums, carnations, lilies and snapdragons. We could add roses. Do you want any other colors mixed in? I can get anything from a deep red to a pale pink or a yellow."

"Rose's dress is blue," Jane said, studying the flowers and picturing the finished bouquets. "A touch of pink or red would go with the holiday and add a little color variation."

"Sylvia is making her dress. I'll bring in a swatch of the fabric tomorrow, so you can match it for the bows," Louise said."

"Great," Craig said, making notes on a work order. "The Bellwoods have been good friends. Samuel helped me put up my nursery, so I'll be happy to do the arrangements at cost. I'll see what flowers I can get to make these really special." He straightened. "Anything else I can do for you ladies today?"

"Oh yes, can you get fresh rosemary sprigs?" Jane asked.

"For cooking?"

"No. Kristin Casey discovered that a rosemary wreath is a wedding custom, and since it stands for remembrance, we thought it would make a nice touch at the anniversary as a decoration."

"I can take care of that, and add a few other herbs and flowers to dress it up."

"Perfect," Jane said.

"Before we go, I want an assortment of your cut flowers for the inn," Louise said. "We need a little cheer."

Craig opened the case and pulled out several stems of each flower, creating a multicolored bouquet. He added ferns and baby's breath, then wrapped the flowers in green waxed paper. Then he covered the bouquet with a plastic bag. "These are half price because they're a couple of days old. They should last for some time if you recut the stems."

"Thank you, Craig," Louise said, accepting the flowers.

"That's one more item I can cross off my to-do list," Alice said. "This decorating business isn't so hard," she added, straight-faced.

Jane laughed. "Especially when you have experts like Craig and Vera to help you."

"Not to mention you and Louise."

They said good-bye and hurried to the car. The cold was shocking after the tropical climate inside Wild Things.

Chapter Twelve

"Today we're experimenting with cakes," Jane told Kristin Thursday afternoon as they tied on their aprons. "I'll be making three different ones for the Bellwoods' anniversary."

"Wouldn't it be easier to make one kind of cake?"

"Easier, yes, but not nearly as much fun. I received an e-mail from Samantha, saying that her father prefers a dark-chocolate cake, and her mother's favorite is coconut. She also told me that she and her brothers love their mother's raspberry-jam cake. I called Gretchen and got the recipes. We'll try the jam cake today. I'm figuring on approximately one hundred guests, so I'll make a three-tiered cake for the centerpiece, and Clarissa Cottrell at Good Apple Bakery will make a couple of coordinating sheet cakes."

Jane pulled several canisters out of the pantry and set them on the counter. "If you'll grease the cake pans, I'll get out the rest of the ingredients."

"I tried the recipe you gave me for chicken potpie. It turned out really well."

"Did Blair like it?"

"He . . . he didn't have any. He went to visit a veterinarian in Potterston and ended up having dinner with him." Kristin sighed. "I saved him one, but he left early yesterday and was gone all day. He grabbed a sandwich from the mini-mart. He said he didn't want to bother me. I was busy working on a Web design, so I ate it myself."

"Establishing a new business takes a lot of hard work and long hours. I'm sure he would rather be home with you."

"In my mind, I know that's true, but I just feel left out. He comes home so tired, he doesn't feel like talking. If we'd stayed in Georgia, he could have worked for the big veterinary hospital and had regular hours." Kristin shook her head. "I didn't mean to start talking about my problems. What do we do next?"

"You can cream the butter and sugar together until the mixture is light and fluffy."

"All right." Kristin got right to work. Jane measured the dry ingredients into a bowl, then began adding eggs to Kristin's mixture one at a time.

"Keep beating it while I add the rest of the ingredients," Jane said. Kristin nodded.

They had just poured the batter into three cake pans when Louise came in.

"What are you cooking up?" she asked.

"We're experimenting with a cake for the reception. Gretchen gave me the recipe. Evidently it's a family favorite. I have to improvise a bit. The original icing recipe doesn't lend itself to decorating. I'll use a filling and a different frosting."

"Do you decorate cakes too?" Kristin asked.

"She makes beautiful cakes and pastries," Louise said.

Jane arranged the cakes in the oven, then shut the door. "Half the requirement of a gourmet dish is presentation. A professional chef must be artistic."

"I'd love to learn how to decorate a cake."

"You can help me decorate this one. It won't be as elaborate as the one for the reception. This is just for us to test and sample."

"I will be glad to act as a judge. I have very discriminating tastes, you know," Louise said, smiling.

"You'll have to wait until after dinner," Jane said, then started at the sound of a loud knock on the door. She went to answer it.

"Oh, Samuel. Come in."

Samuel removed his hat as he entered. "Hi, Jane. Hello, Louise. Kristin. I came by to see how things are going. I went to the hardware store and the feed store and a dozen people must have stopped me to tell me they're coming to our anniversary. I sure hope no one mentions it to Rose."

"We made it clear on the invitations that this is a surprise. I guess we'll find out how well this town can keep a secret," Louise said. "Come sit down. Would you like a cup of tea or coffee?"

"Coffee if you have it."

"I made some at lunch. It's still hot," Jane said.

"Cream and sugar?" Louise asked.

"No. Just black." He accepted a cup and took a swallow. "*Ahhh.* Nice and strong. Just the way I like it," he said. He took a seat at the table.

"I saw your husband this morning out at Baker's farm," he said to Kristin. "I stopped in there to deliver a load of hay. Looks like he's making a good impression on everyone."

"That's nice. I hope he can start working out of the clinic he set up in the shop building," she said.

Samuel nodded gently. "Being a country vet is a bit different than being a vet in the city. People can't always haul their big animals to the clinic. He's got to make house calls, or farm calls, I suppose you'd say."

"I know," she said with a sigh. "He told me he'll have to be on call, but he can do some of it from the house. There's a corral, and stalls in the barn, so people can bring their animals."

"He may get some walk-in business. The vet from Potterston called to thank me for sending Blair over to see him. He gets calls all the time to work on horses and livestock, but he has more business than he can handle with people's pets. He said he'd rather concentrate on the smaller animals."

"Thank you for helping him, Mr. Bellwood." She gave Samuel a smile, but Jane caught the defeated look in her eyes.

Poor Kristin, Jane thought. *She's trying to be excited about Blair's veterinary business, but it keeps him away from home. With Samuel's help, it sounds as if he'll be even busier.*

The phone rang, and Louise got up to answer it. An unfamiliar voice offered her two nights and three days at a ski resort in New York. She responded that she wasn't interested. The caller kept asking her questions and trying to override her objections. Finally she said, "I'm sorry, but I must go now. Good-bye." She hung up the phone.

She shook her head as she refreshed her coffee and carried the pot to the table. "Would you like a refill, Samuel?" she asked.

"Thank you." He held out his cup. "You need to be firm with those people, Louise," Samuel said. "They'd take up all of your time and try to sell you the moon. I had one this morning." He shook his head. "This pushy saleswoman says she wanted us to know she got a special deal for an upgrade on our vacation." Samuel laughed. "You know where she wanted to send us?"

Louise looked at Jane, who frowned. "Where?" Louise asked.

"Hawaii." Samuel laughed. "I told her that we are up to our eyeballs in pregnant ewes and that we aren't going to Hawaii or anywhere at this time of year."

"What did she say to that?" Jane asked.

"I didn't give her a chance to say another word. I said good-bye and hung up, like Louise did just now. I didn't want to be rude, but I couldn't stand around all day talking on the telephone."

Kristin pressed her lips together. Jane took a sip of her coffee.

"Yes, those unsolicited sales calls can be a nuisance," Louise said smoothly. "What is it you wish to discuss, Samuel?"

"Oh, I just want to know how things are coming along and see if there's something I need to do."

"I believe everything is under control," Louise said. "Sylvia is working on a dress. Alice has ordered the decorations and flowers."

"I'm working on the reception," Jane said.

"Have you spoken with Pastor Thompson?" Louise asked.

"Yes. He will do a short ceremony with us renewing our vows. He told me to say a few words about what Rose means to me. Nothing formal, he said. I'm no good at speaking in public, but I guess I can do that."

"Perhaps you should write down what you want to say," Louise suggested. "If you'd like, I'll be glad to type it up for you so that it'll be easy to read."

"Thank you, Louise. All of you. I'm truly grateful for all that you have done, are doing. I know Rose will be very pleased."

"She'll be thrilled," Jane said. The oven timer buzzed. She got up and tested the cakes, and then removed them from the oven.

Samuel stood too. "I'd better be going. Thanks for the coffee."

"You're welcome."

They watched him leave. As soon as he drove off, they sprang into action.

"Samuel just canceled Rose's surprise trip." Jane said. "What do we do now?"

"We must contact Rose so that she can call the travel company. I'll try the farm." Louise picked up the telephone and dialed. Jane and Kristin could hear the phone ringing on the other end. It rang four times. Then the answering machine clicked on. Louise hung up. "I can't leave a message in case Samuel listens to it."

"Call Sylvia. Maybe Rose is at her shop," Jane said.

Rose wasn't at Sylvia's store, but Sylvia thought she was teaching a class at the elementary school. Louise called there and left an urgent message for Rose to call her back. "Tell her it's an emergency," Louise told the school secretary. "It's about her surprise."

The secretary promised to deliver the message in person.

After several minutes of staring at each other, Jane got up. "Sitting here won't make the phone ring," she said. "The roast won't cook if we don't put it in the oven. Come on, Kristin."

Kristin put her coffee cup in the sink and went to help Jane.

"My next piano student is due in ten minutes," Louise said, and she left the kitchen.

"What would you like me to do?" Kristin asked.

"First, rub the roast all over with this mixture of spices," Jane said, handing Kristin a bowl.

"What's in it?"

"Let's see. I used onion powder, garlic salt, paprika, celery salt, parsley, dill weed, turmeric, thyme, basil, rosemary and black pepper.

"Goodness. Did you mix them yourself?"

"Yes, I love trying different combinations. When you finish, we'll pop the roast in the oven and then work on the vegetables."

"I wish Blair were around to taste some of these meals. I know he'd love them."

"I'll send some home with you. He'll be in for a treat tomorrow." Jane handed the bowl to Kristin.

"If he's home," Kristin said sadly. "Did your husband appreciate your wonderful cooking?"

Jane's hand stilled in midair. How could she answer? Had Justin appreciated her cooking? He must have, because he took her recipes and claimed them as his own. "My ex-husband was also a chef. We worked at different restaurants, so we rarely ate together."

"That's like Blair and me. Your work kept you apart. At least you worked in the same field. Blair doesn't understand my work, and I don't understand his, so we don't have a lot to talk about. That is, *when* we talk."

"Working in the same field has its challenges too," Jane said. "I think a good marriage comes down to wanting success for your spouse more than you want your own success."

Jane busied herself, her back toward Kristin. *How do I advise Kristin when I failed?* She hoped the Lord would give her the wisdom she needed.

"I know it's hard," Jane said, "but you have to make a conscious choice to work at your relationship. I think all relationships help us understand God's love. We have to try to love others the way He loves us."

Jane knew it wasn't always that simple. It took two people to have a relationship. She prayed that Blair wanted his marriage to succeed. If Justin had been willing to work at their relationship the way Jane had been, the outcome of their marriage might have been different.

Kristin sighed. "I'm sure you're right."

Jane turned to Kristin. "I know Blair loves you. His eyes light up when he looks at you. Remember how he talked about your talent? He wants his business to succeed so he can support you. I know you get frustrated, but try to be patient."

Kristin nodded her head. "I'm not very patient. I know I need to work on that. Do you think God is trying to teach me a lesson?"

"Patience is a lesson we all need to learn," Jane answered. "I think everything in life gives us an opportunity to choose either to learn and grow or to give up and be defeated."

Kristin sighed and nodded, but then, Jane noticed, she straightened her shoulders as if, perhaps, determining to make the first choice.

Chapter Thirteen

Rose pulled into the Grace Chapel Inn driveway at the same time Alice arrived home from work. They entered the kitchen together.

"Oh, Rose, I'm glad you came by," Jane said. "We've been trying to reach you."

"The school secretary caught me just as I was getting into my car. What's so urgent?"

Jane told her about the call Samuel took from the travel agent. "You'd better call and make sure that she didn't cancel your trip because of what Samuel said."

"Oh no! I told them the trip was a secret. They shouldn't have called." She put her fist on her hip and grimaced. "Could I use your telephone? It's a toll-free number. I don't want to call from home and have Samuel walk in on my conversation."

"Sure." Alice gave Rose the portable telephone and took her to the library so she could have privacy while she made her call. Then Alice went upstairs to change. When she came back down, she could hear Rose talking in the library. Alice went through to the kitchen.

"Smells like roast beef," she said. "That's a perfect meal for a cold day, and I worked up a hearty appetite today."

Louise came into the kitchen. "Who's in the library?"

"That's Rose. She came by to use our phone so Samuel wouldn't happen to overhear her conversation," Alice said.

"I see. Poor Rose. I hope Samuel didn't ruin her surprise."

"Well, I salvaged our reservations," Rose said, entering the kitchen. "Better than that, the agency was eager to keep our account, so they are giving us a fantastic deal. They apologized all over the place. The call earlier today had been made by a secretary who hadn't been told about the secret. The hotel is running a promotion, and she was calling everyone who has Hawaii bookings." Rose waved a piece of scratch paper with notes scribbled on it. "We can leave earlier than planned, save the night in Philadelphia and go straight to Hawaii. They have upgraded our room to the honeymoon suite at no extra cost. I can't wait to go. This will be our first romantic vacation since we married. In fact, it's the first vacation I can remember."

"You've never taken a vacation?" Kristin asked.

Rose laughed. "That's the life of a farmer. But it's not like we've never taken a trip. We attend the county fair and the state fair every year and we've visited Samuel's family in Oregon, so I can't complain, but we've never gone anywhere as tourists. That man needs to get away and relax before he works himself into an early grave. He's going to get a vacation this year, because I'm going to hijack him." Rose's eyes danced with her excitement.

"You said you'll leave earlier. Aunt Ethel told us you promised to lead a craft and give your testimony at the retreat. How will you manage that?" Alice asked.

"I'll have our bags packed. We can leave as soon as I get home from the retreat." Rose seemed so pleased with herself she didn't notice the dismayed looks on her friends' faces. Louise, Alice, Jane and Kristin just stared at each other.

"Now I'd better get home before Samuel wonders where I've gone. I can tell he feels neglected lately, but I'll make it up to him." Rose put on her coat. "Thanks for giving me the heads-up and letting me use your phone."

Rose left them all staring after her.

"Now I remember why I don't like surprises," Louise said. "All this subterfuge creates too many complications. If we tell Rose the truth, it'll spoil Samuel's surprise. If we tell Samuel that his surprise is about to be ruined, it'll spoil Rose's."

"Perhaps Samantha can intervene," Alice said.

"I don't see how. What can she say that will make Rose change her plans?" Jane said.

"Why not call Gretchen?" Kristin asked. "She's local, so maybe she can do something."

"Good idea." Jane reached for the telephone book and looked up the number. "If I ever want to get involved in someone's secrets again, remind me that it's a bad idea."

Louise gave her a stern look. "The anniversary celebration is not a bad idea. Nor is Rose's second honeymoon trip. We're merely experiencing a little technical difficulty."

"I think it's romantic," Kristin said. "Whatever happens, it's obvious they want to make each other happy. They'll have a wonderful time no matter what."

"I agree," Louise said.

Jane dialed Gretchen's number and was soon explaining the situation.

The gloom lifted Friday morning. Although the temperature remained in the twenties, sunshine made it seem warmer. The streets and sidewalks were dry. Jane decided to walk to Sylvia's Buttons for the crochet class. She encountered several others who were out enjoying the sunshine.

As Jane passed Acorn Hill Antiques, Rachel Holzmann beckoned to her to come inside. Jane opened the door, and a wave of warmth welcomed her.

"Do you have time for a cup of tea? I wanted to talk to you about the party," Rachel asked.

"I'm on my way to Rose's crochet class, but I have a couple of minutes. I'll pass on the tea, though. I just had coffee."

"Well, we plan to come to the anniversary, of course, so please put us down. I was wondering if you think an antique quilt square would be appropriate for the memory quilt. Let me show you."

Rachel went behind the counter and brought out several unfinished quilt squares made of little pieces of fabric joined together like a collage with tiny, intricate stitches. The squares were so well preserved they looked almost new.

"These crazy-quilt squares were in a trunk we bought at an estate auction."

"That's a great idea, Rachel. Rose would love to have an antique square in the quilt. Can you embroider your names or some kind of saying on it, so she'll know who it's from?"

"Yes, I can do that." Rachel hugged herself. "This is such fun. Everyone who comes in here talks about the anniversary. It's a wonder Samuel and Rose haven't discovered all the secrets."

Jane looked at her watch and walked toward the entrance. "Keeping them from spoiling each other's surprise is proving quite a challenge," Jane said as she paused by the door. "And now I must get to class."

In a few minutes, Jane entered Sylvia's Buttons, where Sylvia greeted her.

"I can't believe all the requests I'm getting for quilt squares. We'll have enough for a large quilt," Sylvia told Jane in a whisper. "Vera is coming in tomorrow night to do a workshop for those who need help. Can you come to help as well?"

"Sure, but I don't know what good I'll be. I'm not a quilter," Jane said. "Alice has done a little."

"She can come too. You can all come if you'd like. I'm thinking of your artistic abilities. You have lots of ideas, and you can help those who want to paint a scene on a square or do an appliqué."

"All right. It sounds like fun."

"Good. Seven o'clock."

Jane walked to the back of the shop, where the class met. Kristin was sitting in her usual seat with her yarn and crochet hook in her lap. She looked up and smiled when Jane sat next to her.

"Hi. I was afraid you weren't coming."

"I stopped to chat with Rachel Holzmann at the antique store. Isn't it gorgeous outside?"

Kristin looked at her with surprise. "I don't know about gorgeous, but at least the sun is out. I did think it was pretty with the sun shining on the frosted trees. It looked like a diamond fairyland."

"God's reminder that He is here even on the coldest days."

"That's neat, Jane. You have such a great outlook. I need to see the beauty in things here, instead of thinking how nice it is back home."

"Looking backward doesn't help, unless it's to see our mistakes so we don't repeat them. It's important to remember that today is filled with possibilities and hope."

At the front of the room, Rose clapped her hands. "Good morning, everyone," she said. "Most of you have the main part of your blankets done, so we're going to learn to crochet the edging today." She held up a lovely, lacy rectangular blanket and began demonstrating how to start the edge.

Kristin had completed the body of her blanket.

"Wow! You did a great job for your first crochet project," Jane told her. "And the babies in the nursery will appreciate being snuggly and warm."

"Luckily babies aren't critical."

Everyone chatted and laughed as they spent the morning finishing their blankets, and class came to an end with all in an upbeat mood.

As Kristin and Jane were gathering their things to leave, Rose came over. "I just wanted to thank you for setting up my Web site," she told Kristin. "All of my sweaters and most of my scarves have sold, and I downloaded a stack of special orders. I may have to assemble a group of knitters and crocheters to help me fill the orders."

Kristin beamed. "I'm glad I could help."

"That's wonderful," Jane said. "You'll be starting a whole new industry in Acorn Hill."

"You might be right. If the interest holds, it will keep several of us busy. Fortunately I know many talented women who'd like some extra income. In fact, I have someone working now to fill orders until I get home from our trip, which, by the way, has changed again." She shook her head.

"What happened?" Jane asked.

"Gretchen called me last night. She and Caleb are going to watch the farm while we're gone. I told her about the earlier departure, and she had a fit. She and Daylene and all the grandchildren have planned a surprise for our anniversary and they planned it for the weekend, when the boys are out of school. They want to have a family party at noon, so we can't leave or we'll spoil it."

"Goodness. Your trip gets more and more complicated," Jane said.

Rose sighed. "What could I say? I can't disappoint the grandchildren. So I must call and change the plans again. My travel agent is going to give up on me."

"No she won't. That's her job. I think you're making the right choice."

"I don't really have a choice. Sometimes I think our children run our lives."

Jane laughed. "And you wouldn't have it any other way."

Chapter Fourteen

Jane hadn't expected Ethel to join them for the quilting evening, but her aunt came out of the carriage house when Jane and Alice got in the car.

"Wait for me," she called, waving her gloved hand. The tote bag she carried bounced as she hurried over and climbed into the backseat of Jane's car. "There. I was afraid I would miss you."

"I didn't realize you wanted to come," Jane said.

"My square is nearly finished, so I don't need help. I want to see what everyone else is doing."

Of course, Jane thought. Aunt Ethel couldn't stand being left out of anything. "We're happy to have you come with us, Aunt Ethel."

Light poured out of Sylvia's Buttons. Cars lined both sides of the street. Jane dropped Ethel off at the door. Alice stayed in the car with Jane, who had to park across the street and down the block in the Town Hall parking lot.

"We might as well have walked," Alice said.

Jane laughed. "Silly, isn't it? We only saved a block. We could have cut through from the church."

"True. Did you see that crowd? I can't believe all the people at Sylvia's."

"Amazing. Just a few weeks ago, everyone had the after-holiday blahs. Now the whole town is excited. Rose and Samuel's anniversary has captivated Acorn Hill."

Alice laughed. "We'll have to think up something intriguing for next January."

They arrived at the store. "Patsy already has a poster up for the retreat," Alice said, pointing to a colorful flyer with large red letters taped to the inside of the window by the door.

Jane opened the door. The sounds of laughter and chatter spilled out, warming her before she stepped through the entrance. She waved at Sylvia, who was taking coats and piling them on the cutting table. Vera Humbert and Justine Gilmore were arranging worktables.

Sylvia hurried over to Jane. "Have you ever seen anything like this? I wish I could have this kind of response to one of my sales. Come help me. I only set up one table, but we'll need six of them with this crowd."

"I'm glad Justine came to help. Do you have enough supplies?"

"I will if I dip further into my inventory."

"You can't do that." Then Jane snapped her fingers. "I know. Don't worry about a thing. Just clear some work spaces. I'll take care of the rest."

Alice went off with Sylvia. Jane found a wicker basket, climbed up on a chair and clapped her hands for attention. Conversation gradually stopped and some two dozen pairs of eyes turned to stare at her.

"Wow, what a fantastic turnout. Thank you all for coming. We're going to have a great time. But we have one little problem. We had no idea that we'd have so many people show up. Sylvia generously offered her shop and her supplies so everyone could make a square for Samuel and Rose. Trouble is, with so many people, the cost of the supplies will be much higher than she anticipated. It would cost us a lot if we each had to buy the supplies we'd need to make a square. So, I suggest that we each contribute, say, five dollars toward the supplies we're going to use. That's a bargain for us, and it keeps Sylvia from losing a lot of money. If you can't afford five dollars, just give what you can."

"Great idea, Jane," Carlene Moss announced as she stepped forward and dropped some bills into the basket. Nellie Carter was right behind her, then Betty Dunkle, Nia Komonos, Viola Reed and Patsy Ley. After that, Jane lost track. The noise level rose as people returned to their conversations.

Jane saw Sylvia hand Alice several packages of supplies. Alice and Vera placed them at the workstations, then Vera came over. She had a handful of quilt squares.

Jane clapped her hands again. When everyone quieted, she said, "Thank you, ladies. I'm turning the chair over to Vera, who will give us instructions. Have fun." Jane stepped down and Vera took her place on the chair. Jane made her way to Sylvia and handed her the basket, which brimmed with money. The women had been generous.

Sylvia's eyes widened. She took the basket. "Wow! This will more than cover my costs."

"I hope it will provide a little profit. Look at what you've done for the community. These ladies are having a great time. And Rose is going to love the quilt."

"Yes, she will."

Vera's voice caught their attention.

"Before we get started, I want to show you some examples of what you can do," Vera said, holding up a square with many small pieces of fabric creating a picture.

"These squares are appliquéd. This one has animals." She held up a square with wild animals on it. "And here's a square with a cornucopia." She held up another square. "This shows a woman sitting at a quilt frame, working on a quilt. I'm part of Rose's quilting group, and this is my memory square. I made my picture out of bits of fabric sewn onto the square, and I embroidered a saying and my name on it."

"I can't sew," Betty Dunkle said.

"Me either," someone said.

"Don't worry, there's something for you," Vera said. "We have fabric paint." She held up a flower garden, a tree done in autumn colors and a picture of a barn. "I tried to use examples that are generic, so you can get the idea. "Just think of something that reminds you of the Bellwoods. It can be anything: an activity you attended at the farm, something they did for you, a holiday, a town celebration."

"I can't draw," said Mabel Torrence, a clerk at the General Store.

"No problem," Vera said. "Jane Howard is here to help with designs and drawings. If you can color in the lines, you can make a beautiful square. We're not trying to be professional here. We want to make a quilt that'll tell Rose and Samuel how much we care about them. Are you ready to get started?"

"Yes!" resounded around the room.

"Great. Go to a table. If you aren't ready for paint or fabric, you can sketch your design on paper. Jane, Sylvia and I will go around the room to help you. Justine can help you find fabric or notions that you might need." Justine Gilmore was a single mom who worked part-time for Sylvia and helped at the inn on special occasions. Her eight-year-old daughter Josie was sitting at the front counter, drawing on her own quilt square.

The women moved to the worktables. Within minutes, the shop was a beehive of activity.

Jane stopped to help Mabel first. "Do you have an idea for your design?" she asked.

"Vera suggested something that reminds me of the

Bellwoods, and I remember that after Harold died, I wanted to put in a vegetable garden. Samuel found out, and he and Rose showed up one day with a rototiller, a hoe and a box of plants. Samuel dug up two nice rows and put fertilizer in, then Rose helped me plant a garden. Oh, it was glorious. That was the nicest thing anyone ever did for me."

"What a wonderful story," Jane said. "We can draw your garden." She took a square of paper and began sketching. Mabel told her where to place different plants. Soon they had a beautiful picture. Jane showed her how to transfer the image to the fabric, and Mabel went to work. Jane moved on.

Jane put her arm around Josie's shoulders. Josie turned and gave her a hug. Jane and the eight-year-old had become buddies when Josie's mother helped out at the inn. "What are you making?" Jane asked.

"A circus wagon," Josie said. She proudly displayed the primitive picture she'd sketched on the square of fabric. The red boxcar wagon had wheels and bars. Inside, she'd drawn a tiger.

"That's beautiful, Josie. Did you go to the circus with the Bellwoods?"

"Yes. And I got to feed the baby elephant, but I don't know how to draw an elephant, so I drew the tiger."

"That's a very fine tiger. Mr. and Mrs. Bellwood will love it."

Jane lost track of time as she went from table to table, sketching an amazing assortment of pictures. A tractor. A hayride wagon. A pumpkin patch. A corn maze. A jar of pickles. Even a sketch of Daisy, Clara Horn's miniature potbellied pig, nose-to-nose with a large sow. Evidently Clara had taken Daisy to the farm for a visit. Jane chuckled at that image.

At nine o'clock, Sylvia appeared beside Jane and told her it was time to quit. "Can you do this again next week?" she asked Jane.

"Sure." Jane stood and stretched, reaching back to rub the small of her back. *"Phew*, I'm stiff."

"I would think so. You've spent two hours bent over, drawing pictures for people."

Jane looked around. The ladies were cleaning up, gathering their things and chatting as they got ready to leave. Tiny scraps of fabric littered the floor and tables. Scissors and pincushions lay scattered on the tables.

Hope Carter and Betty Dunkle stayed behind to help Justine clean up. Several ladies stopped to talk to Jane and Sylvia on their way out, thanking them for their help. Justine began vacuuming as Alice emptied wastebaskets into a large trash bag.

"I think it was a success," Sylvia said.

"More than a success. Judging by the noise level and activity, I'd say the women had a wonderful time. You may have to hold craft parties on a regular basis," Jane said.

"Oh no," Sylvia said, groaning. "I'm exhausted."

Jane laughed. "Me too, but it was worth it. From what I saw tonight, there are enough memories to make a king-size quilt."

After church Sunday, Alice saw Florence Simpson and Ellen Moore standing outside talking. Florence was showing Ellen something that looked like a quilt square. Glancing around, Alice saw Rose approaching them. Alice hurried toward the women, but Rose got there first.

"Good morning, Florence, Ellen. I have a question about the retreat," Rose said. Then she saw the square as Florence moved it behind her back.

"Are you working on a quilt? I didn't know you made quilts. You should come to our guild meetings."

Florence appeared to be speechless for the first time that Alice could remember.

"I don't," Florence blurted out. "I'm . . . this is . . . I'm trying to make . . ."

"May I see it?" Rose asked.

"It's a surprise," Ellen said just as Florence brought her hand around. Both women looked as if they'd been caught with their hands in the collection box.

"It's for . . . one of the ladies who helps so much at church," Ellen said.

"Really? How nice. I'd be happy to make a square for your surprise," Rose said.

Florence and Ellen stared at Rose. Alice jumped in. "I couldn't help overhearing. That would be lovely, Rose. You do such beautiful work."

"So does Florence," Rose said, holding out Florence's square. "This is beautiful."

Florence took it back, stammering, "It . . . it's not finished yet. I may not use this one for the, uh . . . surprise."

Alice realized Florence felt trapped, and so she said, "Rose, I haven't had a chance to talk to you since you were at the inn Monday. How are your plans going?" Alice asked.

Before Rose could reply, Florence and Ellen excused themselves.

Rose looked a bit puzzled by their sudden departure. She shrugged and answered, "I don't know, Alice. This is getting so complicated. Caleb was going to watch the farm for us, but he has injured his ankle, and the doctor told him he might have torn a tendon and need surgery now. Ben is taking care of his own place and Caleb's, so I can't ask him. I can probably arrange for help during the day, but I really need someone there at night as well. Can you think of anyone who might be able to stay out at the farm that week while we're gone? It would have to be someone Samuel can trust with the animals." Rose's gaze implored Alice. "I'm getting desperate. Our anniversary is only two weeks away."

"No one comes to mind immediately, but I'll ask Louise and Jane if they can think of anyone."

"Bless you, Alice." Rose gave Alice a hug. "I'll keep looking. There shouldn't be any surprises at our farm. The ewes aren't due to lamb until mid-March."

"We'll put our thinking caps on," Alice assured her, giving her hug. "I'll call you if we come up with anything."

Chapter Fifteen

R ose has to find someone to watch the farm while they go on vacation," Alice told her sisters as they ate Sunday dinner. "Caleb injured his ankle, and Ben is helping him and taking care of his own place."

"What about Blair and Kristin Casey?" Louise asked, cutting a green bean in half. "Entrusting the Bellwood farm to Blair would be a powerful endorsement."

"That's not a bad idea," Alice said, chewing thoughtfully. "But maybe I should talk to them before I suggest the idea to Rose."

"Why don't you invite them over for dessert this evening, so you can talk to them in person?" Jane said. "I'll make something special."

"Good idea." Alice said, nodding. "I'll do that."

Jane sensed distance between Blair and Kristin as soon as they entered the inn. Alice ushered them into the living room while Louise helped Jane carry in tea and generous slices of peaches-and-cream pie.

"It's good to see you, Blair. You've been so busy lately, we've missed you," Louise said, handing him a piece of pie.

Beside him, Kristin gave Jane a halfhearted smile when she took the pie and tea Jane offered her.

"I missed you at church this morning," Jane said as she sat next to her.

Kristin turned to her. "I overslept."

"My fault," Blair said. "I left early to check on a cow, and I didn't wake Kristin when I left." He gave her hand a squeeze.

Kristin turned toward Alice. "I brought a couple of printed squares with me. Would you like to see them?"

"Oh yes. I'm eager to see how they turned out," Alice said.

Kristin opened the bag she'd set on the floor by her feet and pulled out several quilt squares. One was larger than the others. She passed it to Alice.

"Oh my." Alice gazed at the square. "This is amazing." She handed the cloth to Louise.

"It's beautiful. How did you do it?"

Jane took the square from Louise and held it up. Then she looked at Kristin. "I know *how* you did it, but how did you manage such vibrant colors? I doubt if the photograph looked this good."

Kristin smiled. "I enhanced the colors a bit."

"A bit?" Jane said. "A lot, I'd say. This will be fabulous in the middle of the quilt. Do you have others?"

"Yes." She held up another cloth picture of a young Rose. A lamb was trying to eat the end of one of her long braids while she bottle-fed two other lambs. She was laughing. In the third square, Samuel was helping two young boys shear a large ram. The fourth was the scene that Kristin had photographed for Rose's Web site.

"These are wonderful, Kristin. And they will be perfect with all the other squares. I wish you could have come Saturday night. I couldn't believe how many memories people came up with," Alice said.

"I'm afraid that was my fault too," Blair said. "I promised to take Kristin out for her birthday, and . . . uh . . . I was attending a cow after a difficult delivery." He gave Kristin an apologetic look. "I didn't forget, I was just late," he said as if to excuse himself.

Oh boy, Jane thought. *No wonder Kristin is upset.* "Happy birthday, Kristin. We didn't know." She gave Kristin an understanding smile. "You'll just have to pretend the pie is a cake. Or that the cake we made Thursday was for your birthday. Did she tell you about the decorations she made, Blair?"

Blair frowned and looked sideways at Kristin. "I don't think so. I appreciate the leftovers you sent home with her, though. Thanks."

"We were practicing for the Bellwoods' anniversary cake. Kristin picked up the techniques as if she'd been doing it for years. She's very talented," Jane said.

"I keep telling her that," Blair said, putting his arm around her shoulder, clearly trying to encourage her.

"Speaking of the Bellwoods," Alice said, "Rose told me this morning that none of her sons can watch the farm while she and Samuel take their surprise trip to Hawaii. She's tried everyone she could think of, but no one is available to help. She's getting desperate. Samuel won't go unless he knows the farm is in good hands." Alice paused, then said, "I promised her that we would brainstorm solutions for her problem, and Louise thought of you. Would you be able and willing to stay at Bellwood Farm and take care of their animals for a week?"

"Sure. We could do that," Blair said without hesitation. He glanced at Kristin. "Couldn't we, honey?"

She looked shocked at his response. "I can't take care of a farm. I don't know anything about animals."

"I'll show you. It'll be fun. You won't have to do anything. I'll be there," Blair said.

Kristin let out a sigh and shook her head. "You aren't there now. Why would being at the Bellwoods' be different? Someone'll call, and you'll take off, leaving me with a bunch of animals."

"Kristin . . ."

"Rose feels that she'll be able to find day help," Alice said. "And if Blair has to leave you alone, Jane or I could come out and stay with you until he gets back."

Kristin stared at Alice for a moment. Then she sighed. "Y'all have been so nice to me. I'll do it for you and Rose. Just don't leave me alone out there. I'd be afraid I'd do something wrong and kill a sheep or something."

Blair gave Kristin a reassuring hug. "It will work out fine," he said. "You'll see. You might even like it."

"I doubt it," she said. She sounded almost petulant, but Jane saw something—fear?—in her eyes. Whatever was bothering Kristin went beyond unhappiness at a missed birthday dinner.

Jane put away the bucket of cleaning supplies and gathered the laundry. She paused on the landing and called to her sisters. "I'm going to run a few errands in town. Do you need anything?"

"No, thank you," Alice said as she plugged the vacuum into the hallway socket. "I'm going to work on my quilt square. It's almost done, and I want to finish before we go to Sylvia's tonight."

Louise stopped making the bed to come to the doorway and say, "I ordered a book at Nine Lives. Would you check to see if it's in?"

"Sure. Maybe I'll find something to read. When the anniversary is over, I'll need something to do."

"Have you planned dinner yet?"

"No. Do you have a special request?"

"We could have supper at the Coffee Shop before we go to Sylvia's. That would save your having to cook tonight."

"I don't mind cooking, you know."

"I know, but you haven't had a night off in weeks."

"All right then, it's a date. See you later."

Jane enjoyed the brisk walk into town. She stopped at Nine Lives first. As she reached for the door latch, she noticed a bright retreat poster taped in the window. The door jingled when she entered the shop, and three cats scattered out of the way. Tess, an orange, black and white calico, came over to sniff Jane's pant leg. She stooped to pet the cat, which began to purr loudly and rub up against Jane's leg.

"Hello, Jane," Viola Reed said as she came sailing out of the back room, the green crocheted scarf around her neck shimmering as she walked.

"What a lovely scarf," Jane said. "It sparkles."

"Thank you. I bought it at a craft fair before Christmas. The yarn has iridescent threads woven in. Speaking of thread, you came just in time. I need your advice. Come to the back." She turned around and walked toward the storeroom.

Curious, Jane followed her. Boxes of books were on the floor and on chairs. An open box sat on the table, halfway unpacked. Books were scattered all over the table. Viola picked up one, then another, set them aside and moved several others.

"I know it's here somewhere," she said.

Jane thought she was referring to Louise's book, but Viola suddenly exclaimed "Aha!" and picked up a quilt square.

"Rose comes in for cookbooks and gardening books, like you, and books on quilting. She often comes to my readings, so I thought I would put a book on the square, but I can't decide what kind, and whether it should be open or closed. What do you think?"

The square was completely empty. Jane looked at the

table. A stack of three books with different colored spines sat on the table, each book slightly off-kilter.

"Doesn't Rose wear reading glasses?" Jane asked.

"Yes, I believe she does. Why?"

"Let me borrow your glasses."

Viola seemed to think Jane's request odd, but she removed her bifocals and gave them to Jane.

Jane set them on top of the books and stood back. "There's your picture," she said. "A stack of books with glasses on top. You can title the books Cooking, Gardening and Quilts."

"Why, Jane, you are a genius! Would you sketch it for me?" Viola gave her paper and a pencil.

"All right. While I draw, would you see if Louise's book is in? And do you have any new books? I need something to read when all this excitement dies down."

"Yes, Louise's book arrived yesterday, and I have just the book for you. I'll go get them." Viola went out front. Jane sat and began working on her sketch. She finished and held it up when Viola returned.

"That's perfect, Jane. Will you be at Sylvia's tonight to help me decide on colors?"

"Yes. We're all going."

Jane paid for the books and walked briskly to Time for Tea. The sun peeked through the high clouds, hinting at a break in the weather. The exercise in the crisp, cold air raised her spirits. Jane liked to jog most of the year, but the recent weather had kept her indoors.

The bell jingled as she stepped inside. Jane recognized Pachelbel's "Canon in D" playing as Wilhelm Wood waited on Mona Kramer, a weekend guest who had checked out of the inn earlier that morning. Three other customers browsed the shelves.

Jane stood behind Mona at the counter.

"I'd like one ounce of the jasmine pearls tea and four boxes of Madeleine and Daughters chocolates. They served them at the inn, and I've never before tasted such delicious truffles."

"I only have three boxes of the chocolates left," Wilhelm said. "They have been very popular this week."

"Oh dear. I want them for Valentine's Day gifts. Are you expecting more soon? Perhaps you could ship a box to me," Mona said.

Wilhelm looked past his customer's shoulder at Jane and winked.

With Valentine's Day, the retreat and the anniversary less than two weeks away, Jane was thankful that she had contracted with Exquisite Chocolatiers of Philadelphia to make and market her recipes for the line of Madeleine and Daughters chocolates she had developed. She gave Wilhelm a smile.

"I'll be getting a new supply tomorrow or the next day," he told Mona. "I'll be happy to ship an order to you."

"Wonderful. I'll take the three boxes you have and order two more. That way I can have some for myself." She opened her purse and took out her wallet.

Jane wandered over to look at the new assortment of English biscuits displayed in a picnic hamper while Wilhelm completed his transaction, then rang up a sale for one of the other customers. As they left, she went up to the counter.

Wilhelm looked up. "Hi, Jane. How is everything going?"

"Very well. I'm sorry I didn't return your call from last week. I didn't remember about it until just now when I walked to town."

"Last week? Oh yes." He lowered his voice. "The anniversary. Wait here." He disappeared in the back room, then came out carrying an envelope. "I found this and thought about the Bellwoods."

He took out a small square card. He unfolded it at the
bottom like a little easel and stood it on the counter. A teabag
was attached with a satin ribbon. The teabag envelope held a
picture of a teapot with blue and white flowers. On the flap
were inscribed the words: Forty Years of Tea for Two. Below
the picture of the teapot, it said: Samuel and Rose.
February 14.

"That's lovely, Wilhelm." Jane said, but she wasn't certain what he had in mind.

Wilhelm beamed. "I knew you'd like it. I ordered one
hundred. I hope that'll be enough to give one to each guest."

"Oh, I'm sure that will be enough. What a nice idea. We
can put one at each place on the tables."

"Precisely what I had in mind. I wanted to do something
special. Rose has been one of my most faithful customers for
years. Did I tell you I plan to travel to Brazil after the anniversary?"

"Have you made arrangements then?" Wilhelm loved to
travel and had talked about going to South America for a
long time.

"My travel agent is checking for me. I've had enough of
this cold. Brazil should be wonderful this time of year. I
found an article in one of my travel magazines—"

Jane glanced at her watch. "Goodness, look at the time. I
must get back to the inn," she said, heading for the door. Jane
knew she'd be there for an hour if Wilhelm started talking
about traveling.

Chapter Sixteen

I'm glad we got here early," Sylvia said as she slipped into the red faux-leather booth next to Jane at the Coffee Shop.

"Yes," Louise said, glancing around at the crowded room.

Hope Collins hurried over to their table. She pulled an order pad out of her pocket and reached for the pencil perched over her ear. "Whew! What a crowd," she said. "I hope the meatloaf holds out. That's the special tonight. What can I get you?"

"That sounds good," Alice said. "I'll have that and save me a piece of raisin pie."

"Make that two," Sylvia said.

Jane ordered the fried-chicken dinner.

"I'll have that as well, but no gravy, and a salad instead of mashed potatoes," Louise said. Jane rarely cooked fried foods. Louise knew she was trying to keep them healthy, and she appreciated that, but every so often, she enjoyed fried chicken.

"Looks like business is booming," Jane commented.

"It's that quilting night at your place, Sylvia," Hope said. "We'd been dead since Christmas until this started. All of a sudden, people came crawling out of the woodwork. That was just what we needed around here." A little bell sounded at the kitchen counter. "Well, gotta get moving. Customers waiting." Hope pushed the pencil back above her ear and hurried off.

"Jane said you had a large turnout last week. Are you ready for another onslaught tonight?" Louise asked Sylvia.

"I'm much better prepared than last week," she said. "The tables are already set up with the materials."

"I hope everyone will finish her square and turn it in tonight, so Gretchen can put the quilt together," Alice said. "I need to feather stitch around the appliqués on mine yet."

"I'm not certain I'll finish mine in time," Louise said, shaking her head. "I decided to use cross-stitch to make my picture, and it is taking longer than I expected. Perhaps if I burn the midnight oil all week, I'll complete it."

"Why is it everything seems to pile up at the last minute?" Jane asked. "Our Valentine's weekend at the inn is in four days, and the retreat is in ten."

"Yes, and all of the guest rooms are booked for this weekend," Louise said. "But we're empty on the anniversary weekend."

"I should have taken time off work this week to help you," Alice said.

"We'll do fine," Jane said. "We always do."

Hope arrived with their dinners. Louise gave thanks, and then they conversed companionably while they ate. Most of the women at the restaurant would be at Sylvia's in a half hour, and the men would head home.

June Carter came out of the kitchen when there was a lull in orders and brought her quilt square over to show them. "I can't leave the restaurant, but I definitely need help," she said, sighing. "I tried to sketch a picnic table, and it looks like a box."

"Are you going to paint it?" Sylvia asked.

"I'd like to, but I have to buy the paints."

"If you can come over to my shop sometime tomorrow, you can use my supplies. Maybe Jane could sketch a picture for you and then you could paint it," Sylvia suggested.

"Would you, Jane? I'd be ever so grateful."

"I'd be happy to."

June went back into the kitchen and Hope brought them their desserts. "Would you mind looking at my quilt square?" she asked.

"We'd love to see it," Alice said.

"I'll go get it," she said and disappeared into the back. She returned a moment later with an appliquéd square that had bits of fabric fitted on like a mosaic. The scene showed two silhouetted figures in a Coffee Shop booth with a pie in the middle of the table.

"I couldn't think what to do, but I remember Samuel used to bring Rose in for blackberry pie every Saturday night during the summer, like it was a date. I always thought that was so sweet. Maybe it'll bring them some good memories."

"This is beautiful, Hope," Louise said. "You even put the Coffee Shop on the window in the background and wrote it backward, as it appears from inside. I'm impressed."

Hope blushed and looked a bit embarrassed, but pleased. "I used to make collages out of scraps of paper. I used iron-on backing to make the pieces stick, but I don't know how to finish it. Should I stitch the pieces to make sure they stay down?"

"I would recommend it," Sylvia said. "You don't want to make the stitches obvious, though. The picture is wonderful. I'd use a dark thread and barely catch the edges, like a hem stitch or a very small blanket stitch."

"Could you show me?"

"Sure. If you can drop by the store tomorrow sometime, I'll help you."

"Oh, thank you. I'll come on my lunch break. That's about two o'clock. Is that all right?"

"Perfect. And now we'd better get going so we can get to the store before everyone else does. I left Justine alone."

As they walked to Sylvia's Buttons, they could see a retreat poster in nearly every shop window.

They entered the shop to a hum of activity.

"This reminds me of an old-fashioned sewing bee," Louise commented, looking around the store. "Everyone is working, and yet listen to the laughter and conversations."

"I suppose this is a good example of multitasking," Alice said. "Women can work together on individual projects and have a grand time while they do. I hope the women's retreat has this same congenial atmosphere."

"I don't see many here who are Kristin Casey's age," Louise commented. "We hope to attract those younger women to the retreat. They need to discover the sense of belonging these ladies have developed."

Louise looked around and saw that Jane was already working, bent over a quilt square, paintbrush in hand. Sylvia sat on one side of her and Nellie Carter on the other. Vera and Patsy looked over her shoulder. Their affection for each other showed clearly on their animated, smiling faces as they watched and talked, like most everyone in the room.

Her pen poised over a notepad, Louise watched Jane roll small scoops of creamy chocolate into balls and place them in precise rows on parchment paper. How like their mother she looked. Youthful, energetic, filled with the joy of life. Madeleine Howard had been in her midthirties the last time Louise watched her make truffles. Louise and Alice had helped, dipping the filling into the rich, molten chocolate.

The tantalizing aroma of dark chocolate mixed with the pungent scent of fresh grated orange peel and diced candied ginger made Louise's mouth water. Earlier that morning Jane had grated zest off of a dozen oranges. The naked oranges went back into the refrigerator to be juiced for their guests on the weekend.

Louise marveled at her sister's talent. Watching Jane's efficiency and concentration, she remembered the baby who had changed her life fifty years earlier.

At fifteen, Louise had been too young to take over the role of mother to an infant, but their mother's death after childbirth had given her no choice.

At twenty, Louise had decided she was not cut out to be a mother. She adored her little sister, but raising a child required great wisdom and fortitude. And their father, bless his soul, rarely played the disciplinarian, although his three daughters had no doubts about his authority and high moral standards.

Daniel Howard was a true spiritual shepherd, loving and guiding his flock and his daughters. The thought of rebelling never occurred to Louise. Nor to Alice, she was sure. Jane was a little more headstrong. Louise remembered spending considerable time praying for her little sister. She smiled to think how her prayers had been answered.

"Louise, where are you?"

Louise shook her head. "Did you say something?"

"You were a million miles away. I asked if you wanted more tea," Jane said.

"Oh yes. I'm sorry. I was reminiscing."

"It must have been quite a memory. You had a very sentimental expression on your face."

"I was remembering Mother making truffles when I was a teenager. She used to let me help. May I help you?"

"You bet. After all, these are Madeleine and Daughters chocolates. Want a taste?"

"Certainly." Louise took the teaspoon with a small bit of filling that Jane offered. She let the creamy mixture melt on her tongue. "*Mmm.* The ginger gives it a little piquancy. I like it. How do you come up with these flavors?"

Jane shrugged. "Something triggers an idea. Like today—I was in Time for Tea and saw a tea blend with orange and ginger. I just put the things together. Chocolate with orange and ginger."

"My mind would never have made that connection." Louise washed her hands, slipped an apron over her head and tied it.

"Here's another scoop," Jane said, handing Louise a utensil the size of a melon baller. "Dust your hands with a little powdered sugar so the chocolate won't stick to your fingers."

Louise's first few tries came out flat, but she finally got the hang of it and picked up speed. Soon she had several rows of neat little brown balls.

"How is your list coming?" Jane asked.

Louise stopped for a second in the middle of a roll. She cleared her throat, then continued rolling. "I'm afraid I forgot about the list."

Jane laughed out loud. "Chocolate has that effect on people. I think the fumes from melting chocolate can lure us to a different level of consciousness."

"I read recently that dark chocolate is good for one's health," Louise said.

"I don't doubt it, but as you have shown, it is distracting. After all, you are one of the most single-minded, task-oriented women I know."

"Do you think so?" Louise glanced at Jane, surprised by her sister's opinion.

Jane nodded. "Definitely. I wish I could cultivate that quality. Perhaps I wouldn't be trying out a new idea when I should be doing something more productive. There's something therapeutic about the motions of cooking and the smells and textures of food. So how are we doing, discounting myself, of course?"

"You are doing fine, although I don't doubt you could use a little therapy at the moment." Louise placed the last ball on the parchment paper.

Jane laughed. "I'll pop these in the freezer while the chocolate coating melts." Jane carried the tray of chocolate-orange balls to the freezer, then took out a block of dark chocolate.

"I'll go back to making a task list for the anniversary celebration and the retreat," Louise said. "I believe we have everything under control. Experience, however, tells me there's always something left undone. I want this to be perfect for Rose and Samuel."

"We've received tons of positive responses to the invitations, right?" Jane worked as she talked, quickly and deftly chopping the chocolate with a butcher knife.

"Ninety-two affirmatives so far and only three negatives, because of previous commitments and travel."

"Wow! We'll have standing room only. How will the house handle all those people?"

"I considered asking Samuel to move the ceremony to the church, but the farm is where they've lived all their married life and where they raised their family. Samuel wants it there, and I suspect Rose would feel the same way. What would you think of moving the ceremony and reception to the barn?"

Jane stopped and turned toward Louise. "Why, I think that's absolutely inspired. Everyone in town has been to their living crèche in the barn at Christmastime. What better place to renew their vows?"

"Do you think Samuel will agree?"

"Call him and find out. Rose is teaching spinning and weaving cloth at the elementary school today. If Samuel doesn't answer, don't leave a message."

"Good idea." Louise washed her hands and picked up the phone. She let it ring four times and hung up when the answering machine came on. "He's not there," she said.

After a moment's hesitation, she picked up the receiver again and dialed. "Hi, Fred, this is Louise Smith . . . I'm fine, thank you . . . Oh yes, that's good news. Would you do me a favor and call Samuel Bellwood? I must talk to him . . . Yes, about the anniversary. If you have to leave a message, have him call you. Don't leave my name on the answering machine. Rose would wonder why I'm calling Samuel . . . Thanks." Louise said good-bye and hung up.

"What's the good news?" Jane asked.

"Fred said we will have clear weather next week and the temperatures will jump to the midfifties."

"Wonderful. That'll help a lot."

Chapter Seventeen

I hope Samuel calls us soon. His thoughts about the barn will have an impact on my list." Louise poured a cup of coffee and sat down with her notebook.

Alice had ordered the decorating supplies, but if they used the barn, they might want to add a few items. They'd ask Samuel to put fresh straw on the floor, and then they could sprinkle dried rose petals and other flowers and get a runner to create an aisle. She wrote "additional decorations" and put Alice's name next to the notation.

She made a note to herself to talk to Fred about transporting chairs and tables from the church.

"What about mints and nuts?" she asked Jane.

"Covered. I've ordered the nuts, and Kristin will help me make the mints Thursday. I'm making several other dishes ahead as well. I've planned a buffet luncheon. I'll give you a copy of my menu later."

"Is anyone helping you?"

"Yes. Daylene is supplying relish trays and hams. Gretchen is cooking turkeys. I asked Clarissa to make dinner rolls and some of her wonderful marbled rye bread, as well as two sheet cakes. I'll make scalloped potatoes, salads and finger foods."

"That sounds wonderful. I wish I could be here to help you. I feel obligated to attend the women's retreat."

"Several people have offered to help. Don't worry. We'll manage. I suspect you will have your hands full keeping Rose occupied and keeping the peace between Aunt Ethel and Florence."

Louise groaned. "Don't remind me. I'm hoping they'll behave and that the retreat will draw the women together."

"Especially the younger women like Kristin," said Jane.

"Indeed. That reminds me. Several young mothers have said that they'd like to attend the retreat. We're looking for after-school care so they can come."

"Perhaps the teenagers at church would volunteer as a service project."

"Good idea," Louise said. She pulled out another piece of paper. "I need a retreat list too." She wrote "retreat" at the top of the page and jotted a note to have Alice ask the ANGELs about babysitting. "Oh, before I leave the anniversary plans, Sylvia called earlier about the quilt squares. So far, she has forty-five finished squares. That doesn't count Gretchen's and Daylene's squares or Kristin's and ours. Vera said she'd take the squares to Gretchen and help her lay them out after school tomorrow. I hope I can complete mine tonight."

"I need to finish mine too." Jane filled a large pot with water and set it on the stove to heat, then poured a cup of coffee and sat down next to Louise. She leaned over to see her sister's list. "Goodness. You have a lot to do."

"This isn't *my* to-do list. Only a few of these jobs are my responsibility. I merely want to make sure we don't forget something important."

"Never fear. With your organizational skills, the anniversary celebration and the retreat will come off without a hitch."

Louise shook her head. "I hope you're right."

"Now here's my list," Jane said as she took a blank sheet of paper and wrote "Anniversary Menu" across the top.

Beneath it she wrote all the dishes for the luncheon reception. "Kristin and I can make the scalloped potatoes and cakes Thursday and freeze them."

"I'm glad you're working with her. She's such a sweet girl and so willing to help. You're giving her quite an education. She couldn't find better culinary training."

"She's so eager and willing, she makes teaching fun. I only have two more sessions with her before she goes to visit her parents."

Louise shook her head. "The way she talks about going home, I get the feeling that she's running away. I hope she and Blair will realize that they must work at their marriage to make it successful."

After dinner, Jane set up her paints at the kitchen table to finish her quilt square. Alice and Louise took their squares into the parlor where they could be more comfortable.

Louise rubbed her arms. "It's a bit chilly in here. Shall we have a fire?"

"I'll start one," Alice said. "Why don't you pick out some music—something to stitch by?"

Louise walked over to a stack of CDs. "Something soothing, but not too slow," she murmured. She made her selection and put it in the player.

Flames danced around the kindling, reflecting off the cut facets of the crystal chandelier as the lilting sounds of flute, fiddle and drums filled the room with the haunting harmony of Irish folk music. Alice sat on one of the Victorian Eastlake chairs and picked up her square. She slipped a thimble onto her finger and began the small feather stitches to outline and secure her pattern.

Louise sat on a matching chair and picked up the hoop holding her quilt square. "Sylvia said Gretchen is picking up the finished squares tomorrow afternoon."

"Then I have to finish tonight. I'm working tomorrow."

"I made a list of all the things left to do before the anniversary party and the retreat. It would be nice if we could supply after-school care for some of the young mothers so they can attend the retreat. Do you think some of the older ANGELs would be interested in babysitting as a service project?"

"They might. We've been looking for a service project. Now that the holidays are over, there hasn't been much need for help. I'll ask tomorrow night."

The telephone rang, then stopped ringing before Alice could get up. A moment later, Jane came into the room. "That was Samuel. I asked him about using the barn. At first he was hesitant, but then I told him how many are coming and he changed his mind. I asked him about heating it. It has big heaters on thermostats, so it should be all right, even if the weather stays this cold. I told him that we'll decorate and it'll be really pretty."

"I hope the decorations I ordered will work out there."

"They'll be fine," Jane said. "We'll get extra streamers and maybe some of those three-dimensional paper bells, and we can string them from the rafters."

"I think you should order a runner," Louise said to Alice. "Samuel can put fresh straw down, but that would make it seem more formal."

"All right. I'll call Fred tomorrow and see if he can order one for us to rent."

"Between the three of us and our lists, we just might get through all this," Jane said, laughing.

"I can't believe these mints are so easy to make," Kristin said as she pressed a small heart-shaped cutter into the rolled-out pink dough. "They taste so good."

"Most of the time, the best recipes come from the simplest

combinations. These are a good example. From three basic ingredients—cream cheese, sugar and flavoring—you get melt-in-your-mouth mints."

"I'm so glad you're letting me help. I never enjoyed cooking before, but I'm really catching the bug." Kristin slid a stainless-steel spatula beneath the dough and carefully peeled away the scraps, leaving a dozen small hearts, which she scooped up and placed on parchment paper. "I've started working my way through the cookbook I got as a wedding present. This week I made meatballs one night and a roasted chicken another. They came out pretty well. Blair even seemed to like them, at least he said so. He gobbled them down so fast, I don't know how he tasted them. I worry about his working so hard. He had a Grange meeting one night, and he's been working on our barn in the evenings, putting up insulation and drywall to make it into a clinic. I tried to help him, but I'm not good with a hammer."

"At least you're trying. Good for you. I suspect learning carpentry is a little like learning to cook. Knowing all the terms and methods doesn't do any good unless you put the knowledge to use. You have to practice. Not every attempt will be great, but each time, you get better. With a hammer, you start hitting the nails on the head. With cooking, you learn how foods will mix together and cook, and then you can begin experimenting and varying the recipes."

Kristin laughed. "You make it sound so easy, but you haven't seen my runny Jell-O or watery scrambled eggs."

Jane smiled. "I have stories like that too. Cooking, like life, requires a little TLC—a little tenderness, a little love and a lot of care. Success with gelatin requires boiling water, patience to make sure it is fully dissolved, and exact measurements. Eggs, well there are variables: good fresh eggs, not too much liquid, and an even heat as they cook. Certain ingredients can make them runny."

Jane looked at the trays of pink and white mint hearts. "Very nice. And one job finished." She set aside the trays to dry. "Now we're going to make a very complicated recipe."

Kristin looked at her so seriously that Jane had to laugh as she took a package of miniature sausages and several packages of refrigerated corn biscuits out of the refrigerator. She turned on the oven before she opened the packages.

"We're going to make corn-dog appetizers. We could make a corn batter and deep-fry them, but we'll do this the easy way." She took out a squeeze bottle of Dijon mustard.

Jane showed Kristin how to squirt mustard on the sausage, then roll little coils of pastry around it. Before long, they had several trays of tiny sausage bits ready to bake. "We'll prebake these and freeze them. Then I'll reheat them before the reception. Voilà!" She said with a flourish. "Instant appetizers."

Kristin grinned. "Oh sure . . . 'very complicated,' but your secret is safe with me," she said, crossing her heart.

"Good. You can do the same thing with hot dogs," Jane said. "Use craft sticks to hold them and add cheese."

"I'll have to try that." Kristin's voice trailed off, as if she had gone somewhere else in her thoughts.

Jane knew something was troubling her friend, but she didn't want to pry. *Lord, I need help here. Give me wisdom to encourage Kristin. Give me the right words to say. I know she needs a friend. Help me to be that friend.*

"That's two items off my list. We're doing great," Jane said. "Now we'll make scalloped potatoes for the anniversary party. Normally, I'd make everything just in time to be served, but we're cooking for a crowd, so we have to take some shortcuts. That's why we are precooking part of the food."

Jane took a large bowl of cooked, whole red potatoes out of the refrigerator. "For instance, I cooked these potatoes this morning while I was cleaning up from breakfast. Now it's easy to slip the skins off and slice them for baking. They're just barely cooked, so they still will absorb the sauce while they're baking, and precooking keeps them from turning brown. Plus, the scalloped potatoes will bake faster and more evenly. Making them ahead gives the flavors a chance to fully develop."

Jane removed the puffy corn-dog appetizers from the oven and set them aside to cool. Then she and Kristin began building the potato casseroles.

They made white sauce and sautéed sliced mushrooms and onions. She added Dijon mustard and they layered the potatoes, onions, mushrooms, sauce and grated cheese in aluminum baking dishes.

"I wouldn't use disposable aluminum pans with raw potatoes," Jane told Kristin. "A reactive pan can turn the potatoes black. Also, potatoes can turn black because they are stored at too low a temperature or because they are high in iron. If your potatoes are cold, let them sit out until they come to room temperature. I always add a quarter teaspoon of cream of tartar to the water while they cook. That prevents discoloration. A quarter of a fresh lemon or a teaspoon of white vinegar will work too."

"How did you learn all that?" Kristin asked, shaking her head. "I'll never remember all your tips."

"I take lots of notes. I discover some things by trial and error, and I learn from other people. My mother's cookbook is filled with little notes of her wisdom, and I find a lot of things by researching in trade journals and cookbooks or over the Internet."

When four pans of the potatoes were in the oven, Jane suggested a break. She washed her hands and made a pot of decaffeinated coffee.

"I have a treat to go with our coffee," she said. She set a box of truffles on the table.

Kristin sat down and glanced at the tempting chocolates but didn't take one. At a loss for a topic of conversation, Jane busied herself getting out cups and cream and sugar. When the coffee was ready, she poured two cups and took them to the table, sitting next to Kristin.

Kristin slowly stirred cream and sugar into her coffee, watching as her spoon swirled around in the caramel-colored liquid. Still stirring, she looked up at Jane.

"If you'd had a child, do you think your marriage would have lasted?" she asked, pinning Jane with a searching gaze.

"You really ask the hard questions, don't you?"

Kristin just stared at Jane, waiting for an answer.

Help me, Lord, Jane thought. "I can only guess that I'd have tried harder to salvage something for my child's sake. I believe I'm grateful that a child wasn't involved."

"That's what I think too. Blair says we should look into adopting a child. I was kind of surprised he brought it up. He always said he wants a big family, and he talked about having a place in the country with a bunch of little Caseys running around. I just assumed he meant his own children. He thinks I'm unhappy because I can't have a baby, but that's not it. I want a child, but I want a strong marriage first, and I don't think we have that. Adding a child won't close the distance that's growing between us."

"Oh, Kristin, no wonder you're troubled." Jane reached over and took Kristin's hand. "What are you going to do about it?" she asked gently.

"Do?" Tears sprang to her eyes. "What can I do? He's so busy that I might as well be in Georgia."

"Have you tried going out on calls with him? Maybe you could help him."

"I can't. I . . . I'm not cut out to be a veterinarian's wife. I wish I'd realized that before we got married. He needs someone who can relate to the animals and his work. I just don't." Emotion deepened Kristin's drawl. Her lower lip quivered. "I don't know what I expected, but it wasn't this." Her shoulders shuddered. "I don't think I can be what he needs. Sooner or later, he's going to figure that out."

Jane felt absolutely certain that Blair loved Kristin. She'd seen the adoration in his eyes when he looked at his pretty wife, and she heard the pride in his voice when he spoke about her. He clearly believed she was what he needed. Was Kristin willing to try to save their marriage?

"Kristin, have you ever had meringue?"

"Meringue? You mean like lemon-meringue pie?"

Jane nodded.

"Yes. My grandmother makes fabulous lemon-meringue pies. Why?"

"Do you have any idea how hard it is to make a perfect meringue?"

Kristin shook her head. "I don't think Grandma ever has any trouble."

"Perhaps not, probably because she's had lots of experience and she knows the secrets. You see, a meringue will fall or weep for many reasons. Old eggs, rainy weather, too much beating, too much sugar, too little sugar, too coarse sugar, a little grease on the bowl or the beaters, the wrong oven temperature, or cooking it the wrong amount of time, and sometimes even when you get all that right, it can still fall apart."

"That sounds like way too much work."

"But it's worth it. And it gets easier with practice. Oh, and there's a secret ingredient to make it last."

"There's always a secret ingredient."

"The point is, Kristin, it takes work and the right ingredients to make a really fine meringue. Relationships are like that. They take work, practice and the right ingredients. And if you give up and walk away, you'll never have the satisfaction of making something wonderful. Besides that, you'll go hungry. I don't know how to help you. I don't have any wise advice. But you have everything you need—all the right ingredients—to have a wonderful relationship."

Kristin stared at her. Jane could almost see her mind trying to make sense of the meringue example. *Please, Lord, let it make sense. Let Kristin see the possibilities.*

"What . . . what is the secret ingredient? Is it love?"

Jane gave Kristin a wistful smile. "I used to think that. I used to think enough love could overcome anything. I guess I still think that's true, if it's the right kind of love. But the secret ingredient is prayer, Kristin, because God has the answers. If we rely on the Lord and follow His examples, then we have the secret ingredient."

A tear spilled over and trickled down Kristin's cheek. "I love Blair," she whispered.

"I know that. Does he know?" Jane asked gently.

"I . . . I hope so."

Jane squeezed Kristin's hand. "I can't advise you on working with Blair and helping him with the animals, but Rose is an expert. Why don't you go talk to her? Tell her how you feel and ask her how she does it."

Jane got up to check the potatoes, leaving Kristin to her private thoughts.

Chapter Eighteen

As Jane mixed kippering ingredients with water in a heavy zippered plastic bag Friday morning, the Wild Things van drove up and parked in back of the inn. "Craig's here," she said to Louise, who was drying the breakfast dishes.

Louise opened the door for him. He carried two beautiful red-and-white bouquets into the kitchen.

While Louise held the door to the dining room open for Craig, Jane added thin fillets of salmon to the bag and set it in the refrigerator to marinate until the next morning, when she would bake the fish for breakfast.

Alice came downstairs from checking the guest rooms and helped Craig carry in more flowers and wreaths. Their Valentine Special guests would arrive in the afternoon.

Jane took a chilled mixture of her unusual orange shortbread out of the refrigerator. She was rolling out the dough when Alice came back into the kitchen.

"Each guest room has a Valentine bouquet and a dish of heart soaps, and I hung the Valentine wreath on the front door. Craig outdid himself. That wreath is beautiful, with the balsam fir, red berries and lacy white ribbon. I almost hated to hang it outside." Alice washed her hands. "Put me to work."

"You can fill the dishes with truffles for the rooms."

Louise came in just then. "What can I do to help?"

"If you'll fold the napkins in the rosebud design, we'll use them for tomorrow's breakfast. Use the pink and the green ones."

Jane made two trays of heart-shaped cookies and put them in the oven, then started cleaning up her utensils. She loved the activity of holiday weekends. Four couples were booked through Wednesday to take full advantage of the holiday package, which included Jane's gourmet breakfasts each day, and a romantic high tea at the inn.

"Are you going to Rose's crochet class this morning?" Alice asked.

"Yes. I think I have just enough time to fit it in."

"Go ahead," Louise said. "I'll finish cleaning up."

"I will as soon as the shortbread comes out of the oven."

Just then the timer went off. Jane pulled the trays out of the oven. The delicious aroma of buttery sweetness filled the kitchen. The cookies were perfectly golden.

Haley Gorman didn't make it to crochet class Friday morning. Mila Babin excitedly announced that Haley had gone into labor that morning and was on her way to the hospital. All of the women were excited about the advent of a new baby and began relating their own experiences. Kristin smiled politely. She sat in her usual chair and picked up her blanket, which she had completed. Jane sat next to her.

"Your blanket looks great," Jane commented.

Kristin gave her a wry look. "Well, at least I finished it," she said.

"And some lucky baby in the church nursery will love snuggling up under it."

Kristin's lips curved up in a hint of a smile. "Thanks," she said. "I don't think I'll go into business making blankets. I need to find something more to do, though. My Web business has slowed down. I hope it's just the time of year."

"That could be it. Everything seems to slow down during the winter," Jane said. "But keep in mind that we've made it through January, and February is a short month that's packed with activity. Spring will be here before you know it."

"It's already springtime in Atlanta. Mom said her daffodils and hyacinths are opening up. I can't wait to see them."

"Trees will start budding out here in March, and we have gorgeous flowers in May," Jane said. Kristin just nodded.

Rose started the class on booties, but gave the option of picking another project. Neither Jane nor Kristen was interested in making the tiny footwear, so they decided to pick out something different. They went to talk to Sylvia.

"I'm thinking of making a scarf," Jane said. "Viola had one she bought at a craft fair. The crafter used a special yarn, so it came out looking like it was made of long-haired fur."

"I have a pattern for those," Sylvia said. "You use eyelash or fun-fur yarn." She took a skein of yarn from a shelf. The soft lavender yarn had fine, hairy filaments. She showed them a picture of a finished scarf.

"Oh, I like that," Kristin said.

"Even better, it's considered an easy skill level. I'll take that pattern," Jane said after examining it. "Do you have other colors? Like bright red?"

"I'll check."

"I'll take the lavender," Kristin said. "I can make this while I travel. I can't wait to show my mother."

Sylvia came back with two balls of cherry red yarn.

"That's perfect," Jane said.

Sylvia rang up their purchases. Then she looked over

toward the class. Rose had her back to them, bent over someone's work. "Do you want to see the dress?" Sylvia asked in a low voice.

"Yes," Jane and Kristin both whispered, then laughed conspiratorially.

"Come on." Sylvia ushered them to the back room. She took a plastic-covered garment out of a closet, looked around to make sure no one else was watching, then removed the plastic.

"Oh, it's gorgeous," Kristin said, drawing out her pronouncement.

The sky-blue woolen dress and jacket were trimmed in periwinkle-blue satin. The suit looked like an expensive designer garment.

"Rose is going to flip over this, Sylvia," Jane said. "And Samuel will love it."

Sylvia looked relieved. "I'm glad you think so. I like it, but I wasn't sure."

"We are down to the wire, ladies," Ethel said as the members of the retreat committee finished their peach tarts that Ethel had made. They were sitting around the dining-room table in Grace Chapel Inn.

"I compiled a list of everything we've discussed," Louise said, looking down at the paper in her hand. "We seem to be on schedule. The posters are in store windows all over town, and the churches all promised to put the registration form in their bulletins."

"We have thirty-three registrations, not counting our speaker," June Carter said.

"That's wonderful," Sylvia commented. "I'll tell Rose. She wanted to know how many craft kits to put together."

"So we'll have our speaker, then a time for asking

questions and sharing testimonies. We've scheduled devotions after dinner and after breakfast, and Rose will give a craft presentation. What about music and singing?" Louise asked.

"You can handle that," Ethel said.

When Louise raised her eyebrows and peered over the top of her glasses at her aunt, Ethel stammered, "Of course, I just assumed . . . after all . . . you are the only one qualified."

"What kind of music do you want?" Louise asked.

"Some familiar hymns," Florence said.

"Could you also play some fun camp songs?" Sylvia asked.

"I imagine I could. I'll go through my music to see what I can find."

"That's settled then," Ethel said.

"And our meals?" Florence asked.

"Jane is taking care of that," Ethel said.

"You know, Jane has a lot going on at that time," Louise said. "I don't know how she'll handle the reception and the food for the retreat.

"I'll get together with Jane," Patsy said. "We can work out the menus together."

"Thank you, Patsy. Now what are we missing?" Ethel asked.

"Alice arranged for the ANGELs to babysit some of the children after school Friday until their fathers can take over," Louise reported.

"I'll call the younger registrants to let them know about that," Florence volunteered. "What have we forgotten?"

"We could play some games," Patsy suggested hesitantly. "I was thinking we should do some icebreakers. Like charades or the one where you collect other people's nametags," Patsy said.

"Patsy is right," Ethel said. "We need to help everyone relax. Patsy, you'll be in charge of the games."

"All right," Patsy said. "I'll think up something fun."

Louise heard the front door and stood. Straightening her wool skirt, she said, "I believe our guests have arrived. Excuse me. I'm sure you can finish without me."

She went out to the foyer. Jane poked her head out the kitchen door. Seeing Louise, she disappeared back in the kitchen.

Two couples came through the door just as Louise got there to welcome them. The women looked very chic and professional in slacks, long wool coats, dressy scarves, and soft leather gloves. Their carefully coiffed hair and artfully applied makeup made them look like models. The men were dressed more casually in slacks and jackets.

"Welcome to Grace Chapel Inn. I'm Louise Smith," she said, smiling graciously. "You must be the Graysons and Hartleys."

"Conn Grayson," the taller man said, reaching out to shake hands.

Louise shook hands with him and each of the others and checked them in. Then she escorted them to their rooms. Louise learned that the women were executives with a cosmetics company. They were in town for special meetings with distributors in Potterston and were taking advantage of the long romantic-weekend package to mix pleasure with their business.

The retreat committee meeting was breaking up when Louise came back downstairs. She went into the kitchen, shut the door, and breathed a sigh of relief. Jane turned and gave her a sympathetic look. "Grueling meeting?"

"It had its moments," Louise said.

The door opened behind Louise, and Patsy poked her head in. "Excuse me, am I interrupting?"

"No, come in, Patsy. What can I do for you?" Jane asked, smiling warmly.

"I wondered if we could discuss food."

Jane looked puzzled.

"For the retreat?" Patsy said.

"Oh. I'm supposed to come up with meals, aren't I?"

Jane answered so calmly that Louise marveled at her sister's composure. Three separate events to cook for in a week's time would be enough to send Louise running for a hiding place.

"That's what Ethel said, but I know you are busy, so I thought maybe I could help."

"Bless your heart, Patsy, your help would be wonderful. What meals do they need?"

Louise listened to them talk as she put on a kettle of water for tea. Alice carried a load of dishes in from the dining room, and Louise went to help her clear the table.

"Did I hear our guests arrive?" Alice asked her as she returned to the dining room for more plates.

"Two couples. We have two more reservations tonight, and they're all staying until Wednesday. I have a feeling it's about to get hectic around here."

Alice smiled. "Feast or famine. I guess I'd rather have the feast."

Louise nodded in agreement.

They picked up the rest of the dishes and carried them into the kitchen, where Jane and Patsy were huddled together at the table, writing out a list.

"I'll order trays from the General Store for sandwich fixings and a veggie tray with dips," Patsy said. "Shall I buy the ingredients for the breakfast casseroles?"

"No. I can do that," Jane said. "I have to buy for the reception, so I'll just add it to my order."

"Keep track so the retreat committee can reimburse you. I'll get dinner rolls and sweet rolls from the Good Apple Bakery," Patsy said. "That'll save us some baking. Would you . . . do you think you'd have time to make brownies? No one can match your brownies."

Jane smiled. "I believe I can squeeze that in. You're taking such a load off my shoulders taking care of this."

"It won't be as good as your luncheons, but it'll do."

"Sometimes it's what you put with the basics that makes a meal special. For instance, instead of plain mayonnaise for the sandwiches, we can make special spreads. They aren't hard. I can make them or give you the recipes."

"That would be wonderful," Patsy said. "I'll be glad to make them."

Jane pulled out a long wooden file box. Inside were three-by-five cards filed by category. She rifled through to "Sauces and Spreads" and pulled out several recipes and some blank cards.

"Here are some of my favorites," Jane said. She handed a card to Patsy. It contained recipes for Basil Mayonnaise and Cranberry Cream Cheese Spread.

"These are good too." Jane handed Patsy recipe cards for Chipotle Cheese Spread, Cucumber-Dill Spread and Olive Tapenade. "You can decide how many you want to serve. Then you might add a pasta salad or fruit salad or just fruit slices to round out the meal."

"These all sound wonderful," Patsy said.

"I can make up the breakfast casseroles and bring them out on Friday night. Then you can cook them in the morning."

"That's too much running around for you to do, Jane," Patsy objected.

"I have to take things out to Bellwood Farm Friday night, so I'll just make a side trip to Rolling Hills. It's not far out of the way."

"All right." Patsy finished copying the recipes and put the cards in her purse. "I'd better let you get back to your cooking. Thank you, Jane. I'm really excited about the retreat and the anniversary." Then she giggled. "So's Henry. It's so romantic." She put on her coat and let herself out the back door.

Jane smiled to herself. Patsy would do a wonderful job with the retreat food, leaving Jane free to concentrate on the anniversary. She set her coffee cup in the sink and put away the recipe box. Back to work. She had food to prepare for the weekend breakfast and Valentine tea.

Chapter Nineteen

Alice carried the chili-relleno potato pie to the dining room, followed by Louise with the kippered salmon and dill hollandaise. Jane took a quick look at her menu. The ruby-red grapefruit and orange compote with pomegranate sauce had been served with the assorted sweet breads and raspberry-apple kuchen.

"I think that's everything." Jane stepped out of her clogs and slipped her feet into a pair of black pumps. She rarely wore them, except when she served special meals, and today was the special Valentine breakfast they'd advertised. Setting her apron aside, she picked up the platter of savory baked eggs in crepe cups and carried it out to the dining room.

The table looked festive with the white lace tablecloth over a red liner and the red-and-white floral centerpiece.

"Oh, that looks delicious," Edwina Stockwell said. The elderly woman exuded energy. Her husband seemed completely opposite, almost dour and bored. She nudged him, and he inhaled and sat straighter as if pulling himself together.

"This is delightful," Tanya Grayson said. Her makeup and hair were perfect. Although she wore a casual outfit, everything was beautifully coordinated. Charlene Hartley looked equally fashionable.

"My compliments to the chef," Conn Grayson said.

"Thank you," Jane said. "Is there anything else I can get for anyone?"

Mrs. Tiptons raised her hand. "Do you have any flavored creamers? I always use vanilla-toffee-caramel creamer in my coffee."

"I'm sorry I didn't point it out," Alice said. "It is in the little pitcher next to your cup."

Mrs. Tiptons beamed. "How thoughtful. Thank you."

Jane glanced at Louise, who smiled serenely at their guests. Louise had suggested asking for preferences and dietary restrictions when people made reservations. The extra service had been received enthusiastically.

Jane returned to the kitchen to begin cleanup while Louise and Alice attended their guests. Soon they were bringing dirty dishes and leftovers to the kitchen.

"It always amazes me how much time it takes to prepare a meal and how quickly it disappears," Alice said, stacking plates and silverware next to the sink. "Isn't it a little disheartening?"

"Oh no. Only untouched food is disheartening. My joy comes from seeing our guests' pleasure in what I create. Definitely worth it."

Caleb and Gretchen Bellwood weren't in church on Sunday. Alice knew Caleb couldn't drive with his injured ankle, but Gretchen and the boys rarely missed Sunday services, so she was a bit concerned, especially with the anniversary only a week away.

When they got back to the inn, a telephone message awaited them.

"Hi. It's Gretchen. The boys are sick. Between that and taking care of the new calves, I'm having trouble finding time to work on the quilt. I'm getting a little worried. I don't know if I can finish it by Saturday. Daylene offered to help, but she is not a seamstress, trust me. Any chance you can help me out? Give me a call." The message ended.

"Oh dear. Perhaps I had better take a couple of days off this week," Alice said. "Vera and Sylvia are working. I don't know who else could help."

"Louise and I can help," Jane said.

"It'll have to wait until we've served the tea this afternoon. If we had the quilt here, perhaps we could work on it. We can't all leave with a houseful of guests," Louise said.

"Maybe I'll see if Vera and Sylvia could come help us tonight," Alice said.

"Excellent idea," Louise said. "Then we can plan a strategy from there."

"All right. I'll call them as soon as I change." Alice dressed quickly in jeans and a red sweater and went back downstairs to make phone calls. She called Vera, then Sylvia, and at last, Gretchen.

"I'm so sorry," Gretchen said. "I didn't know who else to call."

"You just concentrate on getting your family well for the anniversary party. I'll come get the supplies. Vera and Sylvia are going to help us."

"Thank you."

Alice heard a sneeze in the background. She was glad germs could not transmit over the telephone lines.

Louise and Alice set up for the Valentine tea, arranging individual tables, one in the parlor, one in the library and a larger one for the Graysons and Hartleys in the living room. The sisters draped the tables with white linen cloths topped with lace scarves. Louise added floral centerpieces, and Jane sprinkled red and silver heart confetti on the tables for accent.

"Very pretty," Louise pronounced as they took a critical look at the settings.

While Alice and Louise laid fires in the living room and parlor fireplaces, Jane went to finish preparing the food.

Jane arranged truffles, pink meringue kisses, shortbread hearts and chocolate-dipped fruit on the top plate of the tiered serving dishes. She mixed and shaped almond-cranberry scones, ready for the oven. The chicken salad for finger sandwiches was chilling in the refrigerator. Knowing the men would want something substantial, Jane sautéed diced steak, onions, potatoes, turnips, carrots and spices to make meat pasties. She was filling small rounds of pie dough for the little meat turnovers when Alice came in.

"Louise went up to change. I'm going to change too."

Jane looked down at her stained apron, jeans and clogs and grimaced. "I'd better change too. I'll be along in a few minutes."

Alice left the kitchen. Jane glanced at the clock. Three o'clock. How had it gotten so late? One hour until teatime. Jane picked up her pace, filling and sealing the bite-sized meat pasties. She still had the sandwiches to make.

"These truffles and meringue drops are delicious," Edwina Stockwell said, closing her eyes and popping another truffle in her mouth.

"So were the meat pies and chicken sandwiches," her husband said.

Jane smiled. "I'll be happy to bring more when I refill your tea," Jane said, picking up their teapot. She left the parlor and went to the kitchen, where Alice was refilling the teapots from the living room.

"How's the tea holding out?" Jane asked as Alice finished.

"I thought you made enough to fill a bathtub, but we're out of the mango tea and low on the green mint. I put on the kettle for more hot water. Do you have any more of those meat turnovers? They are a hit with the men."

"I have a request for more too. I have one more tray to cook. It only takes a few minutes. Meanwhile, here are some more Swedish meatballs. I have plenty of them." Jane spooned out two small bowls full. Be sure to take some of the tasseled toothpicks."

"Great. The Graysons and the Hartleys raved about your shortbread and scones," Alice said.

As Alice went out with the teapots, Louise came in with two empty serving plates. She opened the refrigerator and took out covered plates. "Are you making more meat pasties?" she asked as she used tongs to fill the plates with chocolate-dipped fruit and dainty sandwiches.

"Goodness. It's a good thing I made plenty." Jane opened the oven and removed a sheet of pasties. "Warn them these are hot."

A few hours after the tea things had been cleared and the tables put away, Vera and Sylvia arrived at the inn. Alice had just returned from Gretchen's house where she had picked up the quilt materials. She took everything into the dining room, so they could spread out all the pieces on the big table.

"Gretchen laid out the squares and sewed on some of the sashing," Alice told them as she began to unpack the material.

Louise and Jane joined them, and they soon had brightly decorated squares covering the table.

"I think we can get them all on a king-size quilt," Sylvia said.

"Excuse me," a voice from the doorway said. They all turned around. It was Tanya Grayson, one of the guests. "May I use the telephone? My cell phone doesn't seem to work here."

"Certainly," Alice said. She started to show her where the phone was, but Tanya came into the room and walked over to the table.

"Is this a memory quilt?" she asked.

"Yes. One of our local couples is celebrating their fortieth wedding anniversary on Valentine's Day," Jane said.

Tanya stared for a moment, seeming almost overcome. She reached out and touched one of the squares. "My family made a memory quilt for my grandmother's eightieth birthday. It wasn't this large. I remember how she hugged the quilt and cried. 'Tears of joy,' she said, that God had blessed her with such a loving family. This couple must be very special to have so many people want to honor them. What a fabulous gift."

"They've touched the lives of nearly everyone around here. I hope they'll feel as blessed as your grandmother did," Alice said. "The telephone is out here at the reception desk." She led Tanya to the telephone.

"Thank you for the phone and for letting me see your quilt project. I'm glad we came to stay here. The cosmetics business can seem so superficial sometimes, it's good to get away and see how people really live."

Alice thought about Tanya's comments as she went back into the dining room. The quilt, the anniversary, the retreat were all labors of love. Alice gave thanks that she shared in the loving community of Acorn Hill.

"I think we should place the photograph squares on angled backgrounds to get diamond shapes like the squares Florence and Jane made," Vera suggested, standing back, one hand on her hip, gazing at the arrangement of squares. "That would highlight the pictures and give the quilt some variety." She reached over and put the squares at an angle to the others. "See? If we add triangles of fabric to the sides, we'll have diamonds."

"I like that," Jane said. Do we have extra fabric?"

"I have more at the store," Sylvia said.

"Does it have to be the plain muslin?" Alice asked. "I have pieces of muslin in various colors. I'll get them."

She hurried upstairs, dug around in a box of fabric in her closet and grabbed several pieces, which she took back downstairs.

The sashing fabric to connect the quilt squares was a print of small blue and red flowers on a white background to go with the wedding colors and the traditional red for Valentine's Day. Alice pulled out a piece of red fabric and a piece of light-blue fabric. She laid them on the table, and Vera put the picture squares on top.

"Lovely," Louise said, nodding thoughtfully.

"Genius," Sylvia said, smiling at Vera, who looked satisfied.

"I can't wait to see this put together," Jane said. "And I can't wait to see Rose's reaction. These squares are priceless."

"I have one more square, and I'm not sure what to do with it," Sylvia said.

"Why? Who made it?" Louise asked.

"Rose brought it to me. She said it was for the special quilt the chapel ladies were putting together."

"Oh dear, I'd forgotten about that," Alice said. "Rose saw Florence and Ellen talking about a quilt square last Sunday. They told her it was for a surprise for someone at church. Rose said she wanted to make a square too. That must be it."

"What should we do with it?" Vera asked.

"We should include it with the other squares. It'll be another testament to Rose's caring, giving spirit," Louise said.

Jane picked up the square and looked at it, then handed it to Alice. The square depicted a pair of hands holding a Bible. The inscription under the hands read, "Always Helping Others."

"Well, it certainly fits Rose, although she intended it for someone else. I agree with Louise. We must include it," Alice said. She looked at the various squares. Many she had seen at Sylvia's. The Bellwood grandsons had painted pictures of the farm: a barn with a fuzzy sheep in the doorway; a very young cowboy riding a horse, with a man leading it; a boy swinging on a tire swing suspended from a big tree; a small set of bright red handprints; a tractor. Gretchen's square had three aprons with the names Rose, Gretchen and Daylene embroidered on them. Daylene's square held a tabletop with three teacups. The square Samantha sent from college was covered in lavender velvet with tiny pearl beads and a rhinestone tiara embroidered on top. The note with it explained that it was from the prom dress Rose had made for her in high school.

Alice blinked back tears. She didn't usually get sentimental, but the love in the quilt squares touched her heart. What a legacy this family shared, and they blessed everyone around them by sharing their lives with others.

Vera set up a fabric cutting board on the kitchen table. Using a rotary cutting wheel and a quilter's ruler, she began making short, narrow strips for the sashing. Sylvia brought in a small portable sewing machine from her car and went to work stitching squares and sashing pieces together. While Jane and Louise pinned the pieces together for the next two rows, Alice took a row of squares and sashing pieces upstairs to her room to assemble on her sewing machine. She came down for more rows. An hour later, all that remained was connecting the rows together with the triangular pieces and the center square, which Vera volunteered to do at home.

"Wow," Vera said as she placed the last row on top of the others. "I'm bringing all of my quilts over here to assemble. You ladies are fast."

"That's because five of us worked on it," Jane said. "Anyone for tea or coffee?"

They all wanted a break, so they carefully folded all the quilt pieces and put away the cutting board. Then they gathered around the kitchen table.

Vera took a sip of tea, then said, "Once I put in the diamond-shaped pieces and stitch the rows together, we'll need to attach the backing and tie the quilt. Are you free to work in the evenings on this?"

They all agreed to meet the following night at the inn.

"I'm amazed that we accomplished so much tonight," Louise said after they'd gone.

"Yes, but there's still a lot to do," Alice said. "I hope we can finish it."

"We will," Jane stated positively. "We must. The town is counting on giving the quilt to Rose and Samuel for their anniversary."

"Can you imagine Rose's face when she realizes she made a square for her own memory quilt?" Alice asked with a chuckle.

"It's hard to believe this quilt is nearly completed," Louise said Tuesday evening as Sylvia and Vera spread the backing fabric on the living-room floor.

"All I had to do was sew on the border strips. Tonight we need to attach the top to the back and batting. Then we can tie it. If we finish tying the quilt tonight, I'll sew on the edging tomorrow," Sylvia said.

With the fabric smoothed out, wrong side up, Vera sprayed a temporary adhesive on the backing. Then they carefully laid the batting down on top of it.

"Now it gets tricky," Sylvia said. "It'll take all of us to get this straight. We have to lay the quilt top on the batting, getting it exactly centered and smooth." She sprayed the backside of the quilt top with the adhesive. Jane, Alice, Vera and Louise held the corners of the quilt top over the batting. With Sylvia guiding the top, they carefully lowered the center first. Sylvia smoothed the center against the batting, then worked out in circles from the center, carefully smoothing the top over the batting until the quilt top adhered to the batting and backing.

Using curved safety pins, Sylvia pinned the bride's bouquet in the wedding photograph to mark the quilt's center point, then began working outward. "We need to put a pin everywhere that we will tie the quilt," she said. "Then we need to decide if we want to use cheddar or something else.

Jane laughed. When they all turned to look at her, she said, "Sorry, I was picturing tying cheese all over the quilt. I'm sure that's not what you mean."

"No," Sylvia said. "Quilt makers often use cheddar-colored yarn or accent pieces to draw the eye. That's why a red quilt often has bright orange yarn ties. We can use cheddar or something else, like red or white. Since the basic quilt background is blue, with only small amounts of red and white, either color would provide a clear contrast."

"Really? I never knew that, but it makes sense." Jane laughed. "I would have used a color that blended in, so you wouldn't notice it."

Jane helped Vera and Sylvia pin baste the quilt. By the time they finished, they had used dozens of pins. Then they transported the quilt to the dining-room table.

Louise stood back to get a full view of the quilt. "With all the amateur quilt makers involved, I imagined a hodgepodge of primitive squares. This quilt is absolutely beautiful," she said.

"We'd better get busy and tie this beautiful quilt before it gets too late," Sylvia said.

The ladies sat around the table with the quilt spread out between them, tying the quilt and reminiscing about the various events depicted in the squares.

Chapter Twenty

Thursday dawned cold and damp, with a thin layer of fog blanketing Grace Chapel Inn and the town below. All of the guests had checked out Wednesday, and Jane was relieved to have the day free to prepare for the upcoming weekend's events.

Kristin knocked on the kitchen door just as Jane and Louise were cleaning up from lunch. When Jane opened the door, she saw a welcome sight. "Hey, the sun is trying to shine. Did you do that, Kristin?"

"No, but it sure raises my spirits to see it. The forecast for the weekend is sunny and warmer."

"Hallelujah and thank You, Lord," Louise said.

"I brought a sample of the cover for the retreat book." Kristin set her laptop on the kitchen table, then from her briefcase pulled out a piece of heavy tan paper with "Acorn Hill Ladies Retreat, Sponsored by Grace Chapel" across the top and a sepia-toned picture of Rolling Hills Youth Camp under the banner.

"This is the front cover. I'll punch all the pages and fasten them together." She opened her computer and brought up a document. "Then I'll make a table of contents like this, with recipes, speaker notes and highlights of the retreat."

Louise looked at the pages, then at Kristin. "This is wonderful. The women will be thrilled to get one of these."

"Thanks. I'll make one for each lady with blank paper so they can take notes. Then they can add the recipe section and I'll make copies of pictures to add to the booklet. I'm taking my digital camera, so I can load the pictures right into my laptop. I'll work on it while we're house-sitting for the Bellwoods. Then I can mail out the extra sections."

"Sounds like you have it handled," Jane said. "I'm glad you're here today to help me get the food under control."

"What are we making today?" Kristin asked.

"The cakes. I'll decorate them tomorrow, but I will freeze the cakes so they'll be easy to work with. And we need to make brownies for the retreat."

"I'd better put this away. I just wanted to make sure the retreat booklet will work."

"It's perfect," Louise said. "I hate to leave you with all the cooking, but I'm expecting one of my adult students."

"No problem, Louise. Kristin and I have it covered."

When Louise left, Jane turned to Kristin. "You've done a wonderful job of everything, Kristin," she said. "The invitations, Rose's Web site, the retreat booklet, the quilt squares. And now you're helping me cook. I hope you realize how much we appreciate everything you've done. If you receive as many blessings as you are giving out, your cup should be running over by now."

"I like helping people." Kristin put on an apron and washed her hands. "So what's first?"

"You can chop the pecans for the brownies while I start the cakes," Jane said, getting out the ingredients.

"My grandmother made delicious cakes and cookies for Christmas every year. She let me mix the sugar and butter. I loved the way it got so fluffy and creamy." Kristin looked up from chopping and grinned. "I liked the way it tasted too."

Jane laughed.

"I never stayed in the kitchen very long. I would lose interest and run outside to play with Grandma's cats." Kristin scraped the chopped nuts into a bowl. "Actually, it's funny. Grandma said I'd never be a cook, but I'd make a fine veterinarian." Kristin frowned. "I'd forgotten about that. She was wrong. I'd never been around big animals before moving here, and I've just realized that they scare me. That's why . . . well, I don't go with Blair on calls." She took a deep breath and looked at Jane. "I checked out several books about sheep and cattle and horses from the library. If I learn more about them, maybe I can get over this silly fear."

Jane wasn't afraid of animals, but she'd faced her share of fears over the years, so she knew how crippling they could be. "That must be difficult for you, considering Blair's work. Have you told him about your fear?"

"No. I can't tell him. He'd never understand. He teased me when I went on one of his calls with him and got scared trying to pet a horse. He said the horse liked me, but I tell you, I saw murder in that horse's eyes, and he was so big. He would've chomped my hand if I hadn't pulled it away." Kristin shivered, remembering the frightening experience.

"You suggested I talk to Rose. I asked her to help me after she and Samuel get back from their trip. She said she'd be happy to. She was so nice. She told me she struggled with adjusting to their life together when she and Samuel first married. She said adjusting is part of learning to love."

"Rose would know. She and Samuel have one of the most solid relationships I've ever seen," Jane said.

Kristin nodded. "Rose told me they've had their share of disagreements and hurt feelings, but working together to keep their animals alive and healthy puts other troubles in perspective. I've never been around death, except when my dog Bitsy died, and Blair really helped me then."

Kristin looked up at Jane. "Blair saves lives. I mean, I knew that, but I didn't realize how important his work is. It isn't just a business to him, like my computer business. I guess I need that kind of perspective."

"That's like Alice's job as a nurse. She helps so many people. That takes special compassion."

"I think Rose and Samuel are like that too. I told Rose about the horse. She didn't think I was crazy. She said horses can get pushy. She thought it was looking for a treat. She said I have to be firm with the animals, so they'll know I'm in charge. I can't imagine ever doing that, but she said she'd show me how to handle their horse and the cows. I'm going to do chores with her when they get home and get to know her animals. I don't know, Jane. If I could get over this fear, maybe I could be part of Blair's work too."

"You know, Blair could help you better than anyone. Besides, he might be relieved to find out about your fears. Otherwise, he might think you don't care about his work."

"He can't think that, can he?"

Jane just raised her eyebrows.

"I'm such a doofus." She sighed. "I guess I'll have to tell him. I'm terrified that he'll leave me with the animals at Bellwood Farm next week and I'll do something horrible and make the animals sick or something."

"You'll be fine, and Alice and I will help you."

"I don't know what I'd do without you, Jane. Thanks."

"You've helped me more than I've helped you. And now we'd better get this cooking done, or we'll be in hot water."

Jane's heart filled with gratitude as she mixed the cake batter. Somehow, in spite of her shortcomings, the Lord was using her to help Kristin. Jane felt relieved that words of encouragement and advice had come to her when she needed them, and she felt incredibly humbled that the Lord had entrusted this sweet young woman to her clumsy care.

∽

Louise came into the kitchen from her last piano lesson just as Alice arrived home from work. Jane and Kristin were taking pans of brownies out of the oven. Three large, square cakes were cooling on racks.

"That smells heavenly," Alice said.

"We can have some brownies. I made an extra." Jane filled the teakettle with water and put it on the stove.

"I'll change and be right back." Alice went out to the hall.

"I'll take a few minutes to have a cup of tea, but then I need to pack for this retreat," Louise said. She took cups out of the cupboard and carried them to the table. "I can't believe I'm going to sleep on a cot at a camp while you and Alice sleep in your own beds. You should be the one going, Jane. You're the youngest of the three of us."

"If I went, you'd have to do the cooking for the anniversary reception."

"I know, and that is the only reason I agreed to go."

"I'm glad you're going," Kristin said.

Louise put her arm around Kristin's shoulder. "We'll help each other. I can introduce you to the women you don't know, but you'll have to help me fit in. I hate to admit it, but I am dreading the games Patsy has planned and the whole slumber-party atmosphere. I may just disappear to bed early and let you younger women have your fun."

"Now, Louise, you are going to have a great time," Jane predicted.

"I doubt that very much, but I'll put on a good face so I don't spoil the fun for others."

Jane hugged her. "You're a good sport. So did you find a sleeping bag to take?"

"Certainly not. I'll take sheets and blankets like a civilized person," Louise retorted, making Jane hoot with laughter.

The kettle whistled, and Jane poured the boiling water into the teapot. Alice returned and they sat at the table with their tea and samples of hot, moist brownies with dollops of whipped cream.

"I shouldn't eat this," Kristin said. "It will ruin my appetite for dinner. I left barbecue short ribs cooking in my Crock-Pot. The recipe is one of Blair's favorites. I got it from his mother. I just hope it turns out as good as hers. I made coleslaw too. All I have to do is add the dressing."

"That sounds wonderful. I'm sure it will be delicious," Jane assured her.

Kristin smiled. "I wouldn't have dared cook it a few weeks ago. I've learned so much from you, Jane, I'm getting brave."

"Bravery is half the battle, Kristin. In everything."

"That's true," Louise said. "And I'm going to need a big dose of bravery tomorrow."

Kristin giggled, then looked embarrassed. "I'm sorry. I didn't mean to laugh, Louise."

"No need to apologize, my dear." Louise sighed dramatically. "We all have our crosses to bear." She stood and carried her plate to the sink. "Now I'd better pack my bag and collect my linens. Then perhaps I can relax and sleep well tonight. It's a good bet that I won't get any sleep tomorrow night."

Friday dawned sunny and clear, and by breakfast the temperature had climbed to the midforties. Louise sat with Alice at the kitchen table, eating hot cereal, while Jane busied herself at the stove. The delicious smell of Jane's caramel-fudge pecan brownies filled the kitchen. "It doesn't seem right for me to go off and leave you two with all the work. Perhaps I could go to the camp for part of the day and come back this afternoon. They don't really need me at the retreat," she said.

"But you need to be there to make sure Rose stays away from home," Jane said. "If you leave, she'll want to leave too. Besides, you're involved in the program, and who knows what Aunt Ethel and Florence will do if you're not there to mediate."

Louise sighed. "I suppose you're right. What can I do to help you before I go?"

"I think everything is under control with the decorating," Alice said. "Fred is going to deliver all the rental pieces and supplies to the farm this afternoon. I just have to go out tonight and set up."

"I'll spend most of the day baking," Jane said. "We'll be fine. You could copy this recipe for me, though, for the potluck tonight. I'll bake it now, and you can reheat it at the camp."

"Since you're making my potluck dish, that's the least I can do," Louise said, getting a blank recipe card and a pen. She picked up their mother's cookbook and copied the recipe for corn casserole.

Jane put the casserole in the oven. Louise double-checked the recipe, then helped to tidy the kitchen. When she was finished, she took her retreat list out of her pocket. "Music. I almost forgot," she said to no one in particular. "Here is the recipe, Jane. I need to gather my music." She handed the card to Jane and went to the parlor. She leafed through a stack of music and put her selections in a folder. A glance at her watch told her it was time to go. She collected her overnight case and the duffle that held her linens, blankets and pillow. After donning her coat, hat and gloves, Louise took her things out to her car. When she went back into the kitchen, Jane was packing the hot casserole in a box with a towel around it.

"Perfect timing," Louise said. "I suppose I am ready to go." She smiled, but it was a halfhearted effort. She silently contemplated her lack of enthusiasm. *How bad could it be?* she asked herself. The weather forecast called for clear skies. The camp was not far from town. The committee had done an excellent job planning the program. *Lord, help me to stay focused on the purpose of this retreat. Help me be an encouragement to the women who attend. Help me forget about my comfort and instead try to make others comfortable.*

Louise picked up the box with the casserole. "I guess I'm off, then. Pray for me," she added. "And I'll pray for you."

"Everything will be fine," Alice assured her.

"Relax and have fun, Louie," Jane said, giving her a kiss on the cheek. "I'll see you tonight when I bring the breakfast casseroles."

"All right. You know how to reach me if you need me," she said, half hoping they would call and beg her to return home.

Jane opened the door for her, and Louise carried the box to the car. As she set the casserole on the backseat, Ethel came out of the carriage house.

"Yoo-hoo. Louise." Ethel waved from her front porch. "I'm ready." Ethel pulled a large suitcase out onto the porch and began dragging it down the steps.

"Let me help you," Louise said, heading for the carriage house. When she picked up the suitcase, she felt the strain in her back.

"Goodness, Aunt Ethel, what did you pack?"

"Just a few essentials," Ethel said. "It doesn't hurt to be prepared."

Louise noticed the mischievous sparkle in her aunt's eyes and couldn't help wondering what her aunt had planned. She carried Ethel's suitcase to her car and stowed it in the trunk. "Anything else?"

"Yes. I have to get my linens and the peach tarts for tonight's potluck. I made one for everyone."

"Wonderful," Louise said, then quietly added, "at least we'll eat well." Louise helped to put the rest of her aunt's gear in the car.

Ethel turned to Louise as they pulled out of the driveway. "This is so exciting! I can't wait. I feel like a young girl going away to summer camp." She giggled, and her Titian Dreams red hair seemed to bounce with her enthusiasm. "That wasn't so long ago, you know. I was a counselor at church camp when Francine was young." Ethel grinned. "I think I had more fun than the children," she said.

Ethel suddenly burst into song at the top of her lungs, exuberantly if not melodiously. "Oh, Lord, I want two wings to cover my face . . ."

Startled, Louise glanced at her passenger. She tried not to laugh. Ethel kept on singing, oblivious to the effect she was having. Louise took a deep breath and kept driving. She had a feeling the next hours would be interesting. Very interesting, indeed.

Chapter Twenty-One

After Louise left, Jane glanced at her menu. Thanks to Kristin's help, she had already crossed off quite a few items. Some of the recipes couldn't be made ahead, so she noted the ones that could.

She would make the tortilla cream-cheese wraps and prepare the ingredients for a salad, which she could assemble at the last minute. She took fresh broccoli, sweet onion and celery out of the refrigerator and began making inch-long strips from the broccoli stems.

When she finished preparing those ingredients, she mixed them with two cups of dried cranberries and put them in the refrigerator, ready to add shredded apples, pine nuts and the slaw dressing at the last minute.

Alice came through the door. "I'm ready to help. What can I do?"

"Oh good, I have just the job for you—making tortilla pinwheels."

The sisters worked side by side, concentrating on their tasks while soft jazz music played in the background. Alice spread salsa cream cheese, sliced olives and pimientos on large flour tortillas and rolled them up like jelly rolls, while Jane made sauce for another batch of scalloped potatoes.

"I'm relieved that we don't have guests this weekend. I'm running out of room to store all this food. It's a good thing June suggested using the cooler at the Coffee Shop."

"What about cooking everything and keeping it hot?"

"Most of it is precooked," Jane said. "June said she'll sneak away from the retreat early tomorrow and reheat all of the potatoes and the hams from Daylene. Gretchen and Daylene are cooking and slicing the turkeys. Nothing else requires cooking."

"You make it sound easy. I know it's not."

"Actually, I have so many helpers I don't know what to do with myself."

Alice laughed. "You have plenty to do, but it's wonderful how everyone wants to help. I love seeing the town get excited about the anniversary party," Alice said. "I haven't seen such joy around Acorn Hill in weeks. Honoring some-one else seems to bring out the best in people. It's like Father used to say: 'Kindness to others is the best antidote for a heavy spirit.' Then he would quote Philippians 2:3–4, 'In humility consider others better than yourselves. Each of you should look not only to your own interests, but also to the interests of others.'"

"Father would know. He lived those verses." Jane turned to look at her sister. "Alice, you remind me so much of Father. You shower light and love on everyone. That's why you make such a terrific nurse."

Alice blushed, then busied herself washing spatulas, beaters and mixing bowls. Jane smiled. Alice shied from attention. Jane wished she were more like her sister. Perhaps in a few more years, some of Alice's gentle spirit and humil-ity would rub off on her, and that would be a good thing.

∽

Louise pulled into the driveway to Rolling Hills Youth Camp and parked in front of the main building next to June

Carter's car. "I'll take out our bags later," she told Ethel. "Let's find out where we're sleeping first."

"I've been told we can sleep in the lodge," Ethel replied. "One of the dormitories houses thirty-six people."

"Thirty-six people in one room?" Louise asked, alarmed.

Ethel laughed. "Won't it be fun?"

Louise decided to keep her opinion to herself. She opened the heavy pine door and stepped into the dining hall. The cold followed them in. She shivered, realizing the room had no heat.

Shelly Hackenbauer, the camp administrator, came rushing over. She had on a heavy wool sweater. A few wisps of red hair poked out of her navy-blue stocking hat. Her rosy cheeks almost camouflaged her freckles.

"Louise, it's so good to see you," she said, smiling. "Mrs. Buckley, welcome to Rolling Hills. I'm sorry it's so cold. I turned the furnace on a couple of hours ago, but it takes a while to heat the hall. The dormitories are much warmer."

"Good," Louise said, rubbing her hands together. "The lodge looks wonderful, Shelly. I haven't been out here since last summer."

"The addition is a real asset. Here. Let me help you bring in your gear." Shelly went out to the porch, so Louise followed her. As they came out, Florence went in, followed by her husband, Ronald, lugging a large suitcase. Ethel stayed inside.

Louise waited until the Simpsons were inside. "My goodness, Florence's suitcase is as large as Ethel's. I can't imagine that they need so much for one night."

Shelly laughed. "You'd be surprised what some people bring to camp. They seem to think they are going to a foreign country and need extra provisions." As they took the suitcases out of the trunk, she said, "I'm so excited about this retreat. This makes our third winter group. So far, everyone has had a great time."

Shelly insisted on taking Ethel's suitcase and bag. Because Shelly was young and athletic, Louise did not argue. She followed Shelly inside and upstairs. A long hallway stretched the length of the building, with three large rooms and two restrooms off the hall. Shelly carried the bags into the middle room.

"This is the nicest room. It doesn't have as many bunks, and the bathroom is right next-door. Which bed do you want? I assume you'd like a bottom bunk?"

Louise looked around the room. Two of the lower bunks and one upper bunk had bags and linens on them already.

"June Carter and Shannon Walsh took the two lower beds. Patsy Ley took the top bunk."

"They should be good roommates," Louise said. That left two bottom beds. Louise refused to climb to an upper bunk. All the mattresses seemed pretty hard and thin. Finally she decided on the bunk behind the doorway, thinking it would be somewhat shielded, yet close to the bathroom. She set her overnight bag and linens on it.

"I think you'll be pretty comfortable here. It stays warm, and a women's group should be pretty quiet. The youth group we had recently was very, uh, active." Shelly chuckled. "They stayed up until four in the morning. I think you could hear them all the way to town."

"Most of us will be in bed by ten, I'm sure," Louise said.

Ethel poked her head in the doorway. "Is this your room, Louise?"

"Yes. Shelly brought your bags up. There is one lower bunk left if you want it."

"Oh, I want to be in the big room. It will be much more fun. Would you take my bags down there, Shelly? Thank you." Ethel sailed off down the hallway.

Louise felt embarrassed that her aunt treated Shelly so cavalierly, but Shelly merely smiled, picked up Ethel's bags and went down the hall after her.

Louise shook her head and went downstairs to bring in

the food. She put the casserole in the large walk-in cooler and set the brownies and Ethel's tarts on a counter. She heard voices and went to investigate.

Patsy Ley stood on a chair in the theater, hanging a banner from the ceiling. June stood below, holding one end of the banner, and a young woman in jeans and a sweater with shoulder-length blonde hair stood on the other side. Patsy looked up first and saw Louise. She waved her hand, jiggling one end of the banner.

"Hi, Louise. Look and tell us if we have this centered," she said. She held up her end, but June's end still hung down. They were in front of a small stage.

"I can't really tell, Patsy. I think it needs to go a little to the right on your side."

Patsy reached as far as she could.

"Yes. That looks better."

Patsy wrapped a piece of string around a hook in the ceiling and pulled it tight. Then she got down and moved her chair to the left of the stage and got up again.

June handed her the banner. As she stretched it out, Louise read the words. "This is my command: Love each other. John 15:17."

"That's a lovely banner, Patsy," Louise said, looking up at it.

"Thanks, Louise, but I didn't make it. Kristin Casey made it for us. Isn't she talented? And so eager to help."

"Yes she is. I'm glad she'll be coming."

"She's already here. She's in the craft room, helping Rose set up."

"Oh. I didn't see their cars. They must have parked in the staff lot. Do you need help in here?"

"You can take my place. I have to go to work. But first I want you to meet my niece," June said. "Shannon, this is Louise Howard Smith. She's the one I told you about who plays the piano so beautifully."

"I'm so glad to meet you, Louise. I'm Shannon Walsh. I'd

love to see what music you've picked before the retreat gets started."

"I'm finished with the banner," Patsy said. "Thanks for helping me, June. We'll see you later."

"Are you coming back?" Louise asked.

"I sure am. I wouldn't miss a chance to spend time with Shannon. I'm closing the Coffee Shop tonight. No dinner and no breakfast or lunch tomorrow. I made a sign. Gone Fishing." June laughed. "No one will believe that, but it will get the point across."

Louise was surprised. As far back as she could remember, June had never closed the Coffee Shop, except on Sundays. June winked at her.

"I didn't want someone else running my kitchen. Besides, I wanted Hope to be able to come to the retreat too. I'm serving lunch today, then we'll close up and come out here."

Louise nodded. "Good for you. I'm glad you can join us."

June took her jacket from a chair and slipped it on. "I'll see you later, Shannon. You're in good hands here."

"Bye, Aunt June." She turned to Patsy. "Do you have something else to put up?"

"Not in here. You two go ahead with the music. I'm going to decorate in the dining hall."

Patsy picked up her jacket, and Louise suddenly realized the room was comfortably warm. Perhaps the dining hall would warm up soon too.

"Let me get my music. I left it upstairs in the dormitory."

"I'll come with you. I have a couple of pieces I'd like you to play if you can," Shannon said. "Have you heard the song, 'I Am a Friend of God'?"

"No, I haven't. If you have sheet music, I should be able to play it," Louise said.

They went up the stairs together. They passed Kristin and Rose. Shannon had already met them and greeted them by name. Kristin had a lively sparkle in her lovely brown eyes.

If Kristin could feel at home here among these women, then Louise would count the retreat a complete success.

By lunchtime, twenty-eight women congregated in the dining hall. Louise helped Patsy set out the lunch spread.

Florence brought the group to order and asked a blessing on their meal and on the retreat. After that, a line quickly formed on both sides of the food table.

The ladies chose between stacks of various deli meats and cheeses, fresh breads and rolls from the Good Apple Bakery, salads and chips. Brownies and cookies were in plentiful supply for dessert.

After waiting until everyone else had been through the line, Louise made a sandwich and took a serving of vegetables and dip. She passed on the pasta salad, although it looked delicious.

She looked for an empty seat. Each of the three tables had room for her. One table held all young women. She could hear snatches of talk about discount stores, fashions and computers.

At another table, Ethel and Florence sat on either side of Shannon, both talking to her at once, bending her ear about something. She nodded politely as they talked. Louise considered rescuing her but decided against it. Perhaps Florence and Aunt Ethel would calm down as the retreat got underway.

Louise sat at the third table.

"Louise, how nice to see you," Pauline Sherman said with a welcoming smile. "Isn't this wonderful? I've been cooped up since Christmas, so it's nice to have a retreat just for us ladies."

"I agree," Betty Dunkle said. "I get to visit plenty in the shop, but I just decided to do something for myself for a change. I worked late all week so I could close the beauty shop for the weekend."

"I had serious reservations about coming, but we needed to get out of the house," Clara Horn said. "I miss our daily walks and so does Daisy. We hardly get a chance to visit anyone these days. It's been such a long winter, and Fred Humbert predicts more snow in March. Poor Daisy is suffering from cabin fever, I'm afraid."

Louise looked around but didn't see Clara's miniature potbellied pig.

"You're looking for Daisy, aren't you?" Clara asked. "It nearly broke my heart to leave her, but Florence insisted I should support the ladies by attending the retreat. She talked Ronald into babysitting. The dear man promised to keep Daisy bundled up so she wouldn't catch cold. I hate to be away from her, but I know she is having an adventure too. I do tend to coddle her, you know."

Chapter Twenty-Two

Alice ran errands after lunch, picking up the tea favors from Time for Tea, a guest book at Nine Lives Bookstore that Viola Reed was donating to the anniversary celebration, and some of the decorations from Fred's Hardware. Her car was loaded when she pulled into the driveway at Bellwood Farm and parked by the main barn. Gretchen Bellwood was helping her brother-in-law Ben unload folding tables from the back of a pickup truck.

"Hi, Alice," Gretchen said.

"Hi, Gretchen. How are the boys?" Alice asked.

"Much better. And thanks for all your help. You and Jane and Louise are lifesavers."

"Is everything going as planned? No hint your in-laws have caught on to the secrets?"

"Oh no, not at all. In fact, all of us thought it would seem strange if we ignored Mom and Dad's anniversary and didn't do anything, so we sent them to Zachary's for dinner Tuesday night to celebrate. Neither one suspects a thing." Gretchen gave Alice a conspiratorial wink as Samuel came out to help Alice carry in her cargo.

He picked up a box and carried it into the barn. Looking over his shoulder at her, he asked, "Where do you want this?"

"Can we set up a table to use while we decorate?" she suggested. She was surprised how warm it was inside the barn. She looked around. Two large heaters warmed the large structure from each end of the building. Caleb was shuffling along, one foot in a soft cast, pushing a large broom across the floor. Another young man who looked a lot like Ben was moving bales of hay with the prongs of a Bobcat tractor. The barn looked neat and smelled of clean hay.

"Here's one," Ben said, carting a folded table under his arm. He and Gretchen opened it. "Where do you want us to set up for the ceremony and the reception?"

Alice glanced around, then looked helplessly at Gretchen and Samuel. "What do you think?"

Samuel looked back, his expression just as helpless. He shrugged. "I'm not the best person to ask."

"Let's arrange the chairs near the main door, so Mom won't have far to walk when she gets out here," Gretchen said. "We can set up the reception farther back. I'm guessing we'll need three or four tables for the food, then tables for everyone to eat. Should we arrange it like a wedding reception?"

"How is that?" Alice asked, trying to think of all the wedding receptions she'd attended.

"Have a table for the cake, and a head table for Mom and Dad and the family facing the other tables," Gretchen said.

"That sounds like a good idea. Why don't you go ahead and set it up that way," Alice suggested.

"We'll get Travis to help us before he has to go to work," Ben said. He headed for the Bobcat.

"That's Travis?" Alice asked, watching the two young men converse. "I haven't seen him for so long, I hardly recognized him. There's no mistaking that he and Ben are brothers, though."

"He works nights, so he came out to help us get ready," Gretchen said.

Caleb hobbled over just then. "Hi, Alice. It's a good thing Travis was available. I'm not much help with this crazy cast on my foot. I feel like an old man limping around, having to let people do my work." He went off to help Travis.

"He's having a fit that he can't come watch the place while the folks are gone," Gretchen said.

"I'm sure that Blair and Kristin will do a great job," Alice said.

"I'm so glad they chose Acorn Hill for their home. They are a godsend. Blair comes by almost every day to see how Caleb's doing and to give him a hand."

"Kristin has been helping Rose and Jane," Alice said. *Unfortunately,* she thought, *all Kristin's and Blair's kind deeds are keeping them from spending time together.* "I have to get back to the inn, but I'll be back this evening to decorate, and Jane will bring some of the food."

"Put two chocolate kisses bottom to bottom and wrap them in red cellophane, twisting it together with a pipe cleaner at the tip," Rose instructed. "It should look like this." She held up her neatly wrapped candies with the gathered end down.

The slick red plastic kept slipping, but Louise finally got hers together and twisted the end. She looked around. Several other women were struggling, but most of them had nice, neat red bundles.

"Excellent. Now attach a leaf on each side and wrap the stems with wire, like this, then with florist tape." She deftly demonstrated.

Louise felt like she had ten thumbs. *How can fingers that play the piano so easily be so clumsy?* she wondered. She didn't possess the talent her sisters had for crafts and frankly didn't care. She was quite happy to leave the crafts to others. Betty leaned over to help her, getting the green stretchy tape started.

"Thank you, Betty." Louise wound the stem just as Rose instructed. She held the finished flower and inspected it critically. Not too bad for a first attempt. It looked somewhat like a rosebud.

Rose praised everyone's results and instructed each woman to make six of the candy flowers for their table centerpieces. Louise sighed and picked up two more candy kisses. This was not her idea of a good time, but everyone else seemed thrilled by the endeavor. She had not attended to have a good time, but to support the church committee and encourage the women of Acorn Hill. If making candy roses would accomplish that end, then she would twist until her fingers were numb and hope that her efforts resembled flowers.

"I love holidays, and Valentine's Day is one of my favorites," Shannon told the women who were seated in the camp's theater. "Especially this year. When my dearest friend took me out for dinner on Valentine's Day, he told me he wanted to ask me a special question. As you might have guessed, he asked me to become his wife. I'm thrilled to tell you I said yes." She held up her left hand to show off a diamond sparkling on her ring finger.

Shannon's announcement was received with applause and cheers. *What an appropriate way to begin a celebration of love,* Louise thought.

"This isn't the first time I've been asked to join someone's family," Shannon continued. "The first time, I was three years old. I was an orphan. The people in my foster home were very kind to me, but I didn't belong to them. Then this wonderful man and woman came to see me and they asked me if I wanted to become their daughter." Shannon smiled. "They tell me I just nodded my head and stuck my thumb in my mouth. But I remember that day. They brought me a doll that was almost as big as I was, and they had to pry it away from me later so I could take a bath. And they put me in this enormous bed in my own bedroom, and I was afraid to go to sleep, so I got up and went to sleep in their room on their rug. The woman got up and picked me up and held me and rocked me until I fell asleep in her arms. I remember that night. I felt secure for the first time in my life.

"I'm telling you this because I want you to know why I understand love."

Louise tried to imagine the lonely three year old. Glancing down the row, she caught a glimpse of Kristin staring intensely at the speaker, her eyes wide but no readable emotion on her face. Louise remembered the conversation at the inn when Kristin told them she couldn't have children, and they had talked about adoption. They had prayed with her. Could this retreat be an answer to their prayers? Louise closed her eyes and silently prayed, *Lord, I'm sure Kristin and Shannon are here together for a reason. Please open Kristin's heart to Shannon's message and give her hope. Be with Shannon and give her the words You want her to speak. In Jesus' name. Amen.*

With a little smile, Louise sat back to hear Shannon's message.

Chapter Twenty-Three

The potluck spread looked delicious. Louise went through the line, taking scant spoonfuls of June's chicken divan, Vera's creamy penne primavera, Florence's stuffed pork loin, Jane's corn casserole, Sylvia's Oriental coleslaw, Nia Komonos' stuffed grape leaves, and at least a half dozen other dishes. Despite taking only a small sampling of the dishes offered, her plate was full. She glanced at the dessert table. Normally Louise passed up sweets, although Jane's creations often enticed her to take a small sample. Tonight everything on the table looked tempting, especially Hope's pumpkin-pecan cake and Nancy Colwin's apple-raspberry cobbler. Louise looked at her plate and sighed. If she ate everything on her plate, she doubted she'd have room for dessert.

Louise was surprised to see Viola Reed sitting at one of the tables across from their speaker. The bookstore owner did not attend church and had her own ideas about religion. A women's retreat didn't seem like her type of event. Louise took a seat between her and Kristin.

"Hello, Viola. I didn't know you were coming tonight."

"You can blame Patsy Ley for my presence," Viola said. "First, I let her put a poster in my window, then she wanted suggestions for love sonnets. Then she asked me to read some to your group, so here I am. I'm not staying, however. I can't leave all my friends alone." Viola's friends were her cats. Some lived at her bookstore and some lived at her house. She left them with plenty of food and water, so they would be fine for one night, but Viola's feline friends were more like family than pets. Besides, that gave her an excuse to go home and sleep in her own bed, which Louise thought sounded like an excellent idea.

"So you are reading for us?"

"Not a full reading like the ones I put on at Nine Lives. I brought Elizabeth Barrett Browning's love sonnets," Viola said.

"Wonderful." Louise enjoyed Viola's readings. She and Viola had similar tastes in literature. A poetry reading interested Louise much more than candy roses and games.

"Delicious food," Viola said. "I told Kristin I want one of the recipe books she's making from all these dishes. Acorn Hill has some fine cooks."

Louise looked down at her plate. "Indeed. My eyes were bigger than my stomach, I'm afraid." She leaned over to Shannon. "I enjoyed your talk this afternoon. My father was a pastor, and one of his favorite passages was Romans 8:14–17: 'Those who are led by the Spirit of God are sons of God. For you did not receive a spirit that makes you a slave again to fear, but you received the Spirit of sonship. And by him we cry, "*Abba*, Father." The Spirit himself testifies with our spirit that we are God's children.'"

"That is one of my favorite verses," Shannon said. "I understand God as my heavenly Father because of my earthly adopted father. It took some time before I believed that I truly belonged and I lost my fear that they would get tired of me and take me back to the foster home. Once I truly understood my adoption, I just blossomed."

"You didn't feel like you were less of a daughter because you were adopted?" Kristin asked Shannon.

"No. Never," Shannon said. "Oh, I was teased at school by some of the children who didn't understand, but my father called me his little princess and told me he and my mother chose me because they loved me at first sight. Now how many natural children can claim that?"

Kristin smiled at Shannon. "I never thought about that, but I've seen my baby pictures. I looked like a prune."

Clara Horn laughed. She was sitting on the other side of Kristin. "My Audrey was so wrinkled, I was sure something was wrong with her. I was afraid to ask, but my concern must have been obvious. One of the nurses told me she was perfectly healthy and she would grow into her skin in no time. I was so relieved."

Vera joined the laughter. "Someone should warn first-time mothers. I remember thinking that about Polly."

"So you don't . . . regret that you were adopted?" Kristin asked hesitantly.

"I thank God every day for parents who cared enough to give me a loving home. And for a birth mother who loved me enough to give me life. Over the years, I have become so much like my adoptive mother, no one can believe we are not related by blood. I know I have emulated her because she is so special, but I love it when people are amazed to learn I'm adopted. Isn't that so, Aunt June?"

June smiled fondly across the table. "I like to think you're a little like me too. The best part, of course," she said with a laugh.

While the conversation continued around her, Louise sat quietly thinking about Shannon's words. *Kristin has such a giving nature, she would make a wonderful adoptive mother.* She hoped Kristin could see that too.

Jane checked the kitchen clock. Five forty-five. She poured a mixture of eggs and spices over bread cubes, ham, cheese and asparagus in several casserole dishes and covered them with plastic wrap. Alice helped her carry them to her car, along with a box of food and supplies for the reception.

"I'll run out to the farm in a bit to start arranging the decorations," Alice told Jane. "I hope I can make the barn look festive enough."

"Are you sure you don't want me to help you?"

"You have enough to do tonight getting the food ready. I just wish I had your talent for decorating."

"Alice, it's going to be beautiful. You helped Father decorate the church for years." Jane gave Alice a hug. "And just think. In twenty-four hours we will be relaxing over a cup of tea, and everything will be history."

Alice laughed. "I just hope the results justify all our plotting and scheming."

"They will. Now I'd better go." Jane started the car and drove carefully so that the soupy egg casseroles wouldn't spill.

The house was dark when she pulled into Bellwood Farm. She parked and looked around.

"Samuel?" she called. Missy, the farm's black-and-white sheltie, came to investigate, then ran back toward one of the outbuildings. Jane followed the dog, which led her to the lambing shed. Missy ran to Samuel's side and stood as if to protect him, although her tail was wagging. Jane went to a corner inside the building next to one of the enclosed lambing pens that Samuel called *jugs*, where they kept their ewes with their newborn lambs. Samuel was kneeling beside a shorn white sheep with a large, distended abdomen.

"Is it sick?" she asked.

Samuel looked up. "Ah, Jane, I didn't hear you come in. She's about to give birth, and she's very early." Samuel wiped his brow with his forearm. When he looked up, Jane saw the concern in his eyes.

"Do you need help?"

"Rose usually helps me." He shook his head. "I should have expected this, you know. With a farm full of animals, it seems like something always happens to ruin our anniversary. Rose says it doesn't matter, but this year it really does."

"How about Blair Casey? I can call him for you."

"I don't know. I should be able to handle this alone. After all, we've been birthing lambs for decades. I could use another pair of hands, though."

"I'd be happy to help you, but I'm afraid I don't know a thing about sheep. Let me call Blair."

"Yes, I guess that's the best idea."

"Do you need blankets or something? With the clear weather, the temperatures have dropped below freezing again."

"I have supplies, but some hot coffee would be great. It might be a long night. There's a thermos in the kitchen, if you don't mind."

"I'll make coffee and call Blair. Have you eaten?"

"No. Don't worry about me. I'm not hungry."

"Perhaps not now, but you will be. I'll bring out something. I'll be in the house if you need anything."

"Thank you, Jane." Samuel leaned down and ran one of his large hands gently over the ewe's abdomen. The animal made a bleating sound and raised her head but didn't try to get up. "She's Rose's favorite."

"Oh, Lord, keep that sheep safe," Jane muttered as she hurried to the house. Rose would blame herself for not being at home if something happened to the ewe and its lamb. Jane turned on the kitchen light and grabbed the phone. She hoped Blair was at home. Jane had memorized Kristin's number, but she didn't know Blair's cell-phone number. The phone rang four times, and the answering service picked up.

"Blair, this is Jane Howard. I hope you get this message. I'm out at Bellwood Farm, and Samuel needs your help. He is having trouble with a ewe that's in labor. Please come if you get this message. Thanks."

Jane hung up and called Alice. "Hi. Samuel has a ewe in labor and he thinks there might be complications. Rose usually helps him. I tried calling Blair Casey, but he wasn't there, so I left a message."

"Perhaps I can help him," Alice said.

"Can you come right out?"

"Sure." Alice said. "I just finished loading my car with the rest of the decorations."

"I'm going to make something for Samuel to eat, then I'll drop these casseroles off at the camp and go home to do some more cooking. Hurry, Alice."

"All right."

Jane made coffee and threw together two sandwiches from leftover pot roast that was in the refrigerator. She cut a large wedge of apple pie, piled everything on a tray and took the makeshift dinner to Samuel.

"How is she?"

"She's all right for the moment, but I think she has triplets, and as near as I can tell, the legs are all entwined. I'll have to manipulate the lambs."

"I left a message for Blair, and Alice is coming out. Her nursing experience might be of help. Should I call Ben?"

"He and Daylene took the boys to Potterston tonight, and Caleb really couldn't help much with that injured foot. I'll be all right. Thanks for your help. And for the coffee and sandwiches."

"All right. I'll see you in the morning."

Jane prayed for the ewe and for Samuel as she drove to Rolling Hills Youth Camp. She didn't want to disturb the women, so she went in through the kitchen door and put her casseroles in the walk-in cooler. She heard laughter coming from the theater as she left a note with baking instructions and quietly went back to her car.

☙❧

Before she left the inn, Alice called Gretchen Bellwood, hoping to get Blair Casey's cell-phone number. Fortunately, Blair was helping Caleb and promised to go straight to Bellwood Farm. When she pulled into the driveway, she saw Blair's pickup truck parked by the birthing shed. She parked next to his truck, jumped out of her car and entered the shed.

A radiant lamp on a tall stand shone on the corner of the shed next to one of the lambing jugs, emitting warmth as well as light. The scent of fresh sawdust and straw gave the shed a pleasant, earthy smell. Samuel and Blair stood conversing a few feet from a very pregnant ewe, which lay motionless in the straw.

"Hi, gentlemen. How's she doing?" Alice asked when she got next to the men.

"Hi, Alice," Samuel said. "Thanks for coming. She's restless and getting close to delivery, but it could be some time yet. She's carrying at least twins, and I'm thinking she may have triplets."

The ewe tried to get up. Then she flopped down, making a pitiful bleating sound.

Alice looked up at Samuel. He seemed calm, but Alice sensed his awareness of the ewe's every move.

"If possible, it's best to let her deliver on her own," Blair explained. "We should know soon whether the lambs are positioned normally."

As Blair spoke, the ewe lurched to her feet, danced around a bit, then lay back down.

"Her size could be a problem," Blair said. "She's not very large."

"This is her first lambing," Samuel said. "Lilybelle is one of Rose's bottle-fed lambs. I wouldn't have bred her this early, but one of the rams got in with the ewes before breeding time. Rose will shoot me if anything happens to her."

"She'll be all right," Blair said.

"I know you need to fix up the barn for tomorrow," Samuel told Alice. "If you want to, go ahead. I'll call you if we need help."

"All right. I'll check back in an hour if you haven't called."

Leaving the men, Alice walked to the main barn. She flipped the light switch, and a party scene materialized before her eyes. To her left, folding chairs sat in neat rows on both sides of an aisle. At the end of the aisle, a white arch stood, looking a bit lonely. *It needs the flowers and bows we ordered,* Alice thought. Past the seating area, groupings of tables were set up in a large semicircle around one head table. Off to the side, serving tables were set up. Boxes were stacked on one of the tables.

The two large electric heaters were blasting warm air into the large room. It was surprisingly comfortable. Alice removed her jacket and began opening the boxes.

Alice entwined wide blue satin ribbons around the arch. Then, standing at the far end of the aisle, Alice eyed the set-up and tried to imagine Rose and Samuel standing together in front of the arch. *Much better,* she thought. She would unroll the aisle runner right before the ceremony. Craig Tracy would bring fresh flowers in the morning. They would make the effect even more festive. Alice sighed. It really did seem as if everything would come together as planned.

"This is called a hand, or drop, spindle," Rose said, standing in front of the women, holding up a wooden dowel with a disk near the bottom. The disk was painted with bright colors. It looked like a toy top with a long handle.

"If you want to spin without investing in a spinning wheel, this works well," she said. "Tonight everyone will make a drop spindle. If you come up to the table, I have the supplies you need to make one."

The women surrounded Rose at the table. She gave everyone a dowel, two used compact disks, two rubber grommets and a hook. "It's fun to use a colorful spindle, so decorate one side of your disks and the dowel with colored marking pens and put your name on yours. In your design, incorporate an arrow pointing to the right. That will let you know which direction to spin. Then we'll assemble them."

After the women finished their decorative efforts, Rose showed them how to assemble the spindles. When they all finished, Rose demonstrated the spinning process. Explaining as she worked, she attached a piece of starting yarn, twisting it around the spindle near the disk and then up the shaft to a hook on the top.

"I'm ready to start spinning. I take a piece of roving, which is a thick rope of fluffy prepared wool. This has been cleaned, machine carded and dyed." She held up the thick rope of wool so everyone could see what she was doing. "I'm going to split off a piece of the roving." She pulled off a strand. "Then I'll unravel a few inches of the end of my starter yarn and overlap it with the end of the roving. I'll hold the ends together while I give the spindle a clockwise spin. See how it twists into a single strand of yarn?" She gave the spindle another twirl and began drafting her way up the length of the roving, pinching and pulling on the wool to even it out as it spun. "I love the drop spindle because it is portable. I can take it anywhere. This gives you one-ply yarn. We usually knit and crochet with two-ply yarn, so this would have to be spun together with another strand of yarn. Now it's your turn," she said.

Walking around the room, Rose helped each woman get started. She had them balance the end of the spinner on the table to make it easier to handle. Within minutes, spindles were twirling awkwardly. Yarn broke or pulled apart. Spindles dropped, flopping over or twirling off the tables.

All the women were laughing at their efforts. The spindles were all tipping, falling and slipping, but spinning nonetheless.

Sylvia put hers on the floor between her feet and started it spinning. Kristin followed suit. They seemed to have better control, and their yarn began to grow. Within minutes, they all had spindles between their feet as they stood and spun. As the women got the hang of it, their yarn got longer and longer. When they had about three feet of yarn, Rose showed them how to wind on, twisting the yarn around the top of the disk in a low, wide cone shape. Winding the yarn smoothly and evenly was another challenge. A few groans of frustration punctuated the laughter. Louise wound her yarn meticulously and slowly to get it perfect, feeling pretty good about her efforts. Then her yarn broke. She overlapped and pinched the ends together and started again. Her yarn came out much more even. Spinning wasn't so hard. And it was rather relaxing, she thought.

"Thank you, Rose," Patsy said as she got up in front of the group. "You ladies can continue spinning later, but now we must move to the next item on our agenda. We are going to play a little game to help us get acquainted."

Louise looked around for an escape. Surely there were dishes to wash in the kitchen, but the kitchen was dark. Sighing, she took the piece of paper and pencil Vera passed to her.

Chapter Twenty-Four

"The object of this exercise is to get to know one another better," Patsy said. "Each of you has a list of questions. You have fifteen minutes to get your answers. Ask each question of a different person and write down her name and the answer. And no fair writing down answers you already know."

"That doesn't sound too painful," Louise said to Vera. "Since we're next to each other, what's one embarrassing memory from your past?"

Vera laughed. "You expect me to admit it?"

"Is that your answer?" Louise asked, smiling as she wrote it down. "Now you can ask me one. How about my favorite color. That's on there, isn't it? You can put down pale blue."

Ethel came up behind them and placed a hand on Louise's shoulder. "You ladies wouldn't be avoiding the game, would you?" she asked. She laughed, patted Vera's shoulder, then flitted off.

"I didn't see a paper in her hand, did you?" Louise said.

"No, but I suppose we'd better join the game. See you later."

As Vera moved away, Louise noticed a big, glowing red heart on her shoulder. She reached back and removed a heart from her own shoulder. Looking around, she saw several people with glowing hearts. Ethel was tagging people. Louise went up to Viola and tapped her on the shoulder, transferring the heart to her friend.

"I think I can guess, but what's your favorite pastime?"

"You probably think it is reading, but my answer is spending time at the cat-rescue center. And now you can answer a question. Let's see. What's something you long to do or have?"

"Oh my. I have every blessing I could possibly imagine." Louise drew a blank. What did she long to have? She did not long to travel. She had a lovely home and a wonderful business with her sisters. She had a ministry through her music at church.

Louise looked around the room at the young women so focused on playing the game, going from person to person asking questions, jotting down answers, smiling and sparkling with enthusiasm. She didn't want to turn back the clock in her own life, but she missed the exuberance her daughter brought into her life. "I'd love to spend more time with Cynthia," she finally said. "I don't know that I long for that, however. She has her life to lead, just as I had a life away from my family. No, I can't wish for any changes on that front. If I've any longing, it's to become more kind." Louise shrugged.

Viola nodded. "Your answer is exactly what I'd expect. You're one of the most contented people I know, and you give thoughtful consideration to everything you do. I don't know that you can become more kind. However, I'll take that as your answer."

"Thank you. And now I've two answers. These party games aren't my forte," Louise said, grimacing for effect.

Viola laughed. "Perhaps you'll win the booby prize."

"Very likely. I suppose I should talk to someone I don't know well." Louise spotted Wilma Hutch, the music teacher at the elementary school, and went to talk to her.

She didn't get very far before Patsy yelled, "Time's up everyone. Let's see how you did."

They all took their seats. Louise was pleased to see Kristin had collected the most answers. The prizes were heart-shaped rhinestone sunglasses. Six pairs were given out. Kristin put hers on and modeled them to much applause and laughter. Louise noticed that Kristin seemed to be at the center of a group of young women her age. Perhaps after the retreat, Kristin wouldn't be lonely in Acorn Hill.

Before Viola's poetry reading, Louise was asked to play a few love songs. She passed out copies of the words so everyone could sing along. To begin, she played "Beautiful Dreamer." Ethel, Florence and Clara joined in. After the first verse, a few others began singing. A glance at the younger women told her they had never heard the song before. She played "You Are My Sunshine," thinking surely the ladies would recognize that song. A few more ladies sang, but the younger ones still listened with bewildered expressions.

Searching through the music she'd brought, Louise pulled out "Unchained Melody." She played the first stanza and suddenly everyone joined in. Relieved, she played it several times, and the voices rose like a beautiful chorus. Smiling, she ended the song. Music was the universal language, *if* you played the right melody.

As Louise returned to her seat and Viola got up to read poetry, the lights suddenly went out. Louise stopped, disoriented. She heard a clunk and Viola grunted. For a moment, no one moved, then she heard chairs scraping and ladies murmuring.

"Everyone be calm," Florence said. "We'll find candles."

"I know a song," someone said, then she started in, "When you walk through a storm hold your head up high and don't be afraid of the dark . . ."

Someone laughed, but other voices joined in. Louise remembered the words from long ago, and she began singing along. When they repeated the chorus, a candle suddenly flickered to life, and then another and another.

Florence set a candle on top of the piano. As she walked away, Louise could see the glow of a bright red heart on her back.

"Oh, look," someone said. "Mrs. Simpson is glowing."

"So's Vera," someone else said.

"And Betsy."

"How cool," Betsy said. "I have a heart!"

Everyone started laughing and talking all at once, as they pivoted in circles, looking for hearts. Louise smiled. Aunt Ethel had caused quite a stir.

"Does anyone have a cell phone to call the utility company and report the power outage?" Ethel asked the group.

"I do," Kristin said. "I'll have to go outside where I can get better reception."

"Take a flashlight with you," Vera said. She held several that she'd found in the kitchen.

"I'll go with you," Nia Komonos said. "It's too dark to be out there alone."

The two young women went outside.

Viola stood and announced, "I can read by flashlight. You might as well be entertained while we wait." She got up in front and opened her book, holding a flashlight on it. "I will read a sonnet written by Elizabeth Barrett Browning for her husband, fellow poet Robert Browning. It is from a longer poem called 'Sonnets from the Portuguese.' The title is misleading. The sonnets aren't translations. The title refers to her husband's pet name for her, 'my little Portuguese,' a reference to her olive complexion."

Viola paused for effect and then began to read. When she came to the end of the sonnet, the only sound in the room was her voice:

I love thee with the breath,
Smiles, tears, of all my life!—and, if God choose,
I shall but love thee better after death.

There was a long silence, then a hearty round of applause. After the clapping died down, Kristin approached Ethel and whispered to her. Ethel stood and clapped her hands for attention. Holding a flashlight to illuminate her face, she announced, "A transformer blew at the substation. They told Kristin that it might take six or seven hours to fix it. I'm sorry, ladies. I'm afraid we'll have to cancel the rest of the retreat. We have enough flashlights to help everyone get their belongings."

Groans of disappointment filled the room.

"I don't want to go home. My husband volunteered to babysit. I hate to waste the night. Do we have to quit?" Kay Penderbeck asked.

"I closed the Coffee Shop tonight and tomorrow morning. I don't want to leave," June Carter said.

"Me either," Betty Dunkle said.

Clara Horn asked Vera for a flashlight. Then she stood on a chair. "Attention!" she said loudly. Everyone turned toward her.

"It took a lot of courage for me to leave Daisy with someone else for the night," she said. "Now that I did, I refuse to give in to a little thing like losing power. We don't need power to continue the retreat. We have flashlights and candles, and I bet the camp has lanterns for emergencies. Why, this will be just like camping out! There. I've had my say. I'm staying."

For a moment, there was silence. Then someone cheered, and everyone started talking at once.

"I should go home," Rose said. "The farm's on the same power grid, and Samuel will need my help."

"No, he doesn't," Kristin said. "I called Blair on his cell phone to see if he was all right, and he's at your farm, so Samuel has help. He said they're fine."

"Oh good," Rose said, smiling. "I haven't had a night out with the girls in ... in as long as I can remember. This'll be fun."

"Is the stove gas?" June asked. "Can we make popcorn and hot chocolate?"

"Great idea," Vera said. "I'll help."

"I'll look for lanterns," Clara said.

"I'll help you," Betty said, following Clara to the kitchen.

Before long, the women all sat in a circle in the dining hall drinking cocoa, passing big bowls of popcorn, talking and laughing. Some of them sat on chairs, but many sat cross-legged on blankets on the floor. Light from lanterns and candles flickered off the ceiling and walls.

Someone had a guitar and began strumming it softly. The chords sounded familiar. Then Wilma Hutch began singing "Be Not Afraid," and everyone joined in. The sweet harmony of women's voices filled the darkness, bringing warmth and comfort. Kristin popped the dark lenses out of her rhinestone glasses and wore the frames. They glittered in the light of the lanterns. Others did the same, and soon the glasses sparkled and the glow-in-the-dark hearts shone bright red, and the women started calling out song requests. They sang "Lonesome Valley" and "Jesus Loves Me" and "Oh, Susanna."

When the song requests hit a lull, Ethel got up and grabbed Florence's hand. "Come on," she said.

She got in the middle of the circle and started singing, "Yes sir, that's my baby . . ." and dancing the Charleston. Florence picked up on it and sang and danced along. Several others got up, and soon the circle was filled with dancers.

When the Charleston dancers sat down, one of the young women got up and pulled several others, including Kristin, into the circle. They belted out, "We Are Family." The words and tune repeated, and Ethel got up to imitate them. Soon everyone was singing and clapping along. Louise even joined in. Laughing and moving her shoulders from side to side, she felt like a teenager at a campout.

Outside the circle, darkness swallowed up the dim lighting, wrapping the group of women in an atmosphere of intimacy.

"This is fun," Clara said. "I love Daisy, but I get lonely since Oscar died."

"I get lonely too," Ethel said. "Living by myself can be nice. No one tells me what to do or when to eat, but I don't have anyone to talk to, either. Sometimes I turn the television on just so I can hear another human voice. I don't know what I'd do if I didn't have the girls living right next door. And Lloyd, of course, is wonderful company."

"Ronald is around the house all day long, and sometimes I still feel lonely," Florence Simpson said.

"Really?" Kristin said. "I thought I was just lonely because Blair is gone so much with his new business. I didn't know y'all felt the same way."

"Loneliness is a universal feeling," Shannon said. "I think it's the God-hole inside of us. God created us to have fellowship with Him, so we have a hunger inside, but we don't always realize it's a longing for God. We look to others for fulfillment, like our parents, friends, boyfriends or husbands, but people cannot meet our needs and expectations. Only God can do that. He is always with us. We just don't recognize His presence, because we aren't looking. God said, 'Never will I leave you; never will I forsake you'" (Hebrews 13:5).

Kristin's eyes shone brightly in the lantern light.

"Can we pray?" Shannon asked.

The group murmured its assent.

She bowed her head and closed her eyes. "Dear Father, You are the One Who fills our hearts with Your love. Besides You, we need no other, but You give us so much more. You give us friends and family. Let our hearts overflow to pass Your love on to each other. Let us shine Your light into the darkness of sorrow and grief and loneliness. Help us to forget our own loneliness and reach out at home and in our community to help others. In Jesus' name. Amen."

Amens echoed around the room.

∞

Alice looked around the barn and was pleased with the effect that had been created. The decorations had transformed it. She glanced at her watch. An hour and twenty minutes had passed, and the men hadn't called her. She wasn't quite done decorating, but she decided to check on Samuel and Blair. Alice slipped on her jacket, flipped off the lights, took her flashlight and walked toward the lambing shed.

As she crossed the barnyard, the big overhead yard light dimmed, surged, flickered and died, plunging the farm into total darkness. Thankful that she had a flashlight, Alice opened the door to the shed and stepped inside.

"Alice, is that you? Bring your flashlight over here. Hurry," Samuel said.

Alice moved quickly. She heard the urgency in his voice, like the firm command of an ER doctor who needs assistance. She shone the light on the ewe in labor.

"We have multiple lambs and they are all tangled up," Samuel said. "At least one is breach. She presented a back leg of one and a front leg of another. I was trying to untangle and turn them when the lights went out."

"This isn't a very powerful flashlight. Do you have a stronger one?"

"There's a battery-powered lantern hanging by the door," Samuel said.

Alice found the lantern and held it. "Do you need me to get anything for you?" Alice asked.

"We might need colostrum," Blair said. "That's the initial milk that contains natural antibodies."

"There are small plastic bags of colostrum in the freezer," Samuel said. "There's also a feeding tube over by the sink. You don't need to get it yet, though. Let's see if she has a normal birth once we get these lambs turned."

Alice watched Samuel work on the ewe. He moved slowly

and gently, and the ewe didn't complain. She seemed to know he was helping her. Blair watched without interrupting. He gave Samuel the space to care for his own ewe and waited patiently in case Samuel needed his help.

Samuel worked for a while, then stopped to let Lilybelle rest. He sat back. "They're still tangled up, but I think I freed some of the legs. I count three lambs."

Blair poured a cup of coffee from the thermos for Samuel. The ewe began pushing and grunting, and a nose and hoof appeared.

Blair took over, checking to see if the nose and hoof belonged to the same lamb. They did not. He gently repelled the head and felt the legs up to the body. It took some time for him to untangle the lamb's other leg.

"I can't turn it, Samuel. Its head is free, though. She's pushing. I'm going to bring it out."

Samuel put down his cup, which tipped, spilling the coffee onto the straw. He squatted next to Blair. "Let's do it."

Blair gently pulled, and the lamb slid out easily and landed on the straw, vigorously shaking its head to break the membrane over its nose. Samuel wiped its nose to remove the membrane and lifted the lamb by its back feet, gently shaking it upside down. "This helps the fluid drain out of its lungs," he explained to Alice. He carefully laid the lamb where Lilybelle could reach it to clean and dry it. She sniffed it, then began licking the wet membrane around its head. The lamb began to wiggle and thrash about. Alice rejoiced when it bleated loudly, protesting its rude awakening to the cold world.

Samuel examined Lilybelle. "The lamb's head is turned backward," he said. He turned the lamb's head, got hold of the feet and began to pull. The third lamb wanted to get in the way, so Samuel had to move it out of the way. It took another forty-five minutes to birth the second lamb. It did not move or try to breathe. The third lamb began coming immediately. Blair stepped in to deliver it while Samuel cradled the small lamb in his arms, working to remove the membrane and get it breathing. He used a small piece of straw to tickle its nose. It didn't resist. He held it upside down and shook it to get the fluid flowing. Then he breathed into its nose to resuscitate it. It did not move.

"Is it alive?" Alice asked.

"Yes, but we may not be able to keep it alive."

Lilybelle began thrashing about as if in pain. Samuel looked at her. Blair was working to deliver the third lamb. Alice could see Samuel's struggle between helping the lamb or Lilybelle.

"Give me the lamb, Samuel. I'll work on it," Alice said.

He handed the bundle to her. The lamb lay in her arms like a rag doll.

"It needs to be warmed up or it will go into hypothermia," he said. "Take it to the house and turn on the stove to low heat. Rub it down in front of the heat. There's a wood box you can lay it in by the oven. It needs colostrum too."

"Got it. Don't worry. Just tend to Lilybelle."

Alice wrapped the lamb in a blanket, grabbed her flashlight and headed for the house. She was glad she knew her way around as she shouldered her way through the back door into the mudroom that also served as the laundry. She grabbed a couple of old towels from a bin by the door and carried the lamb into the kitchen, rubbing the tiny body as she went. Carefully setting it down on the kitchen rug, she opened the oven. The pilot light was still lit. She turned the oven on low. Leaving the oven door open, she pulled a chair in front of the oven, held the lamb in her lap and began rubbing it with the towels to stimulate its circulation. She heard tiny whooshes of air as it breathed shallowly. The sound gave her hope. As she sat there, she prayed for the lamb, for the ewe and the other babies, and for Samuel and Blair as they struggled to save Rose's favorite ewe.

When the lamb was as dry as she could rub it, she set it in the wood box and placed the box on the open oven door. The lamb lay unmoving.

She found a pot and put it in the sink to fill with water. She turned on the faucet. Nothing happened. Then she realized the farm used well water, and without power, the pump wasn't working.

Looking around the mudroom, Alice found a dozen plastic gallon jugs of water. Bless Rose. Of course she was prepared for every situation.

It seemed to take forever, but the water on the stove finally began to steam. Removing the pan from the heat, she placed a bag of frozen colostrum in the water to defrost and warm. Blair had explained that a lamb became hypothermic because it lacked the body fat to warm it. Getting it dry was the first priority, but it needed the protein the milk would provide to get its metabolism going.

As she waited for the colostrum to warm, Alice picked up the lamb and sat rubbing it vigorously in front of the oven. Suddenly the lamb let out a tiny mewling sound. Alice's heart leaped for joy. "Thank you, Lord," she said out loud. She rubbed the lamb until it tried to lift its head. She set it in the crate once again. This time it wiggled, but it was too weak to struggle.

Alice checked the bag of colostrum, squeezing it to break down all the ice crystals. It didn't take long to warm the colostrum in the hot water. When she put a little colostrum on her finger and tried to get it to suck, she got no reaction. The lamb needed nourishment, so she looked for and found a feeding tube and large syringe.

To feed the lamb, she needed to position it so that she had a clear passage from its mouth to its stomach. She put the crate on the floor between her legs and raised the lamb's head. Working carefully, pinching the hollow at the back of

the jaw to open the lamb's mouth, Alice slid the tube carefully down its throat, pausing as it inhaled to make sure she
didn't go into a lung. When she had it down all the way, she
attached the syringe and aspirated to make sure she was in
the stomach. This time she was glad for the lamb's inertia.
She filled the large syringe with colostrum and slowly forced
it down the tube.

As she removed the tube, the lamb opened its eyes and
blinked at her. Alice laughed out loud and tears sprang into
her eyes. With all her years of nursing, she'd helped deliver
many babies and worked to save hundreds of lives. She had
learned to put life and death into perspective, believing life
on earth was but a brief moment in the span of eternity, and
yet she'd never ceased to sorrow when a patient died or to
rejoice when a life was saved. She rejoiced for the life of this
precious little lamb.

Chapter Twenty-Five

Sitting around the circle at the camp, Ethel told a story about the good ol' days, when her husband operated a farm and she had to learn all kinds of inventive ways to make do when the power went out or the snow got so deep they had to dig a tunnel from the house to the barn.

Not to be topped, Florence told about a particularly harsh winter fifty years ago, when Acorn Hill had an early ice storm over Thanksgiving, and the power was out for eight days.

Kristin recounted memories of her Southern childhood when she would stay at her grandmother's house. Others began sharing experiences. By the time they wound down and headed upstairs for bed, the group had come together as friends.

Alice held the lamb after she fed it. Although it was more alert, it immediately curled up and went to sleep. Believing that it needed to bond with its mother, she wrapped it in clean towels and carried it out to the lambing shed.

Samuel and Blair were on their knees working on Lilybelle. The two lambs were in the fenced jug where they would spend a few days with their mother before joining the other sheep. They were bleating loudly, demanding attention. As they were on their feet, nosing around, Alice assumed they were hungry. She went to see what was wrong with the ewe. Blair was suturing her. Samuel knelt at her head, comforting her. He looked up.

"The lamb seems to be better," Alice said. "I dried it and got some colostrum down. It's sleeping now. I thought it should be close to its mother. Do you need colostrum for the other two? How's Lilybelle?"

"Blair's stitching her up, then we'll try to get the lambs milking. Otherwise, we'll have to feed them. They can't go much longer."

Blair stood and rubbed the small of his back. "Done. I think she'll be all right. Let's get her in the jug and see if those lambs will nurse."

It took some time, but the men got both lambs suckling.

"I wish Kristin could see this," Blair said. "I can't wait to bring her over. She'll love these lambs."

"I'm sure she will," Alice said, "but stay with her. Lilybelle might intimidate her."

"Lilybelle? She's as harmless as a kitten," Blair said.

"Well, you know that, but to someone not used to animals . . ."

"Yes, you're probably right. In fact, Kristin just told me that she's afraid of big animals." Blair gestured toward the ewe lying with her new babies. "But look at her. How could anyone be afraid of her?"

"Fear isn't rational," Samuel said. "Some people can rope a calf and throw it to the ground but be terrified by a mouse."

Blair shook his head. "I hope Kristin can overcome her fear. I'd love to have her visit the farms with me, but I don't want to scare her. Besides, the animals can sense fear, and it could upset them too."

"Let's get this little lamb in with her mother," Samuel

said. He took it from Alice and placed it next to its mother and tried to coax it to nurse. It made no attempt to suckle.

"I'll have to watch it. If it doesn't nurse in an hour or two, I'll have to bottle-feed it or tube it again. Anybody got a watch?" he asked.

Alice looked at the luminous face of her wristwatch. "It's twelve thirty. I hate to leave you, but I need to get home so I can help Jane in the morning and get everything out here for the ceremony and reception."

Samuel groaned and ran a hand through his tousled hair. "I'm not going to be in very good shape for a party tomorrow."

"Why don't you go get some sleep, and I'll stay out here with the ewe and her lambs," Blair said. "I don't like to leave a patient until I know it's stable anyway."

"I can't ask you to do that," Samuel objected.

"You're not asking. I'm offering. Now go on and get some sleep. I've got everything here I need. I'll just wrap up in one of those blankets, and I'll be fine. I can keep an eye on Lilybelle and that little one too."

"If you're sure . . ."

"I'm sure."

Alice walked out with Samuel and wearily got into her car. All the way home, she thanked God for sparing the sheep and asked for an extra measure of energy so she could get up and help Jane in the morning.

It was still dark outside when Jane put the anniversary cake together. For the bottom tier, she spread raspberry jam and a whipped-cream filling between the three layers of raspberry-jam cake. Assembling the large, square cake, she smoothed blue frosting over it. Then she rolled out thin strips of white marzipan, which she applied like ribbon, making the cake look like a wrapped present.

Arranging the bottom layer of the second cake on a foil-covered cardboard square, Jane spread a thick layer of bittersweet ganache between the layers of dark-chocolate cake, then wrapped it in smooth white decorator frosting and crisscrossed it with several thin strips of blue marzipan.

A smaller square Italian cream cake with a coconut whipped-cream filling formed the top tier. Jane frosted it in a pale blue.

Now for the finishing touches, she used white frosting to pipe lacy hearts on the periwinkle blue layer and delicate white flowers on the pale-blue top layer. Using pink frosting, she made hearts and flowers on the middle layer. For the finishing touch, she made a big, fluffy bow out of wide blue-and-white ribbon to top the cake.

Just as she piped on the finishing touches of tiny green leaves around the flowers, the door from the hall opened and Alice came in. She was dressed in jeans and a sweatshirt, and her eyes had dark circles under them.

"Good morning," Jane said cheerfully. "You're not just getting in, are you?"

"No. I got home a little before one, and I slept like a rock." Alice rotated her shoulders and turned her head from side to side. "I had to help with the birth last night and I found that nursing a lamb is harder than taking care of a patient. I ache all over."

Alice started to fill her teacup, then stopped and stared at the cake.

"Jane, that's gorgeous! What a great idea. It looks just like a stack of beautiful presents."

Jane stood back and studied her creation with the critical eye of a perfectionist. "It did turn out nice, didn't it?"

Alice laughed. "*Nice* is such a lukewarm word. It's fabulous. Rose is going to be thrilled. And so will Samuel."

"So tell me about the lamb."

"Actually, there were three of them. And miracle of

miracles, they all lived." While she sipped her tea, Alice recounted the entire lambing story to Jane.

"Oh, Alice, that's amazing. All that in the dark too. We had power here in town. I had no idea there was a problem elsewhere. I'm so glad you were able to help them. I can't even imagine taking care of that poor little lamb."

"The Lord gives us each our abilities and talents, Jane. I could not make a cake like that."

"My talents are frivolous compared to yours."

"Not true, Jane. 'Don't forget to entertain strangers, for by doing so some people have entertained angels without knowing it!'" (Hebrews 13:2).

Jane laughed. She'd become accustomed to her sister's ability to recite scriptures. "If our guests are angels, some of them have had very tarnished halos."

Alice nodded. "We have had a few ... uh ... interesting guests, but also some wonderful ones."

When the women began stirring in the dormitory at Rolling Hills Youth Camp, the power was on.

"Hallelujah! Rise and shine," Ethel announced loudly as she went down the hall.

Louise had risen an hour earlier and quietly showered and dressed. June and Rose and a few others also had awakened early. *Creatures of habit*, Louise thought. They talked quietly as they prepared to face the day. But not Aunt Ethel. She had to make sure everyone else got up too.

Groans could be heard coming from the dorm rooms. Then sleepy-eyed ladies staggered into the hall.

Louise went downstairs to make coffee. June had already been in the kitchen, brewing the coffee and placing the breakfast casseroles in the oven. The coffee smelled wonderful, and Louise took a cup and her Bible and found a quiet spot in the dining room to have her morning devotions. She had just finished when Shannon came in and asked if she could join her. Then Kristin arrived and sat next to Shannon.

"If you don't mind, I wanted to ask you some more about adoption," Kristin told Shannon. "You see, I recently learned that I can't have children."

"I'm sorry. That must be heartbreaking," Shannon said. "Jerry, my fiancé, and I have already decided we'll adopt a child, whether we can have our own or not. We'll wait a year to adjust to being married, but then we'll apply. There are so many children who need homes. We want to adopt an older child. Most people want babies, and the older children get left out." Shannon laughed. "I told Jerry to watch out, because I may want to adopt a dozen. He said that was okay, that he has plans for a big house."

"Blair thinks adopting is a great idea, but we have some issues to face first. I wouldn't want to bring a child into an unstable situation." Kristin blushed and gestured with her hands. "I don't mean we're unhappy. It's just that we are still adjusting to moving and starting a new life."

Shannon put her hand on Kristin's arm. "I understand, and you are wise to wait. Shall we pray for you?"

Kristin nodded her head and she, Shannon and Louise joined hands. Shannon said, "Dear God, You are a loving Father, and You know how much Your children need the love and support and discipline of a family. Just as You have adopted us as Your children, Kristin and her husband have opened their hearts to the possibility of giving a home to a child. Help them create a home together here that will give a child love and security. Guide them to the child You have picked to complete their family. Give them the wisdom and love to raise that child to love You. Thank You, Lord, that they are willing to care for one of Your little ones. In Jesus' name. Amen."

"Amen," Louise echoed.

When Kristin looked up, she had tears in her eyes. "Thank you," she said. "I know God is already answering your prayer. I can feel it in here," she said, putting her hand over her heart.

"I'll keep praying for you," Shannon told her. "Please keep in touch and let me know what you decide."

Louise excused herself to refill her coffee and to give the two young women some time alone before the rest of the women filled the dining hall. She thanked the Lord for nudging her to attend the retreat. She, too, felt that their prayers for Kristin were being answered even now.

Chapter Twenty-Six

Jane and Alice loaded their cars with food for the reception. Jane put her change of clothes and Rose's dress in her car, so she could stay at the farm until the ceremony.

"You go on out to the farm. I'll stop at the Good Apple and pick up the baked goods," Alice said.

"All right. Thanks." Jane double-checked her list. Rose had a fabulous kitchen, so Jane wasn't concerned about cooking utensils, and she had rented china for serving dishes and platters. Fred would have everything delivered to the farm.

When Jane arrived at the farm at seven thirty, Daylene's car was parked by the main barn. Jane parked by the kitchen door. The house was open, so she went inside. Samantha Bellwood stood at the kitchen sink, washing dishes. When she saw Jane, she opened her arms to give Jane a hug, then realized her hands were soapy. Laughing, she wiped her hands.

"I am *soooo* glad to see you," she said. "When I got here this morning, I found the usual anniversary disaster. Dad was in the kitchen trying to make coffee. He had more coffee grounds on the counter than in the pot. He looked like he hadn't shaved for a week. Then I found out that he was up half the night with new lambs." She shook her head. "Some things never change."

Jane laughed at the description. "Don't worry. Everything is under control."

"Yes, I think you're right. I fixed breakfast for Dad before he went out to the lambing shed, but I told him I was going to come get him in a half hour, so he could get ready."

Alice arrived with the bread and rolls. Samantha rushed over and gave her a big hug. Alice laughed. "It's good to see you, too, Sam. Your mother is going to be thrilled to have you home."

"Except I only get to see her for a couple of hours." She sighed dramatically. "Oh well. I'll be home for spring break in a month. I shouldn't have come this weekend, but I didn't want to miss the surprise. Oh, you've *got* to see the barn. It is *soooo* neat." Her hands moved as fast as she talked.

"I saw Daylene's car over there. I couldn't finish decorating last night because of the blackout and the lambs. That's why I came early."

"Well, it's done, and you're going to *love* it. Come on. You too, Jane. You gotta see it." Samantha took their hands and dragged them toward the door.

Jane looked over her shoulder. There was a lot to do, but she could take a few minutes. With Samantha there, she'd have help.

Everything was ready. They had moved their cars around back of the barn, so Rose wouldn't get suspicious. Alice had gone home to change and to meet Louise. The kitchen smelled of cooking, but that couldn't be helped. Samuel was stationed by the door to greet Rose and carry in her overnight bag. By the time she saw her husband, all dressed up like Sunday morning, she would know something was happening.

Samantha had straightened her parents' bedroom, and she and Jane had hung the dress where Rose could see it when she walked into the room.

Kristin called to let them know that Rose was on the way. Samantha began to get things ready for a scented bath for her mother. Jane went down to the kitchen. She couldn't resist being present when Rose discovered Samuel's secret. When she got to the dining room, where she planned to watch from a corner, she found Daylene and Gretchen already waiting there, and Samantha came in right behind her. When they heard Rose's car pull into the driveway, they looked at one another and giggled, then shushed one another, then giggled again. By the time Rose was at the kitchen door, they all were composed.

Samuel was standing in the doorway waiting for Rose. When she saw him, she stopped in her tracks.

"Samuel? What . . . why are you all dressed up? It's Saturday, not Sunday." Her brow wrinkled as she looked at her husband.

"I know what day it is, sweetheart. It's the day we're celebrating our anniversary."

"But we did that already Tuesday at Zachary's."

He took her hand. "Well, we're celebrating some more. I have a surprise for you."

Her eyebrows rose. "You do?"

"Yes. Lilybelle had her lambs last night."

That wasn't what Jane expected him to say. She almost laughed but swallowed instead. Samantha looked ready to giggle out loud. Gretchen held her finger to her lips.

"She did? And you didn't call me? But Sam, the power went out." Then her frown relaxed. "Oh, I forgot. Kristin told me Blair was here."

"He stayed here all night. She had triplets, and they're all doing fine, thanks to Alice."

"Alice? Was she here too? Oh, Samuel, you should have called me. I'd have come right home."

"I know, love, but that would have spoiled my surprise."

"What surprise? What are you talking about?"

Samuel dropped to one knee and looked up at his wife. Rose looked so startled that Jane wanted to laugh again, but Samuel's gesture was so poignant, tears formed in her eyes.

"Rose, would you marry me all over again?"

"Samuel, you'd better get up before you ruin your good pants. Of course I'd marry you again, honey." She took his face in her hands and leaned down and kissed him. "And I'm glad you want to marry me again, because I have a surprise for you, and you might not be exactly thrilled about it."

Samuel got up. For a big man, he was surprisingly agile. He reached over to the counter and picked up a tiara of flowers that Craig had delivered earlier with the other flowers.

"This is for you. I want you to wear it today."

She took the rope of delicate blue and white flowers. "They're lovely, Samuel. Are we going somewhere? Gretchen said she had planned something. What is this all about?"

"Go on up to the bedroom. You have time to bathe and change before they get here."

She looked perplexed and started to say something, but he cut her off. "I'll bring your bag," he said. "Go on."

Samantha, Jane, Gretchen and Daylene scrambled to get up the stairs before Rose saw them. They hid in one of the other bedrooms and waited for Rose to come up. They barely made it.

They heard her gasp.

"Oh, how beautiful," she said, her voice almost reverent.

That was their cue. They all hurried into her bedroom. She swung around. "What are you all doing here . . . Samantha! Oh, baby, it's so good to see you!" Rose rushed forward and enveloped her youngest child in a big hug. Samantha towered over her mother too, making Rose look even more petite.

"We heard Dad propose, Mom," Samantha said. "So we're all here to help you get ready."

"Get ready for what?"

"Why, to get married again. That's what."

Louise and Alice arrived at the Bellwoods' a half hour before the ceremony was to start. They found Rose, Samantha and Daylene in the living room. Rose looked stunning in her beautiful new blue outfit as she paced.

"Louise, Alice, what is going on? No one will tell me anything. And look at this." She held her arms out and twirled around. The soft wool suit dress flattered her petite shape.

"It fits perfectly," Louise said smiling.

"You're all in on this conspiracy, aren't you?"

Alice smiled. "I wouldn't call it a conspiracy. We did give Samuel a little help surprising you."

"I was surprised all right, but now I'm a prisoner in my own living room. Gretchen even barred me from my kitchen. My children are plotting against me."

Rose really didn't look upset. It was clear that she was pleased by the attention.

"I have three new lambs out there, and I can't even go see them."

"Your dress isn't really suited to the barn or the kitchen," Louise said.

"I could change in five minutes," she protested.

"And spoil Dad's surprise?" Samantha asked. "You'd better not. He might not try to surprise you again."

Rose's bluster disappeared. "That dear man," she said, her voice affectionate. "I wouldn't spoil his plans for anything. But I'd sure like to know what they are."

Daylene laughed. "You'll find out soon enough, Mother."

Rose gave her daughter-in-law an affectionate smile. "Gretchen told me you all had something planned. Just having my family around is all the blessing I need," she said.

"But I didn't know Samantha was involved in this scheme, and I didn't know you had invited our friends."

Samantha started laughing. Rose gave her a puzzled look. Then her attention was attracted by sounds from outside. "What's that noise?" she asked as she got up and went to look out the front window.

Cars were streaming up the driveway.

"That's the Simpsons' car and the Humberts'. And there's Pastor Ken's car." She turned her bewildered gaze on Louise. "What's going on?"

Louise smiled and gave Rose a hug. So far, the plan had worked perfectly. "A few of your friends want to celebrate with you. That's all."

"That's all? And I wasn't told? How are we going to feed everyone?" She looked out again. A dozen cars lined the driveway.

"Where are they going? They're all parking by the barn." Rose looked at Daylene. "Are we having a hoedown or something?"

"Or something," Daylene replied with a smile.

A few minutes later, Ben came in. "It's time," he said. He gave his mother a kiss on the cheek. "You look beautiful, Mom. Put on your head thing. I'm going to escort you. You might want a coat. It's still chilly out there."

"Pooh. It must be fifty degrees, and the sun is shining. Besides, this dress has a jacket. I'm fine."

Samantha arranged the floral tiara on the dark ring of braids encircling Rose's head. She looked like a queen. They all followed Ben and Rose across the yard to the main barn. The door opened, and they stepped inside.

Chapter Twenty-Seven

"H ello, Mother," Caleb said. He smiled down at her as he took his mother's hand and tucked it in the crook of his arm. "My turn," he said, handing her a lovely bouquet of white snowdrops and blue star-shaped snow glories.

Rose gazed fondly at her oldest child, then looked around and gasped. She stood at the end of a long white satin runner that extended through rows and rows of folding chairs occupied by townsfolk of Acorn Hill.

"Oh my." Rose put her hand over her heart. "Oh my," she repeated. Louise followed Rose's gaze as she looked around. Blue and white streamers hung from the rafters. Big red hearts and white paper bells hung on strings from the streamers. It looked as if the Bellwood grandsons had been busy. Red hearts covered the white lattice arch behind Samuel at the head of the aisle. A rosemary wreath hung from the top of the arch, and tall baskets of blue, white and pink flowers stood on each side. Louise was warmed by the surprise and wonder on Rose's face.

Ben, Samantha and Daylene left them to join their father, Josh, Travis, Gretchen and all the grandsons at the other end of the aisle. Pastor Kenneth Thompson stood with them.

Louise slipped away to sit at the electronic keyboard they'd rented. She began playing the traditional wedding march. Josie Gilmore, dressed in a frilly blue dress with a big sash and bow in the back, walked slowly up the aisle, sprinkling rose petals on the satin runner. Hobbling on his cast, Caleb walked his mother up the aisle.

From her vantage point at the organ, Louise caught a glimpse of Rose's face. She looked as lovely and loving as any bride Louise had ever seen. Samuel stood tall and proud in his best Sunday suit, gazing adoringly at his bride. Louise glanced at the gathering. Rose's and Samuel's extended families took up two rows of front seats on both sides. Farther back sat Kristin and Blair Casey. Blair looked tired but happy as he held Kristin's hand. She sat close to him, obviously caught up in the emotion of the ceremony.

"Dearly beloved," Pastor Ken said when Caleb handed his mother over to his father. "We are gathered here today to celebrate the marriage of Samuel and Rose Bellwood and the love they have shared with all of you."

Rose gazed up at her husband, and he looked down at her tenderly.

Pastor Ken held up his open Bible and said, "Proverbs 5:18 advises, 'Rejoice in the wife of your youth.' Samuel has asked us today to witness and rejoice with him as he honors his wife, Rose Bellwood, the wife of his youth. He tells me Rose is his love and his best friend and that she works harder than he does to make their life successful. As you can see, Rose and Samuel raised a wonderful family here at Bellwood Farm in Acorn Hill. We have all have seen their devotion to each other, their family and their friends. Now Samuel has a few words he wants to say."

Samuel squared his shoulders and looked at all their family and friends. "The Bible says in Proverbs 18:22, 'He who finds a wife finds what is good and receives favor from the Lord.' Rose . . ." Samuel lifted Rose's hand to his lips and kissed it. He looked at her and blinked several times.

"Rose, you have given me everything that's good in life, and the Lord has blessed me beyond anything I ever dreamed. I couldn't decide what to do that would tell you how much I love you." He glanced over at Louise for a moment, then looked back at Rose.

"A good friend suggested that I tell you how much you mean to me. I'm proud to be your husband and I thank you for giving me more than any man deserves." He looked at all his children and grandchildren standing around him. "I'm a very lucky man," he said.

"Oh, Samuel, you big sweetheart. I'm overwhelmed." Rose took a deep, ragged breath and looked around. "I can see now that you all were in on this surprise." She smiled at the gathering. "What can I say? You can see why I married this wonderful man."

Louise felt a tear slip down her cheek. Looking around, Louise saw many ladies with tissues dabbing their eyes. She wasn't the only one touched by the Bellwoods' love.

"I love you, Samuel," Rose said, stretching up and kissing Samuel, who looked totally besotted. She stepped back and took both his hands. "Now I have a surprise for you," she said. "Just remember all those kind words you said a minute ago. This afternoon, after all these wonderful people leave, I'm taking you on a second honeymoon. We're going to Hawaii."

Samuel looked at her as if she'd suddenly lost her mind. "Hawaii? Why in the world would I want to go to Hawaii?" he said.

"Because you love me, and we are going away alone for a week."

Samuel was silent for a moment. "Uh, honey, I think I might have canceled that trip," he confessed, managing to look both repentant and relieved.

Rose laughed. "You did, but my spies warned me. The trip is definitely on. We leave this afternoon." She glanced at her daughter-in-law. "We would have left earlier, but Gretchen insisted they had something planned for us. Now I know what it was."

"We have another surprise for you," Gretchen said. She looked over at Daylene on the other side of Rose.

Daylene stepped behind the arch, then came forward. She held the quilt.

"Mom, Dad, we wanted to show you how blessed we are to be part of your family, and all your friends wanted you to see how special you are, so we all put together this quilt for you." She held it up, and Travis and Joshua spread it out in front of their parents.

"It's . . ." Rose stood speechless and stared at the quilt. "I thought . . . Florence told me it was a surprise for someone at church. I even . . ." She covered her mouth with her hand for a moment, then pointed at the quilt. "Oh dear, there's the square I made."

The boys turned the quilt around so everyone could see it.

"I . . . I don't know what to say," Rose said. "Thank you all. I never imagined . . ." She looked up at Samuel. "We'll treasure this forever, won't we Sam?"

"Yes. We are humbled by all your generosity," Samuel said. "Thank you. I can see now that you were all busy keeping a lot of secrets from Rose and me." He smiled. "I never knew I had such devious friends and family, but we're grateful to you all for sharing this day with us. Now please come break bread with us. Some of the best cooks in Acorn Hill have prepared a feast for us."

The barn exploded in applause as Samuel walked his bride down the aisle as Louise played "The Wedding March."

The guest tables looked wonderful with white linen tablecloths, fresh flowers and red and silver heart confetti. A little square teabag favor with a blue flowered teapot sat at each place setting. To one side, a table held picture albums from the Bellwoods' forty years together, and piles of cards.

The townsfolk of Acorn Hill weren't shy when it came to food. A line had formed all the way around the inside of the barn. The Bellwood grandsons were first in line. Jane warned them to save room for cake. Carol Matthews overheard her and laughed.

"I'm sure they're just like Charles," Carol said, referring to her son, who was standing in front of her. "If there's cake, he always has room."

"I suspect you're right."

The food disappeared rapidly. The warming trays they'd rented were a blessing, keeping the sliced ham and turkey and the scalloped potatoes piping hot.

Jane kept most of the cold food in the tack room, which was not heated. It worked as well as a refrigerator and was close at hand. Alice helped bring food out to replenish the finger foods and salads. The whipped-cream fruit ambrosia was very popular, especially with Samuel, who came back for a third helping.

"I need to build up my strength," he told Jane. "I don't know if I'll survive a week on fish and coconut. It's a good thing I like pineapple."

"Yes it is, because that salad is full of pineapple."

He chuckled. "I knew I liked it." He took a bite to prove it. "Rose told me the Caseys are going to stay at the farm while we are gone. That puts my mind at rest. Blair is a good man and a great vet. I couldn't have delivered all those lambs without his help."

"They're a wonderful couple. Kristin helped me put together this buffet, and she's been helping Rose too. I know they appreciate your support while Blair builds up his business."

"They are going to be a big asset to Acorn Hill. Now, I've

been eyeing that cake over there. Are we going to cut it or just look at it?"

"It's just waiting for you and Rose. I believe Wilhelm is taking pictures, so you and Rose need to pose by it first."

"Good. I'll go find him and Rose."

After Rose and Samuel made the first cut, Jane and Louise took over serving the cake.

"It looks like you have everything under control here," Alice said to Jane and Louise.

"Go get yourself something to eat," Jane said. "You've been working all morning."

"Oh, I'm not hungry. I thought I'd go see how that little lamb is doing. I haven't had a chance to go out to the lambing shed yet."

"By all means go," Louise said. "It's my turn to help Jane. I'm in charge of cleanup, and I have plenty of helpers here," she said, looking at the barn filled with friends.

Alice wasn't the only one to sneak away to the lambing barn. When she opened the door, she saw Blair and Kristin in the jug with Lilybelle and her babies. Kristin was kneeling in the jug, petting the runt of the litter, Alice's little lamb. "I want to learn about these animals," she said to Blair. "I want to work with you like Rose works with Samuel."

"I would like that. But remember, they've been around animals all their lives. We'll take it slow. If you give yourself a chance, you can learn how to handle them safely, but I'll never let one hurt you. If it makes you feel safer, you can watch me work with them from the other side of the fence," he said.

Kristin looked up and smiled at her husband. Alice quietly backed out of the shed and left.

Blair returned a truckload of rental equipment to Fred's Hardware while Kristin helped Jane transport her supplies back to the inn. Most of the leftover food had gone home with Gretchen and Daylene, and some had been left at the Bellwoods for Blair and Kristin that week.

Alice and Louise arrived at the inn at the same time Blair pulled up. They carried in armloads of plastic plates and cups and silverware that Samuel was donating to the church.

"We have enough left to put on another reception," Louise said, instructing Blair to put the boxes in the pantry for the time being.

"We could use it for next year's women's retreat," Alice suggested.

Louise groaned.

"The retreat was wonderful, wasn't it? I got to know everyone better," Kristin said. "I felt as if I belonged."

Jane gave Kristin a big hug. "You do belong. In a short time, you have become an important part of Acorn Hill."

Kristin looked at Blair. "I hope so."

"I'm making coffee and tea, and Samuel insisted I bring home some leftovers. I don't know about the rest of you, but I didn't eat a thing at the party. Now I'm starved."

"Me too," Blair said, and they all laughed.

They set all the food on the table and dived in, making sandwiches from the sliced ham and turkey.

"Do you have more of that whipped-cream salad?" Blair asked.

"Not much, but enough for you."

"Good. Kristin, you'll have to get that recipe from Jane."

"I will," she looked at Jane. "That is, if you don't mind sharing it."

"If you promise never to reveal the secret ingredients," Jane said solemnly.

"Oh, I promise."

Jane laughed. "I won't hold you to that. I found it in my

mother's cookbook. I modified it slightly, but it's an easy recipe." Jane wondered if the sudden intimacy Blair and Kristin shared meant things were better between them. It seemed so.

"Samuel told me he's happy that you are watching the farm for them this week," Jane said.

"He has helped me so much," Blair said. "I owe him a big debt."

Kristin reached over and took Blair's hand, smiling at him. "We both do. I want to be just like Rose and Samuel when we've been married forty years, and I want to be living in Acorn Hill."

"Are you sure, honey?" Blair asked. "I've been thinking that maybe I shouldn't have taken you away from your family. We can move closer to your parents if you want."

Kristin shook her head. "We need to make a life of our own. Especially if we're going to have children. I can't think of anywhere I'd rather be than Acorn Hill with all our new friends." Kristin gave her husband one of those adoring looks Jane had so often seen brides give their grooms. Then Kristin turned to the rest of them.

"Blair and I talked some more about adopting. We're going to take a year to get his business established, then we're going to talk to that doctor you told me about, Alice, the one who works with the adoption agency."

"You'll be wonderful parents."

"Thank you." Blair turned to Kristin. "We'd better get back to Bellwood Farm so Samuel and Rose can give us instructions. I think he's a little nervous about leaving."

Kristin got up and gave each of the sisters a hug. "I am going to visit my folks after Rose and Samuel get home, but I'll only be gone for a week. I want to start planning a garden. I know you're a terrific gardener, Jane. Will you give me some pointers?"

Jane stood and gave Kristin another hug. "I'll be happy

to. And I'll come have a cup of coffee with you this week. I didn't get to see those lambs."

"I'll be out too," Alice said. "I feel like I'm the littlest lamb's mother."

"I might tag along," Louise said. "Now that the retreat and all the intrigue are over, it's going to seem a little dull around here."

"If I remember right, Louise, all the intrigue was your idea," Alice said.

"Yes indeed." Louise raised her eyebrows and gave her sisters her most imperious look. "And a fine idea it was."

Ham & Asparagus Overnight Omelet
SERVES EIGHT

6 slices white bread, trimmed

4 ounces cream cheese, softened

1 pound fresh asparagus, steamed tender-crisp, drained well and cut in two-inch pieces

2 cups diced ham

2 cups grated cheddar cheese

5 large eggs

2¼ cups milk

¼ teaspoon salt

¼ teaspoon dry mustard

⅛ teaspoon cayenne pepper

Spread cream cheese on bread and let it sit uncovered for an hour to make it easier to cut, then cut slices in one-inch cubes. Spread half of bread cubes in bottom of well-greased 9" x 13" baking dish. Layer half of the asparagus pieces (making sure that tips and stems are evenly distributed), one cup ham, then one cup cheese. Repeat the layers of asparagus and ham. Reserve the remaining cheese.

Beat eggs, milk and spices until blended. Pour egg mixture over layers in baking dish. Top with cheese. Cover with foil and refrigerate overnight. Remove from refrigerator one and a half hours before serving time. While casserole comes to room temperature (thirty minutes), heat oven to 350 degrees. Bake covered for fifty minutes. Uncover and bake ten minutes more or until set.

Variations: A light-textured white bread gives casserole a soufflé texture. A denser bread, like sourdough, creates a bread-pudding consistency. Other vegetables can be used, such as broccoli, bell peppers or onions.

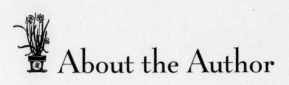 About the Author

Sunni Jeffers calls remote northeast Washington State home, where eagles soar, and elk, deer, moose and the occasional buffalo roam. She and her husband live on a farm with an aging Scottish Highlander cow and an elderly Arabian race-horse. Sunni has won the Romance Writers of America Golden Heart, American Christian Romance Writers Book of the Year and the Colorado Romance Writers Award of Excellence.